CITY OF REFUGE

VERTICAL.

CITY OF REFUGE

Kenzo Kitakata

Translated by Y. T. Horgan

VERTICAL.

Published by Vertical, Inc., New York

Originally published in Japanese as *Nogare no matchi*
by Shueisha, Tokyo, 1982.

ISBN 978-1-934287-12-5

Manufactured in the United States of America

First Edition

Vertical, Inc.
451 Park Avenue South, 7th Floor
New York, NY 10016
www.vertical-inc.com

Appoint out for you cities of refuge, whereof I spake unto you by the hand of Moses: That the slayer that killeth any person unawares and unwittingly may flee thither: and they shall be your refuge from the avenger of blood.

—Joshua 20:2-3

Chapter One

1

It looked like the corpse of an animal. It lay beneath the outside stairs of the apartment building.

Koji flicked the cigarette he'd been smoking.

The corpse got up.

A tall man appeared in the light of the lamp post. The cigarette hadn't landed on him. It had only hit the concrete, scattering sparks.

"Yo, Koji." It was Numata. His hair, which had once touched his shoulders, was now shorn.

"Feeling sick?" Koji peered through the darkness into Numata's face. It was normally unthinkable for the guy to lie on the ground like that. He was the sort who got angry if so much as cigarette ash fell on his knee.

"Why so late? I was waiting for you."

Numata wasn't wearing his usual suit. Today it was a dark blue windbreaker and white jeans, splattered with damp mud. Yet it hadn't rained at all.

"I thought I'd crash at your place tonight," Numata said, smiling. In the darkness the lines in his cheeks seemed more deeply etched.

He wasn't a welcome guest. He usually came with a large bottle of cheap sake and presented it with as much ceremony as Scotch or brandy. Then he'd easily down a bottle of his host's whiskey. Tonight, however, it didn't look like he had his usual offering. He just carried a fully packed duffel bag.

"Come in." It was two in the morning. Too late to tell him to go home.

Once inside, Numata began undressing. He removed not just his windbreaker and jeans but also his shirt and underwear. He was completely naked.

Koji had never seen him like this. Numata was covered with goose bumps, and his dry skin lacked sheen. His long skinny legs, covered sparsely with hair, looked frail.

"I'm all clammy," Numata said. He pulled a gray suit and a dress shirt from his bag. He put on some briefs and spent some time smoothing out the creases in his suit.

Koji put the kettle on the range. He'd had dinner, but that was seven hours ago. If he didn't at least have a Cup o' Noodles, he'd be too hungry to sleep.

"Gimme two of those," Numata said. His hair may have changed, but his brazenness hadn't. Ten or so packages of Cup o' Noodles that Koji had won at a pachinko parlor lay under the kitchen sink.

"Is there something you need to talk to me about?"

"Not really."

"Then why don't you sleep at your own place?"

"Hey, we're pals, aren't we?"

"You in trouble?"

"I just came to crash for a night. Nothing wrong with seeing each other once in a while."

Numata put on the dress shirt over his bare skin, carefully tied a dark tie, pulled on his trousers, and donned his jacket. Now he looked more like his usual self.

"You're hurt," Koji observed. A scar ran from behind Numata's ear down his neck. Caked with blood, it looked as if someone had scratched him with a nail. Koji felt a twinge of regret at having brought it up—Numata might blame it on a woman. Once he started on the topic of women, the guy could go on forever. And most of it was bullshit.

But Numata simply put his hand to his neck and muttered that it was nothing.

Koji poured boiling water into the Cups o' Noodles. "Don't touch that," he warned.

"It's a toy," Numata snorted.

"Don't touch it. I just finished it."

On the wooden crate that served as a table was a model ship. The triple-mast *Eagle*, a barque-class training vessel. It was still sailing somewhere in the world.

"You're still just a little brat, aren't you?"

"Don't make fun of people's hobbies."

Koji pushed the *Eagle*, crate and all, to the corner of the room. He placed three Cups o' Noodles directly on the tatami.

"We get a cup and a half each. You don't get more of my own food than I do."

"Fine."

Numata shoveled the noodles down his throat. He was clearly starved. Yet he was careful to make sure the soup didn't splatter on his suit.

Koji wasn't even halfway through his first cup when Numata reached out for the second, which he quickly polished off. Koji no longer felt like complaining. After all they were pachinko prizes.

"Sorry to come by this late at night."

Seeming to feel better with some food in his stomach, Numata reached out for one of Koji's Hi Lite cigarettes. The guy had stretched out his long legs to spare the knees of his trousers. It seemed to Koji that a wrinkle-free suit, a freshly dry-cleaned dress shirt, and polished shoes were a matter not of mere taste but of life or death for Numata.

"You know, your place always looks like shit. You might want to do something about that, or no woman will want anything to do with you."

"I don't need any lectures from a freeloader," Koji retorted. He poured two shots of whiskey from the double-sized bottle of Suntory Red. One shot each. He always swore to himself to offer no more than that.

The faint noise of late-night radio could be heard through the wall. Koji's neighbor had a habit of falling asleep with it still on. It wasn't a particularly annoying habit as long as the volume wasn't too loud.

Koji owned neither a television nor a radio. It wasn't that he couldn't afford them; he just never wanted those things. He didn't want a suit, a car, a motorcycle, or a stereo, either.

He spent the money he earned as he pleased. On what, he hardly remembered. Yet he regularly saved 10,000 yen every month. He just told himself that he made 10,000 yen less per month than he actually did, so he didn't feel the loss.

He'd saved 310,000 yen and never touched it. Once, when he was ten days from payday and broke, he got by on two Cups o' Noodles per day. He picked instant food as his prizes at pachinko just for such times.

Koji wanted a boat.

Nothing fancy like a cruiser. A second-hand motorboat would do. He knew he couldn't buy even that for 310,000 yen. He still had a long way to his goal, but he would get there, slowly but surely.

"How many of these toys have you made? I'll bet your closet is stuffed with them."

"I told you not to make fun of people's hobbies."

Models were only models, after all. You couldn't board them. They only held his attention while he was building them. Over ten model ships—warships and sailboats—lay in his closet gathering dust.

"Want me to find you a girl?"

Here we go again, Koji thought. That was all Numata ever talked about. On two occasions Koji had said yes; let alone a hook-up, they'd ended in embarrassment. Since then he'd stopped taking Numata's offers seriously.

Koji stood up. He pulled a futon and blanket from the closet. He only had one futon, but he did have an extra blanket. That was enough bedding for two guys.

"I'm going to bed," he said. "Unlike you, I've got to go to work in the morning."

"I know."

Numata curled up in a corner. He tended the bar at a mega-pub in Ueno, so he didn't have to go to work until evening.

Koji and Numata had moved to Tokyo two years and seven months ago after graduating from the same technical high school in Nagano. Numata got a job at a small iron foundry, and Koji at a factory that made electrical machine parts. Since then, Numata had changed jobs twice, Koji once. Of the fifteen or so of them who'd come to Tokyo at the same time, only about half held their original jobs.

Koji felt no solidarity with the others from his hometown. He didn't get along with them, and that was that.

"You ought to come visit my bar. I'll introduce you to a nice co-ed. She's friends with my girlfriend."

Koji changed into pajamas and slid into the futon. The chatter and music from his neighbor's radio mingled with Numata's empty blather.

He closed his eyes and pretended to sleep. The futon was warming up. He felt like he could touch Makiko if he reached out. He could recall every detail, the smell of her hair, the softness of her skin against his. He and Makiko had spent a few hours like that on a hotel bed after sunset.

Numata's women weren't real. They evaporated when you embraced them. They weren't like Makiko. He could make love to her, talk to her, gaze at her.

Koji wanted Numata to meet Makiko but somehow knew that she wouldn't agree to it. Numata continued talking, and Koji fell into a comfortable sleep.

When he woke up, the light was still on. He rubbed his eyes, fumbled under his pillow for his watch, and checked the time. 5:35 a.m. It was absurdly early to get up and still quiet outside.

The room was filled with a white fog. He raised his head, looked around, and saw Numata leaning against a beam, smoking. The ashtray was full.

"Didn't you get any sleep?"

"Not really."

Koji rolled over and lay on his stomach. "You were in them all night? In your suit and tie?"

"I don't feel right unless I'm dressed properly."

"Weirdo. I need a cigarette."

Numata threw the pack of Hi Lites, Koji's own.

Koji couldn't but glance at the sink. The whiskey looked safe.

"Did I tell you about Setsuko?" Numata began, cracking his

knuckles.

Koji was in no mood to talk about women this early in the morning. He blew smoke onto the worn and bristly tatami mat. A white mass lingered over the surface, then faded and disappeared.

"Let me tell you about Setsuko."

"Shut up. I want to go back to sleep. Do you know what time it is?"

Smoke was rising from the ashtray. Some filters were smoldering. It was the kind of smoke that stung your eyes and nose.

Koji crawled out of the futon, filled a cup with water, and poured it into the ashtray. He glanced at the corner of the room and felt the blood rush to his head.

"What the fuck did you do?"

"It's just a toy, but it isn't easy to make."

The *Eagle* was smeared in glue. A replica of an eagle was perched atop the mast. It was meant to be on the prow.

"I told you not to touch it."

"What're you so mad about? You were just going to put it in the closet anyway."

Koji grabbed the *Eagle* and threw it at Numata.

"What the fuck?"

Numata stood up, his voice trembling. He was pretty timid for a guy who acted so tough.

Koji punched him, three times, in the face. Numata's back slammed against the wall and he slid to the floor.

The guy had been on the basketball team in high school. He wasn't weak. If he'd put up even a little resistance, he wouldn't be squatting there with blood gushing out of his nose. The blood stained his white shirt and gray suit, but he didn't even try to wipe it off.

"Get out. And don't ever come back."

"Koji, I…" Numata's voice was feeble.

Koji grabbed his lapels, pulled him to his feet, and shoved him to the door.

"What's going on?" asked a voice from the apartment next door.

"Just getting rid of a rat."

Numata turned around once on his way out. His nose was still bleeding.

The door shut. Koji picked up the fragments of the *Eagle* and threw them in the paper bag he used as a trash can. He got into his futon to go back to sleep.

2

Nakayama, the warehouse caretaker, dragged his bad leg as he approached Koji.

Koji and his work buddy Yonekura had just lifted a washing machine onto the loading platform. Only two TV sets were left.

When Koji jumped down from the platform, Nakayama placed a hand on his shoulder and told him, "You had visitors. Must have been around ten o'clock. Police detectives. Had I.D. and everything."

Koji delivered and installed domestic electrical appliances. His employer's store was in Akihabara, but the merchandise was transported from this warehouse.

"I told them you'd be back by noon," Nakayama added. "They showed up again before one and hung around for ten minutes or so."

Koji had only returned to the warehouse after two. He'd had lunch and napped for an hour on the grounds of a temple on the way back.

"They came twice?"

"What the hell did you do?" Yonekura cut in. He clicked his tongue when Nakayama impatiently brushed him off.

"So what did they want?"

"Just asked if you were around. Those guys don't talk much. Even about stuff it's okay to talk about."

Nakayama lightly stroked his hair. It was almost completely white. Rumor had it that he'd done time. He usually seemed to be ashamed of it, but after a drink or two he'd strip himself to the waist and start shouting how his was a body that had seen the inside. Not that he had a dragon tattoo on his back—all he displayed was sagging flesh and badly wrinkled skin.

"It can't be anything worth getting worried about. I haven't done anything wrong."

"I know that," Nakayama said, bringing his face closer to Koji's. "But that bastard Hatta had just come back and was asking all sorts of questions. Watch out that he doesn't start spreading rumors about you."

"Got it."

Hatta did the wiring in newly constructed buildings. Their company sold electrical appliances, but various employees did a variety of jobs. The Akihabara store sold household appliances on the first and second floors and lighting on the third. The fourth floor served as an interior showroom and as office space. The company not only sold electrical appliances but also provided wiring and repair services.

"When did Hatta say he would be back?"

"Dunno. Probably gone to do the ready-builts in Matsudo. Seems there are almost fifty new houses out there."

Koji took the TV sets to the loading platform. He checked them against the delivery slips, making sure the merchandise was lined up in order of drop-off.

"What should I do if the detectives come back?" Nakayama asked.

"Nothing."

"I see."

Nakayama suddenly seemed to lose interest. He returned to his seat by the entrance.

Koji called to Yonekura. No answer. He'd probably gone to the men's room.

His current job wasn't as easy as he'd hoped. Working on the assembly line at the electrical machinery parts factory had been monotonous but physically undemanding. He'd switched to this job because it paid better. But now he was renting his own place instead of living in a company dorm with meals included, so in the end it was the same.

He didn't regret it. After a year in Tokyo, it was normal to feel that there must be something better out there. He wasn't the type to nurse discontentment, thumb in mouth, eyes glued to the wall.

He was on call to deliver anywhere in the Tokyo metropolitan area. He could be making one to Yokohama today and Chiba tomorrow. Some days he even went to both Yokohama and Chiba. In just over a year he'd learned the roads as well as a taxi driver.

He wasn't too irked by the irregular hours and physical stress, partly because Seta, the manager in charge of deliveries, distributed the workload fairly among the four trucks. Nobody was getting off easy, and that was enough.

Yonekura had been Koji's partner over the past year. Aside from the fact that he talked—and complained—a lot, he wasn't a bad guy. He liked karaoke and dragged Koji to go singing once a week.

Their afternoon deliveries were for a residential area near central Tokyo. They had to deliver two washing machines, two TV sets, a microwave, and one air conditioner. The addresses were near one another so the truck bed quickly emptied out.

A little past four, they took a break in a coffee shop.

"It's a load of shit," Yonekura complained. "I've been with the company for a year now."

He was stirring three lumps of sugar into his coffee. His horselike face looked even longer when he grumbled about the company. Yonekura didn't have a driver's license. This meant he always had "assistant" in his title; his salary was slightly less than Koji's.

"It's obvious how they try to get people on the cheap. I only agreed to work for them because they promised to pay for driving lessons."

Yonekura was deluded to think the company would pay for him to get a license. All they had to do was run an ad in the paper and applicants with licenses would come flocking.

Koji sipped his black coffee and read the paper. He usually read the sports tabloid, but another customer had it, so he'd settled for the freshly delivered evening edition of a major daily. There were hardly any articles he wanted to read. Politics and the economy meant little to him. All he did was glance at the traffic accident reports.

"I'm gonna have a talk with Seta," Yonekura concluded. "No way I'm gonna be an assistant forever."

Once Yonekura got something off his chest, he was satisfied. Making an effort to get a license himself seemed to be beyond him.

The word "robbery" caught Koji's attention. He only noticed it because it was next to the word "mega-pub." The night before, Lucky, in Ueno, was robbed at closing time. The manager was assaulted and 1.2 million yen in sales stolen. Lucky was the bar where Numata worked.

Koji grunted and reached for his coffee cup. He didn't realize it was empty until he brought it to his lips.

He wondered if Numata had tried to fight off the robber. Was that why his clothes had been muddy? But the article said there had been no witnesses. Apparently the manager had been struck on the head with a blunt instrument and was in critical condition.

It was hard to believe that Numata had anything to do with the crime. But the detectives' visit gave Koji pause.

Yonekura puffed out cigarette smoke. He didn't seem to care if Koji was listening to his rambling or not.

Koji folded the paper. Whatever, he thought. Numata was no longer his concern. If he came by again he wouldn't let him in.

He drank some water and stood up.

Back at the warehouse, he saw a glum Nakayama still occupying his usual seat. It was past seven. Normally Nakayama finished at six and went home to his room in another wing of the warehouse. Though he was supposed to be the live-in caretaker, he got so drunk at night he became useless. It was Seta who took and filed the delivery slips—stamped by customers, showing proof of receipt—and locked up the warehouse.

"What's up? Isn't it time for your evening drink?" Koji asked.

"M Electric is sending a truck over. The bastards are an hour late."

The M Electric truck came several times a month to collect old appliances. Koji and Yonekura unloaded and piled against the warehouse wall the old washing machines and TV sets that customers had given them in exchange for the new ones.

"A chill's the worst thing for your waist," Nakayama grumbled. "My neuralgia acts up and I get numb to the tips of my toes." His eyes looked bleary. He got closer to Koji and gave the pile of appliances a kick.

"Can you predict the weather?"

"Eh?"

"They say people with neuralgia can predict the weather. Pain means rain or maybe a typhoon."

"Never heard that before." Nakayama seemed to be giving it

serious consideration.

Yonekura emerged from the warehouse. He had changed out of his delivery uniform and now wore a safari jacket. "How about a drink?" he suggested.

"Sounds good." Koji stuck his hand into his trouser pocket and rummaged for cash. He could only feel coins, which meant he could only afford one drink. Four days until payday. "Can you treat me?"

"You earn more than I do."

"I send money to my mother. Factor that in, and you actually earn more." For Koji, one drink was worse than none.

Yonekura clicked his tongue and left. Koji stuck his mouth beneath a tap used for washing vehicles, drank, then washed his hands and face.

Koji couldn't send money to his mother even if he wanted to. She'd died when he was a sophomore in high school. She'd complained of a headache, collapsed in the kitchen, stayed in a coma for two days, then died. It had happened all too quickly.

You're not old enough to die! his father had sobbed. But not Koji. He only felt like crying days, no, months later. His mother had been fifty. Yet she'd been looking much older than that since about a year before her death.

Koji's father and older brother lived in Nagano. His brother was married with three children. He'd taken over the family business as a plasterer. He was a lout who always made an excuse to beat up Koji since they were little. In middle and high school, Koji played soccer and worked out regularly. By that time he was an even match for his brother.

When Koji graduated from technical high and was about to leave for Tokyo, his brother tossed him an old suit as a gift. The inside pocket contained an envelope of cash. When Koji pointed that out, his brother shook his head, denying any knowledge. He was being shy.

His father, on the other hand, offered neither money nor a word. He only gave Koji a faraway look and a series of little nods. He'd drifted away from work since his wife's death. Koji could clearly see the years taking their toll.

Lights drew closer. He heard Nakayama bellow. It looked like the truck was here. Koji used his uniform to wipe his hands and face and threw on a light-green jacket.

3

Yonekura returned looking pale. Since setting off on the delivery round this morning, they'd stopped the truck four times. Each time, Yonekura would go to the roadside and vomit. His condition didn't seem to be improving at all.

"What the hell did you eat?"

"It's just a hangover."

Doesn't look like it, Koji thought. Just looking at him made Koji feel sick. "Let's finish up here and get back."

Yonekura didn't answer. He sat motionless in the passenger seat, his face still pale and beads of sweat on his brow.

It was eleven. Quitting work before noon meant forfeiting a day's pay, while leaving in the afternoon at least got you thirty percent. Koji knew Yonekura had that thirty percent in mind.

"How can we get any work done if you're carsick all the time?"

Yonekura fared better out of the truck, working. Once back in, he went pale again. The process kept repeating itself.

"Look, how about we just say we left after one? I'll make sure Nakayama's on board."

"Uh huh," Yonekura managed a weak answer.

Koji knew Nakayama was too much of a blabbermouth to rely on. But he couldn't say otherwise to Yonekura. "Take tomorrow off, too. It's Saturday, anyway. You can stay in bed for three days."

Koji had never gotten so drunk that it affected the next day's work. He could hold his drink well. He was in good health, too, never even catching a cold since coming to Tokyo. His only condition to speak of was the occasional aching molar.

Nakayama was napping in his chair, which he'd set in front of the warehouse. The area got a lot of sun in the morning. Perhaps it was good for his neuralgia.

"Goodness, that was quick." The old man rubbed his eyes and

18

stood up. There was yellow mucus between his brows.

"He had to call it a day. He can't stop throwing up, and I can't watch him. Can you tell Seta we got back around two?"

"It's because he drank too much."

Yonekura changed into his own clothes and left, hunched over.

"Is he gonna be okay?" Nakayama asked.

"I can't quit early too just to take him home. He'll take a taxi or something."

"Young men these days don't have any backbone." The old man again sank into his sun-drenched seat. It was almost noon, and the shadow of the warehouse eave had come up right behind him.

Koji transported the used appliances to the junkyard, then flipped through his delivery slips to check what else needed to be done.

The deliveries were mostly TV sets, plus a few washing machines and microwaves. He could manage on his own as long as there weren't any air-conditioning units or large refrigerators.

"You're having lunch, aren't you?" Koji asked after throwing the delivery slips onto the driver's seat.

"If I feel like it."

"Let's have lunch together. I brought two Cups o' Noodles."

"Oh?"

Nakayama promptly got up to boil water. One of the trucks returned, but it didn't belong to delivery staff. It was Hatta from the construction team.

"Ran out of cable," he said. Bringing out a reel from the warehouse, he asked, "Where's Yonekura?"

"Probably in the men's room. Said his stomach hurt," Koji lied.

"So what kind of funny business are you up to?"

"What do you mean?"

"The police were here for you."

"I haven't seen them yet, so I wouldn't know."

"Right."

Hatta studied Koji with a viscous gaze, from behind drooping eyelids. The handyman's face was misshapen, and his nose squashed. He had been a boxer, but his eyes lacked any sparkle, and his warped face looked as sodden as a trashed piece of garment. He was still full of himself and enjoyed spreading malicious gossip.

"Careful you don't stain the company's reputation," he said.

"Are you implying I did something?"

"Fine if you haven't, but you worry me. All of you guys do."

Koji stifled the urge to tell him to mind his own business. Assholes just had to be ignored.

Nakayama came over with the kettle.

Koji and Nakayama gobbled down their Cups o' Noodles. I'll make do with these until Monday, Koji thought. He'd eat plenty of meat once he got paid.

"Hey, Mizui, who do you think Seta will ask to go drinking with him next payday?"

"Dunno," Koji replied. "Last month it was me and Yonekura."

Seta, the delivery manager, made a habit of taking a couple of subordinates out drinking every payday. Nakayama had never been asked, and he was beginning to resent it.

"The place is a real hole," Koji assuaged. "Only three to four thousand yen for three guys to eat and drink their fill? I feel ill just thinking about what they're serving us."

"That doesn't mean anything. When I drank in Asakusa in the old days, lots of places would serve beer at half the going price."

"Where's the money in that?"

"In all of it. They recycled the beer other customers left in their mugs."

Seta was very worried about what his subordinates thought of him. *We all depend on you*—he invited them out hoping to hear such remarks. An honest, timid geezer who was hardly accommodating was not much fun to drink with.

"What do you guys do for women? Buy one on payday?" Nakayama asked.

"Something like that."

"I went to a soapland. That bastard Hatta wanted me to go with him. Said it was an early celebration."

"Of what?"

"He said he was going to be chief of the construction team. You'd think he'd have treated me in that case, but he just didn't want to go alone."

"Chief? Him?"

"He thinks he's hot stuff because the president pays him a lot of attention."

Nakayama was probably bullshitting about having been to a soapland. More likely, he'd balked at hearing the price.

"Hatta was spouting funny stuff this morning. He was telling Seta that detectives were here because you robbed someone."

"He's at it again?"

"Well, it's true about the detectives, so you better report to Seta yourself."

"What a bastard. I should've told him off just now."

"Just don't get into a real brawl with him."

"I know."

Rumor had it that Hatta had been ranked. He himself claimed he'd been on the verge of making headline matches. The president of the company had been his patron, which explained Hatta's attitude. Apparently, he'd quit because of a detached retina.

"Have you ever seen him box?"

"Three years ago. On TV."

"Was it the main event?"

"No, just an opener. Still, he knocked the other guy flat. Really laid into him and then knocked him out with an uppercut and hook."

Hatta's build and beat-up face made it clear he'd been a "fighter." These days he was heavy enough to fight welterweight, but he'd been a featherweight.

Nakayama rubbed his thighs. He described the pain from his neuralgia as a thick wire running from his hips to his feet that periodically budged. All Nakayama needed to say was *the wire*... for everyone to change the subject. No one wanted to hear yet again how little sun he got in his room in the annex.

A car approached. Koji stood drinking the green tea Nakayama had brought.

The car stopped in front of the warehouse. A white Toyota Crown.

Two men got out. Nakayama swiftly left his chair as if he'd completely forgotten about his neuralgia. He bowed several times.

"Mizui, these are the gentlemen."

The balding, older one smiled. The slender, young one had a harsh glint in his eye.

"They're the ones who came to see you yesterday."

It didn't sink into Koji that they were detectives until the older man showed his I.D.

"You're Koji Mizui?" the older detective asked. His tone was gentle but had an intimidating undercurrent.

Koji threw out the remaining tea onto the road and handed the teacup back to Nakayama. He replied, "What is it?"

"You know Hajime Numata, don't you?"

"I do."

"We arrested him three hours ago."

"What's he done?"

The detective didn't reply.

"When did you last see him?" the young one asked, voice bristling.

Koji held a cigarette and lit it with matches from a coffee shop. He'd never spoken to a detective before. "What did Numata do? They say there was a robbery at his pub. Something related to that?"

"You're very up to date, aren't you?"

"It was in the paper."

"I asked you when you last saw him." It was the young one again.

Koji ignored him. His cigarette was still long, but he dropped it and crushed it with his foot. Nakayama was lurking around, trying his best to catch everything, neuralgia totally forgotten.

"We arrested Numata right outside your apartment. We'd appreciate it if you could tell us when you last saw him."

"Yesterday. Yesterday morning." He found it easy to reply to the older one.

"So Numata came to see you?"

"In the middle of the night. I had no choice so I let him stay over."

"Did you notice anything about him? Something different from usual?"

"Yeah, his hair was cut short."

"His hair?"

Koji nodded. Nakayama came closer, but when the young detective glanced at him, he bobbed his head and turned around.

"So what did he do?" Koji asked.

"A certain something. You two were pretty close?"

"Not really. We're just from the same town. Anyway, we're not friends anymore."

"Really. Why?"

"We kind of had an argument. So I kicked him out that morning."

"An argument over what?"

"He just pissed me off. Maybe other people wouldn't think it was a big deal, but it pissed me off."

"Yet Numata showed up at your place again just three hours ago. Isn't that strange, given that you'd just had a fight?"

"Don't ask me. I had no intention of letting him in if he ever came back."

Koji lit another cigarette. The two detectives looked at each other. Beanpole still didn't smile.

"Well, we'd like to ask you a few more questions. Mind coming to the station with us?"

"Why do I have to go? I don't know anything."

"Numata has been to your place twice. We have a lot of things we need to verify."

Baldy was looking at Koji with a calm expression. But the more Koji looked at him, the more unpleasant those eyes seemed.

"I've got to get back to work. My partner went home early so I'm on my own. Why not here? I don't mind it taking some time if we do it here."

"We could have a word with your boss and get his permission. It'd be a great help if you could come over to the station."

Koji exhaled some smoke. What a fucking mess, he thought.

"Can't you see we're requesting you to come?"

Beanpole's oppressive tone grated on Koji's nerves. What had he done to deserve such treatment? He felt an urge to snap back.

"Mizui." It was Nakayama, who had come up behind the detectives somehow. "Go. We can manage here."

"Look, this has nothing to do with me. If I go now, I lose a day's wages."

"Can't be helped. This fellow who got into trouble is a friend of yours. It's your duty to go and tell them what you know. That's why these gentlemen are here to pick you up."

Maybe this was how the police operated. They liked to make a big thing out of it even when it was just a few questions they needed to ask. But it wouldn't have hurt for them to be a little more polite about it. Koji suddenly thought of the tax withholding entry on his pay slip. It was a figure he'd never paid attention to before.

"You should go," Nakayama said, right by Koji's ear. His voice sounded terribly loud.

"All right. Let me just move the truck off to the side. The others will be back soon and it'll be in the way."

The warehouse was partitioned in two. The front was a garage, while the back was for merchandise.

Koji climbed into his truck and started the engine. The white Toyota Crown was in the way, but the detectives stood still.

Clicking his tongue, he turned the wheel sharply. Beanpole was standing near the Toyota Crown and saying something into his radio microphone. Nakayama directed the truck with practiced gestures as it reversed.

4

The building was not as gloomy as Koji had imagined. In fact, it was a modern one that could be mistaken for a ward office if not for the cops in uniform.

He was led upstairs to the second floor and through a large office marked "Criminal Investigation Section" to a small, bleak room.

Sturdy iron bars blocked the small window. Bright light shone in and illuminated the faded old wooden table.

"Try to recall where you were between 11 p.m. and 1 a.m. on the night of the sixteenth," Baldy demanded. Once seated on the other side of the table, his attitude had suddenly changed, the easy manner gone.

Beanpole sat at another table, ballpoint pen in hand.

Koji tensed up as he sensed the hostility in the air. He lit a cigarette. This was indeed an interrogation. Anger began to well up in him.

He didn't attempt a response. Before any words came to mind, his anger began to mix with anxiety. He knew he had to clarify his situation. There would be plenty of time for complaints later.

The sixteenth. That was the night he'd seen Makiko. He'd phoned her at 7:30 p.m. and gone to the coffee shop at eight.

She arrived fifteen minutes late. They talked for a bit, had dinner at a Taiwanese restaurant, and went to a hotel. They left just after 1 a.m., saying bye in front of the hotel. He hailed a cab and went home, and Numata was sleeping at the bottom of the stairs.

He remembered it all clearly.

"You sure about all this?" Beanpole asked as he took notes. "What's Makiko Endo's address?"

"I only know her phone number. We have an agreement that I don't call her before 7 p.m."

"Why?"

"Seems she rents a place with a friend. The friend leaves at seven—as in, she works at night."

"You mean she doesn't want this friend to know about you?" asked Baldy, smiling. It was an unpleasant smile. "She seems very cautious. Is her friend a woman? Or could it be a guy? In which case no wonder she keeps you a secret."

"It's a woman. An older woman who's nagging."

"You know her?"

"That's what Makiko told me."

"Have you known Makiko Endo for long?"

"About three months, I guess. We met during the summer."

"How many times have you seen her so far?"

"None of your business." Four times. Koji had only seen her four times in three months.

"Never mind. Do you always meet in Shibuya?"

Koji nodded.

"So you meet when and how it suits her."

Beanpole stood up. He came up beside Koji and read him the

notes. He went over the names of the coffee shop and the hotel, making sure there was no mistake.

Beanpole left. Koji let out a puff of breath.

"Aren't you going to ask anything about Numata?"

"We'll get to that. After all, you're here because of him."

"But you checked my alibi."

"Don't worry about that. We look into everyone's alibi. We arrested Numata in front of your apartment. That's why we're checking your alibi extra carefully." Baldy laughed aloud, throwing back his head.

Koji was thirsty. His tongue was plastered to the roof of his mouth.

"Just what did Numata do?"

"I thought you knew."

"Was it robbery?"

Koji put a cigarette in his mouth. He didn't believe it; surely Numata, like himself, was the victim of some mistake. Numata was the kind of guy who didn't try to strike back even when he was beaten up and his suit, second only in value to his life, had been ruined by his bleeding nose.

"You said you had an argument with Numata."

"Yeah. It happens a lot."

"You seemed pretty riled up about it."

Koji stubbed out his cigarette. Now his throat was even drier. He remembered seeing cigarette and soda vending machines in the second-floor corridor.

He tried to get up, but Baldy stopped him.

"I just want to get a Coke. I'm really thirsty."

"I'll pour you some tea."

"I want a Coke."

He still had three 100-yen coins in his pocket. Enough to buy cigarettes, too.

"You'll have to do with green tea."

Baldy stuck his head out of the room and said something. A young man soon appeared with a plastic teacup.

Koji had resolved not to drink it, but found himself reaching for it. Tepid, with only a hint of color. Still, it soothed his parched throat.

Baldy resumed his questions. Where in Nagano was he born?

Family? What did his father and elder brother do? First job in Tokyo? Friends in Tokyo? Girlfriends? The guarantor when he got his job? All questions of that nature.

He didn't ask a thing about Numata.

They were investigating Koji, it now seemed clear.

"What's going on here? Are you accusing me of being the robber?" he asked.

"You're just a witness."

Baldy laughed again. He sure laughed a lot for a detective. It was getting on Koji's nerves more than if he had been scowling.

The questions continued. Koji didn't answer. He turned to one side and pursed his lips.

"Ueda was where Yukimura Sanada lived. The samurai," Baldy suddenly changed the subject.

Caught off guard, Koji involuntarily nodded.

"Is the 'ko' in Koji the 'yuki' in Yukimura? It's the same character."

That was right, but Koji didn't feel like nodding.

When his father told him the origin of his name, even though Koji was only a child, he felt less embarrassed than sad. To this day he considered it a simple-minded way of choosing a name and never discussed it with anyone.

"So is it true that when Osaka Castle fell," asked Baldy, "Yukimura escaped to Satsuma with Hideyori?"

"How the hell should I know?"

Koji was intent on remaining silent. He bit down on his lips. Baldy laughed and continued with his questions.

An hour passed.

Exhausted, Koji cast a dazed glance at the floor. The ray of light passing through the small window onto the table had glided to the room's corner. He'd miss the afternoon shift too. What was Beanpole up to? Why was it taking him so long to check the alibi?

He was out of cigarettes. When he asked if he could go buy some, Baldy offered his own Cherry brand. Koji wasn't interested.

The clock arm passed four. The sun vanished into the building's shadow and the room was dim.

Baldy was called out. There were low voices outside the room.

When he returned, Beanpole was with him. Koji felt relieved and looked up at the tall man. A piece of paper fluttered in front of him.

"A warrant for your arrest," Beanpole said, putting his hand on Koji's shoulder.

All Koji caught was his name, Koji Mizui, written with a black ballpoint pen.

"What's going on?" he asked.

Baldy's reply sounded distant. "From here on out, you don't have to say anything that might be held against you."

Koji rose to his feet. "I want an explanation. What's going on?" The chair fell backwards and banged on the floor. That, too, sounded distant. Beanpole grabbed Koji by the arm, and his grip was strong. Koji shook his arm.

"Calm down."

"You've gotta be kidding. Why are you arresting me?"

"You're suspected of being Hajime Numata's accomplice. Watch your words. The victim is still in critical condition."

"Don't mess with me. You think I'm going to fall for this?"

"Just sit down, Mizui."

Beanpole put the chair back on its feet and gave Koji's shoulder a push.

It had to be some terrible mistake. He just needed to stay calm. He reached out for one of Baldy's Cherry cigarettes on the table. Baldy laughed. No matches.

"Ask Makiko. If you couldn't get her, try again after seven." He looked for matches. Baldy was fondling them on his palm. Koji couldn't ask for them and threw the cigarette back on the table. "If you do your investigation properly, I'll be cleared."

Beanpole's words sounded oddly spaced out. "Mizui, there was no such woman. Makiko Endo doesn't exist."

"What?"

"The number you gave us was for an apartment in Yoyogi Hachiman. The resident is a woman who's almost forty."

"Forty? There's another one. There should be two of them living there."

"Yeah, there were two. The other is her daughter. A sixteen-year-old high school girl."

"That's a lie. I've called her at that number and spoken to her several times."

"Yet, she wasn't there. We called them, and we also went to meet the mother and daughter. They've never heard of a Makiko Endo."

"Let me call her. Just let me make the call!"

"It's no use. We checked out the coffee shop, the Taiwanese restaurant, and the hotel. They exist, but nobody remembers you."

Koji began to feel dizzy. Were they pulling his chain? Maybe that was what they were up to so they could have a laugh about it afterwards.

He pulled out his notebook from his jacket pocket. No, he hadn't given them the wrong number. He certainly didn't know anything about an apartment in Yoyogi Hachiman. It made no sense that the number would connect to such a place.

"While you're at it, empty your pockets," Baldy said, still playing with the matches.

"Why?"

"Because that's what you do when you get arrested. Is there something you don't want us to see?"

"Arrested. Give me a break."

"You really don't get it, huh? We showed you the warrant. You want me to handcuff you?"

Yes, his name had been on the warrant: Koji Mizui.

Koji had his hands in his pockets. He was in a stupor.

On the table lay his notebook, a driver's license, the key to his apartment, a ballpoint pen, a supermarket receipt, and three 100-yen coins. He wasn't aware of having pulled them out.

"Call her again, please. She's about twenty-four or -five, on the small side. She's got long hair and wears pearl-pink nail polish. I can give you a detailed description of her face."

"Look, there isn't any woman called Makiko Endo. Don't give us any more trouble."

When the cigarette was offered, Koji's hand automatically reached out to take it. A match flame flickered over Baldy's palm.

Koji inhaled deeply, and dizziness overwhelmed him. He thought for a moment that he had fainted, but he was sitting upright in the chair.

Makiko Endo didn't exist? That was ludicrous. Impossible. Makiko wasn't like one of Numata's women. If you reached out, you could touch her. She didn't vanish when you embraced her.

No, these guys were putting him on. That, or they were trying to lure him into a trap. They were trying to set him up as the culprit. "You won't trick me," he said.

"Give it up, Mizui." Baldy's kind tone made Koji want to shove a shoe into his mouth. "Numata's confessed. You were waiting at the back entrance of Lucky. They handed you the dough and you ferried it."

"That's a load of shit. There's no way Numata would've said that. You're trying to set me up."

"We've got more than circumstantial evidence—we found this in your apartment!" Beanpole yelled.

A big plastic bag landed on the table with a thump. In it were Numata's duffel bag and a double-size bottle of Suntory Red that held something other than whiskey.

Numata must have returned to his apartment to retrieve his bag. Koji stood up and opened it. All he could find inside were muddy clothes.

"Three hundred thousand yen, huh? Since you guys stole 1.2 million that's not much of a share. That's why you and Numata argued."

"You're talking about my savings. And it's not 300,000 yen—it's 310,000 yen. Look at the label on the bottle: six full tallies and one bar. Why are you acting like thieves when you're cops?"

Koji didn't bother to deposit his money in a bank. He saved his cash in an empty bottle because he was sure he wouldn't touch it. It was for buying his boat.

"Fine. Just take your time remembering what you did on the night of the sixteenth." With that, Baldy stood up and left the room.

Koji was now alone with Beanpole, who kept putting the cap of his ballpoint pen in his mouth then putting it back on the pen. He didn't say a word.

Koji fell silent, too. His mind was in disarray; he couldn't find a word to say.

Suddenly the door burst open and a man walked in.

"Sir," Beanpole said, turning around. The man lightly kicked his chair. Beanpole stood up, and the man waved him away.

"Name's Kuroki. I'm the one who nabbed Numata. I was waiting in front of your apartment when he nonchalantly came by. Guess you were the only person in Tokyo he could count on." Kuroki wasn't looking at Koji, but out of the window. It was getting dark.

Koji was feeling thirsty again. He longed for a cold beer. Water with ice cubes would do, too. Then he'd leave this place. His mind was still a blur; he felt as if he could just stand up, bid farewell, and walk out the door.

Kuroki didn't speak. He wasn't interrogating Koji, nor did he seem to be killing time. He simply sat.

Koji looked at his watch—or rather, tried to. It had been confiscated along with the contents of his pockets. He didn't even remember it being unfastened.

Kuroki stood up. He suddenly grabbed Koji by the hair.

The man was strong. The ceiling, then Kuroki's face, came into Koji's view. It loomed in over his, and their eyes met. Koji didn't flinch. He felt as if some force were at work to keep their eyes locked together.

"Did you move the money? Are you really the one who ferried the money?"

No, Koji protested. The word didn't come out.

His head was released. He saw Kuroki's back, which in a moment disappeared out the door.

He was not alone for long. Beanpole came in.

"Stand up, Mizui," he commanded in a low voice.

5

The humiliation and frustration was making him feel like he was peering into complete darkness. Blood spurted from his fist when he punched the floor. He licked it. A salty taste.

The cell was no different from an animal cage. It was in a basement with no light coming in from the outside.

Had Numata really made such a confession? Or rather, had he really committed robbery?

Besides being from the same hometown, they were hardly close. They didn't hate each other, either. Since high school it had been that way.

Maybe he wanted revenge for his ruined suit. Koji remembered how angry he had felt when Numata had ruined his boat. Maybe Numata valued that suit as much as he valued that boat. No, probably more—when he finished a boat he just shoved it into the closet. But that suit constantly covered Numata like a second skin.

But it was outrageous that he'd been arrested, whatever Numata had said.

Makiko?

In the past three months he'd phoned Makiko at least ten times. Only a few times had nobody been home. All the other times, Makiko had answered. When she couldn't come out to see him, they talked about nothing until the public phone had gobbled all of his coins. That was why he always made sure to bring lots of 10-yen coins when he called.

Keep your cool, Koji told himself, licking again the blood from his fist. It was already dry and tasted strange, like iron.

He heard people muttering in stops and starts. He realized for the first time that there were two other men in the same cell.

"So what did you do?" asked a young man in a black leather jacket, crawling up to him.

A uniformed guard was sitting in a chair on the other side of the iron bars. His gaze was hidden by the brim of his hat. Koji looked down at the straw mat on the concrete floor.

"Hey, you crying?"

Koji was wiping his eyes with his jacket sleeve. They were not tears of sorrow.

It suddenly occurred to him that Numata had also been arrested and that he should be in the same underground jail.

"Numata!" Koji shouted, standing up. He sensed people move in the adjacent cells. "Numata! Can you hear me?"

"Quiet," the guard said, rushing over.

"Answer me, Numata. You know my voice. Answer me."

"Hajime Numata isn't here," the guard said. "He was sent to the Public Prosecutor's Office at 3 p.m." He spoke gently as if to calm Koji down.

Koji looked at his face. The hair peeping out of his hat was gray. The guard lightly pressed a white-gloved hand on Koji's, which clutched an iron bar.

"Try to be quiet. You'll be better off that way."

Koji released the iron bars. He heard talking from the cell next door.

"Quiet," said the guard, now from his chair.

The voices stopped.

Koji bundled himself into the two blankets he'd been given and lay on the mat. The cell was not cramped. It was big enough for several people.

He was still worked up, like something hot was racing through his body. But at least his thoughts were starting to take on some coherence. Right now, there was nothing he could do except wait. But for what?

He couldn't fall asleep. He recalled the time when he first met Makiko.

It had been summer. Makiko was wearing a short-sleeved, pale-green dress and sitting alone on a bench at an *oden* stew stall. At first Koji took her for a prostitute; he knew some of them found customers this way.

He'd sat down beside her. Any thought that she may have been a pro vanished. Her makeup was on the heavy side, but her clothing was plain and she didn't have that dissolute air. She didn't even bother to look at him.

"Do you want to go dancing?" was all he said. He couldn't really dance and didn't even like it. She glanced at him. She didn't seem irritated, but he felt she was ignoring him. The eyes she'd turned to him had been moist, lonely.

What was a girl like her doing alone in a stall? Koji was still wondering when he started to get up. He wasn't the sort of guy who found it easy to strike up conversations with girls.

"Would it be cooler by the sea?" she asked suddenly.

Koji lowered himself back onto the bench. He gave a little nod. So she's a prostitute after all, he thought.

But she actually hailed a taxi. They went to the harbor, where she enjoyed a pleasant walk along the wharf. "I love the smell of the sea," she said and laughed. It was a light, singsong laugh. Koji had never met a girl who laughed like that. He could have listened to that laughter forever.

But when he looked at her face a little while later, she was crying. This woman, he thought, nursed something that nobody should touch. His feelings seemed to sway as if he were on a swing.

He couldn't find anything to talk about. They simply walked side by side along the wharf. Koji had to summon up every ounce of his courage to ask for her phone number when they parted.

When he called, he wasn't sure Makiko would pick up on the other end.

"Oh, it's you." It was certainly her voice. She agreed to see him again.

He asked her to go into a hotel with him. More like a prayer than a gamble. She gazed at him, expressionless. He silently went in ahead of her.

Though he didn't know much about women, he didn't think she was particularly experienced. Her moans were small and her movements modest.

As they lay in bed, Koji asked several times if they could see each other again.

Other than her phone number, Koji knew next to nothing about Makiko. When they were together they simply looked at each other. Talk wasn't necessary. Like him, she wasn't much of a conversationalist. She never spoke about herself and never tried to learn more about Koji.

Koji turned over in the cell and felt the hard floor against his shoulders.

He shut his eyes tight. Why couldn't they find her? The question was one he'd asked himself again and again. When he called that number, he could count on hearing her subdued voice. Had Beanpole really even tried?

His head was near bursting. He sat up. He wanted to scream, *Let me dial that number myself!*

He tried to think of something else.

I want to gaze at the sea.

The sea. He saw it for the first time in his third year of middle school, during summer vacation, when he was fifteen. He still remembered that first glimpse. His mother was still alive then, and she'd given him three thousand yen in spending money the night before his trip to the seaside.

It didn't seem that wide or vast. It was both like and entirely unlike what he'd pictured. Something coursed through his body that resembled what he felt when he made love to a woman for the first time. There was a difference, though. He couldn't explain it, but women and the sea were definitely not the same.

He had planned to go to the sea the following year, too, but his mother died. He hadn't had the chance to ask her if she'd ever been in view of the sea. A woman born and bred in Nagano, perhaps she hadn't been.

Koji tried to turn his mind to the boat, but Makiko's and Numata's faces soon intruded. He turned over and shut his eyes even tighter.

Somewhere, someone was snoring lightly. It was the middle of the night. He couldn't tell the exact time.

Morning came.

He was taken to the same room as the day before.

It was Baldy who came in. He went on in just the same way, a man on the cusp of old age, talkative and prone to laughter.

"Numata quickly spilled the beans, but we can't find the money. Except, of course, your 310,000 yen."

That's my money, Koji wanted to protest, but checked himself. He wasn't going to talk. Whatever happened now, he would not utter a word.

Baldy offered a cigarette, but Koji didn't take it.

The room faced west. The window looked out into the building's shadow, but farther away was bright light. It looked to be a sunny Saturday.

Baldy continued questioning him. He never seemed to tire. "You can clam up for as long as you want, I don't care. I ask questions because it's my job. I get paid even if we just sit here glaring at each other. You're the one who's going to suffer for it."

Koji was prepared to glare at him for hours, days. His job, it was not. Something more important was at stake.

What was he supposed to talk about anyway?

The time there didn't feel long to him. He could have sat there forever. He heard shouting in the adjacent room. His was apparently not the only interrogation room. He heard weeping, too.

It was after Koji had eaten his lunch of bread and milk that the detective named Kuroki appeared.

He was a man of markedly few words. For an hour, as they sat facing each other, he didn't utter any. At one point, he simply clipped and filed his nails.

He was a prolific smoker, however. A heap of cigarette butts lay in the ashtray. Koji sometimes filled his lungs with the smoke Kuroki had exhaled. It didn't taste of anything.

"He's weak, that Numata," Kuroki finally said.

Koji felt oddly relieved. There was something about Kuroki that was different from Baldy and Beanpole, and it had made Koji uneasy. Kuroki's face and build were perfectly ordinary; far from sharp, his eyes gleamed feebly and seemed almost to swim. When such a man sat saying nothing, clipping his nails, it was creepy.

"Have you ever heard Numata mention a Matsuda?"

Koji remained silent. The detective had spoken in a way that didn't demand a response. Nor did he repeat his question.

"I heard you beat Numata up. But that didn't irk him as much as how his suit got ruined. He said he still owed monthly payments on it."

Kuroki stood up and stretched. He clicked his tongue and removed his shoes and socks. He was now clipping his toenails. The snapping sounded oddly hollow as it reverberated in the room.

A piece flew onto the table. Koji swept it away with his hand. Only then did Kuroki's eyes, glancing up at him, sharpen.

"See, I don't buy it that Numata did this himself. I think the most he's capable of is theft. He doesn't have the nerve for more." Another piece of toenail flew onto the table. Koji left it. "You, on the other hand, seem to have some nerve. So why have Numata assault the guy? Why wait outside?" Still not expecting any reply, Kuroki remained hunched over trimming his toenails. It was like he was talking to himself.

Beanpole came in. When Kuroki looked up at him, he shook his head no. He stood waiting until Kuroki had put his shoes and socks back on.

"Don't be hoping to get lessons on how to conduct an investigation," Kuroki said, tugging at Beanpole's sky-blue tie. Beanpole looked displeased. "What I asked for—was it such a hassle?"

"No, sir."

Beanpole looked like a scolded child. Koji yawned. Kuroki's Short Peace cigarettes and matches lay on the table. The matches were from a pachinko parlor in Kanda.

"I thought I told you to stake out at night as well."

"But Pops said—"

"Mr. Yabe has his way, I have mine. If you don't like my way, you should have said so from the start."

"I'll go again tonight."

"And tomorrow. And if you find nothing tomorrow, the night after that, too. I asked you to grab that tail 'cause I think there's a tail to be grabbed."

"You're such a slave driver."

With that, Beanpole exited.

Kuroki didn't clip his toenails anymore. It occurred to Koji that the left foot wasn't done yet.

A ray of sun poked through the window and onto the old, worn-down table. It was just like when Koji had come in the day before. He cast a vacant look at his hands, which lay in the pool of light. His nails needed trimming and were black with grime.

"Has he talked yet?" It was Baldy.

"Nope."

Kuroki stood up. He slipped his nail clipper and cigarettes into his pocket and left the room without giving Koji so much as a glance.

Chapter Two

1

It was drizzling.

Koji looked up at the trees along the street. Their leaves were gone. Autumn was coming to an end. He'd never sensed the season like this, from trees lining the street. It got warm, then hot, then cool, then cold—that was how he'd experienced the seasons, especially since arriving in Tokyo.

He had no destination. He simply walked, getting wet. Before he knew it, he'd walked across Ueno Park and was in Yanaka. He hadn't had lunch yet, but he wasn't hungry. All he could think of doing was sleep on his futon. From here it wasn't far to his apartment in Mikawajima, even on foot.

Makiko Endo was a sixteen-year-old high school student according to Beanpole. But that couldn't be true. Without a doubt, Makiko had been a grown woman.

Koji tried to remember his life at age sixteen. He was fifteen when he first saw the sea. So sixteen was when his mother died.

The speed of the city was dizzying. The cars seemed to speed by awfully fast and people couldn't seem to stay still. It was Tuesday, the twenty-second, which meant he'd greeted four mornings in jail.

He hadn't spoken to a soul since Friday. Not only his body but his mouth seemed heavy and sluggish.

His bottle of Suntory Red also felt heavy. The police had rolled it in newspaper before handing it back to him so he couldn't see what was inside. But he knew it wasn't whiskey.

On Wednesday he returned to work.

It continued to drizzle. Installing a television antenna was dangerous in such weather due to the slippery roof tiles. Koji was wearing rubber-soled sneakers.

Seta was in Nakayama's chair. The seat was only really Nakayama's after everyone had left on their delivery rounds.

Seta paused from sorting out delivery slips, pushed down his brown-framed reading glasses a little, and looked up at Koji. He didn't seem that surprised.

"Sorry for taking so much time off," Koji said, bowing his head a little.

"That was some misfortune." It was Nakayama. Seta nodded slightly and went back to sorting the delivery slips.

The staff began to gather. Yonekura was wearing a beige safari jacket and a brown wool scarf.

"Your stomach better?"

"Huh?" Yonekura looked puzzled. It was already five days since he'd been a pale, vomiting mess.

Seta began distributing the delivery slips. Yonekura received a bunch, so Koji didn't extend his hand. Yonekura, however, headed toward a truck with a man who'd been Seta's partner until recently.

It was only then that Koji noticed a new face among them.

"Which truck should I get on?" Koji asked.

"Actually, Mizui…" Seta began, inserting his own batch of slips into his folder. Everyone was already loading appliances; Koji appeared to be one man too many. "We want you to manage the warehouse for a while. We should be getting another truck soon. You'll go back on the road again then."

"Manage the warehouse? What exactly am I supposed to do?" One man—Nakayama—sufficed for that. The merchandise simply went in and out. There was nothing to manage.

"For a start, help unload. Eventually I'll think of other things you can do. Until then, why don't you stay here and give your body a rest?"

Seta was incapable of saying he'd hired a replacement. That was the man's nature, and Koji nodded silently.

Give your body a rest. There was something terribly raw about those words that bothered Koji. It was what you said to a man straight out of prison or a hospital.

What did I do? Koji thought, but said nothing. A weight still seemed to clamp down on his jaws.

When he began lifting and moving some appliances, the others stopped what they were doing to look. If he couldn't handle it on his own, they took turns lending a hand, but otherwise Koji was ordered about.

He felt like he was being punished.

By the time the last truck had left, his shirt was so drenched in sweat he could have wrung it. So much for giving his body a rest—but this too wasn't vocalized.

"Keep your cool. They fired you at first, you know." Nakayama didn't move from his chair. The rain must have been affecting his neuralgia. The place only had one chair.

Koji brought a wooden crate over from the warehouse and sat on it. He took off his shirt, baring his torso. The wet shirt was giving him a chill.

"A new guy showed up as soon as Monday. We could barely manage with four trucks, so how were we supposed to make do with three? All you guys are replaceable."

"I'll bet they can find any number of better replacements for you, too," Koji shot back. He wore his jacket over bare skin; it would have been too cold otherwise. The drizzling didn't look like it would stop.

"You know why you got your job back? The police called. Of course the president didn't refuse. But then there was no truck for you, so Seta was charged to come up with something. Making you my assistant was typical of him."

Why did the police have to call like some busybody? It wasn't as if he'd done anything to justify being fired. He could have sorted things out himself.

The arrest itself didn't infuriate him so much now. If Makiko really turned out to be a sixteen-year-old high school student, then of course they couldn't believe a word he said. He resented getting any help from them.

"Must have been hard being interrogated. It's a piece of cake for those guys to force a confession from an innocent man."

Koji longed for a cup of hot green tea. But his body ached all over and it was a pain even to stand up to set some water to boil. He'd only been in jail for a few days, but he was already out of shape.

Nakayama started talking about how the police went about their work. Koji had heard it from him numerous times—how they sized you up, how swiftly they cuffed you—but the old man was relentless in sharing his knowledge. He'd probably once been a pickpocket. Twisting your arm as they passed by, tapping on your shoulder in a crowd—it all sounded like techniques for apprehending one.

"Hey, assistant," Nakayama said, yanking the cigarette out of Koji's mouth and smoking it himself, "you've become pretty damn taciturn."

Koji took out a fresh cigarette and lit it.

The white Toyota Crown stopped in front of the warehouse. It looked no different from an ordinary car, except that there was a police radio installed beneath the dashboard.

Beanpole stepped out. He was alone. "Back already from your deliveries?"

It was too early for lunch. Koji kicked a cigarette butt near his feet.

"As of today he's in warehouse management," Nakayama explained. Koji kicked another cigarette butt.

"I wanted to see how you're doing. Also, there's something I need to tell you."

Beanpole offered one of his Hope cigarettes, but Koji put one of his own Hi Lites in his mouth. Nakayama helped himself to one of Koji's cigarettes as well.

"Numata made a full confession. The mastermind was one of the other bartenders, a guy named Matsuda. Yoshikawa—the manager we took to be a victim—was an accomplice. The three of them hatched the plan to fake a robbery. It seems Numata hit a little too hard."

"So Mizui here has been totally cleared?"

"He already was cleared when he was released. We went on to interrogate Numata again after that."

Beanpole exhaled smoke. Koji watched it float through the drizzle.

"I did a bad job of confirming your alibi."

Koji didn't want Beanpole to apologize. He just wanted to be left alone. He'd had enough of these people.

"I screwed up, that girl really had me duped. But Mr. Kuroki saw through her instantly. He could tell she used makeup regularly even though she wasn't wearing any then. After that, I noticed her eyebrows were plucked. Still, I found it unbelievable. When I was told to stake her out I thought I'd be wasting my time."

Koji threw away his cigarette and stamped it out.

"Why don't you say something?" Nakayama poked Koji's shoulder. "He's become very taciturn, this guy."

"Can't you let it go, Mizui? I know you've got good reason to hate me. But it was also someone at the police who proved your innocence."

Beanpole cleanly stubbed out his cigarette in the ashtray on the table. Nakayama smoked his right down to the filter. Several yellow stubs lay in the ashtray.

"How much for a small fridge? Mine's broken, I think. It can't even make ice," Beanpole changed the subject.

Nakayama began to answer. Talking to a detective was working the old man up into a lather.

Why had Numata given Koji's name? Did he hate Koji that much? Was it because of the suit? Or was it being kicked out of the apartment? A bit of investigating was bound to bring the truth to light no matter how much bullshit Numata spouted. It took a few days, but in the end it had.

Koji was no longer angry. Back in jail, he'd seriously wanted to kill Numata. Now he was more puzzled than anything.

"The ones with separate freezers use less electricity," Nakayama babbled on. He must have never even read the catalog. While they did handle actual merchandise, the appliances in the warehouse came packed in boxes. Nakayama couldn't have inspected anything but used fridges piled up in the dump outside.

A truck returned.

It was Yonekura's. Apparently he and his new partner had not gotten off to a good start.

"The asshole can't even drive and yet he talks non-stop." The new guy, Kawashima, almost spat out the words, looking at Koji. Yonekura had disappeared into the warehouse.

Koji lifted a used television off the loading platform—part of his new job.

"Is there anything I can do?" Beanpole asked, coming near. "It doesn't matter what, if you need to discuss anything, come to me. That man said they hired a replacement for you."

He didn't need any help. The guy could get lost. But the words didn't come out.

"You can also call if you want."

The word "call" brought Makiko to mind. "What's Makiko's real name?" Koji asked.

"Forget about that girl. She's still in high school. She's just a kid."

"There are middle-school girls who sell their bodies."

"And if they're found, they're detained. The law treats minors differently."

"Tell me her name."

"I can't. Besides, she won't get off scot-free."

Beanpole placed a hand on Koji's shoulder. With a faint smile, he turned and walked toward his Toyota Crown.

"That gentleman has got heart," Nakayama said after the Toyota Crown had driven off. "But he won't get far as a detective. Too much of a softie. People will walk all over him."

Koji unloaded all the used appliances and went inside the warehouse. Loading up the afternoon deliveries was another new task of his.

"We almost had an accident." It was Yonekura, seated on a microwave box.

Koji was reading the delivery slips, checking what needed to be loaded. Nakayama would verify before the merchandise left the warehouse. Although the old man's checking was slapdash, there had never been a mistake. In any case, an error would only mean getting the product turned back at the delivery point, just some extra work.

"Be more careful," Yonekura complained.

"Tell that to Kawashima."

"It was your fault. The truck was off balance because you didn't load it right."

The trucks weren't that big. Ten washing machines, and a truck was full. It made no difference to the driving how you loaded them.

Yonekura was rocking back and forth, his habit when he was angry. He'd had a fight with Kawashima, and he wanted to take it out on Koji? He put the delivery slips on top of a refrigerator.

Kawashima came in. Yonekura's rocking got worse and he piled on: "Light things near the driver, heavy things in the rear. Don't you get that? If we have an accident, all the merchandise gets ruined. It'll cost us over a million yen. Me and Kawashima will have to pay for it."

Koji grabbed Yonekura by the hair.

Yonekura screamed as his butt rose from the box. Koji kicked him in the stomach, lightly, but he still doubled over.

"Stand up."

Yonekura cast up a panicked look. Koji told him again to stand up. Still doubled over, he crawled backwards and knocked his butt against the wooden box.

"Do it, Mizui," Kawashima exhorted from behind. "I'm sick of his yammering. Make it so he can't even stand up."

Yonekura shook his head. He was crying.

Kawashima laughed. "Let's do the afternoon shift together, Mizui. Have this guy work the warehouse instead. He doesn't have a license so it's perfect for him."

"That won't happen." Nakayama had just come by. "Seta makes those decisions, not you guys."

Kawashima clicked his tongue and left.

Yonekura stood up. He was still crying. "What's so great about having a license?" he whined.

Koji put away the delivery slip. He didn't give Yonekura another look.

2

With its torn leather, the electric massage chair was in awful shape. Nakayama had pulled it out of the scrap dump.

"You expecting me to fix it for you?"

"I've always wanted something like this."

Koji had seen one at the public baths. This particular specimen had no coin slot so it had been used at home.

There were two bars protruding from the back with hard rubber balls at their ends. Rotating a handle near the elbow rest was supposed to move the rollers up and down. Only, the rollers didn't move, no matter what they did to the handle.

"I bet the motor is broken too," Koji guessed.

"Should be easy to fix, no? We've got all these old vacuum cleaners and washing machines. There must be some with motors that work. If not, we can take a few appliances apart, get the right parts together, and make a new motor."

"Don't be ridiculous."

"I thought you graduated from a technical high school."

Koji gave the electric massage chair a light kick. Actually, he didn't mind trying to fix it. He hadn't really tinkered with machinery in a while. The necessary circuit testers and tools were there. "How much if I get it to move?"

"Are you trying to fleece me?" Nakayama's face turned thoughtful. "Fine, I'll treat you at that place Seta takes you guys. The damage will be just 1,000 yen each there, right?"

"Don't forget. If you act like you never made that promise, I'll trash this thing all over again."

Fixing machinery would make him feel like less of a loser. Six days in the warehouse and still Seta showed no signs of coming up with any work ideas.

Loading and unloading the merchandise was not a problem now that Koji had gotten back into shape. What he needed to attend to was all the time he had on his hands.

"I'm just trying to take your mind off things," Nakayama pointed out, as if he'd read the younger man's thoughts.

Koji crouched behind the electric massage chair. He noticed what looked like a removable panel.

"You're the one who should be buying me drinks, you know."

"Bring a toolbox."

"You starting already?"

Nakayama coughed as if clearing phlegm. The weather had improved, but his neuralgia wasn't letting up. The old man was suffering considerably. After having spent whole days with him, Koji knew that well.

Nakayama came back with a toolbox.

When Koji unfastened the panel, he saw that the motor was not as damaged as he had feared. There was a cog on the same rod as the handle, and the chain had fallen off it. The chain itself was intact.

When Koji fitted it back onto the cog, resistance returned to the loose handle. The massage rods started moving down.

"Help me take this to your room."

"You want to take it apart there?"

"Just need to check that it works. I need to plug it into a outlet." The warehouse had outlets too, but the contraption would be in the way when the trucks returned.

"Let's see." Nakayama placed his hands on the chair.

Apart from the fact that all the windows faced north, Nakayama's room was decent. Although it was connected to the warehouse, it was a separate annex that had been built against the warehouse wall, and the front door featured a little fixture like a teller's window. There was a six-mat tatami room and a small kitchen. The needlessly large unfloored entrance could be made into another room with some more mats.

Apparently, the annex structure had already been there when the company bought the warehouse. Most likely it had served as a security guard's quarters.

"Wait a moment. I'll just wipe the dirt off." Uncharacteristically, Nakayama kept his house tidy. He cleaned regularly, and he'd even soaped down the used fridge he'd found in the dump. A handy closet, a low table, a small cupboard for his dishes, a 14-inch-screen television, and a kerosene stove—he had all the basic furnishings.

On top of the closet was a framed photograph. It showed a little boy about five, his baseball cap tilted far back. Koji asked who he was but Nakayama didn't answer. Can't possibly be his son, Koji mused.

Nakayama had never mentioned family.

"Try not to make a mess. Dust off your trousers outside. You're always sitting on the ground, so I bet they're covered in dirt."

Koji studied the wiring of the motor and reached for the circuit tester. The machinery wasn't very complex. Moreover, it was lodged inside a huge chair so he had plenty of room to maneuver.

There was no need for dismantling. He only had to reconnect the switch cord for the motor to begin emitting a light whirr. Nakayama had stepped out for a moment to answer the warehouse phone.

Koji sat in the chair. The massage rollers were quite powerful. The way they pounded his back didn't feel particularly good.

"Hey, it's working!" Nakayama exclaimed when he returned.

Koji was disappointed. He'd counted on two days for basic repairs, a week total if the motor was to be dismantled and reassembled. Yet it had taken only ten minutes.

"It's a rip-off. You can't expect me to treat you for that."

"You promised." Koji inserted the screwdriver in his hand into the switch beneath the elbow rest.

"Fine, I'll treat you."

The old man shooed Koji out of the way and sat down in the chair. His chest and stomach began to ripple. His neck became floppy and his gray hair fell on his brow.

His voice was also vibrating when he declared, "This is great!"

Once Koji had eaten lunch and seen off the trucks for their afternoon deliveries, he started going through the scrap pile. He just felt like doing so. If he turned about the junk, perhaps he'd find something he could fix or reassemble.

Yonekura and Kawashima were still not getting along, but neither of them seemed ready to quit.

As Seta had prepared to leave on Saturday, he'd told Koji that he'd think of something new for certain for the following week. But the only new task today was cleaning the warehouse. Seta had had all day Sunday to think about it, but that was what he'd come up with.

"Be patient," Nakayama advised. Koji thought he was already doing a good job at that.

He somehow found an old-fashioned pedal-powered sewing machine amidst all the electrical appliances. It made a nasty rattle—maybe something was caught inside—but it did work.

Koji brought the sewing machine to the warehouse. "Want to buy this?"

"You're asking me to step on that thing?"

"I've seen you sewing with a needle. Anyway, I wouldn't sell it to you like this. I'd remove the motor from an old vacuum cleaner or something and make it electric."

Nakayama studied the sewing machine as if to appraise its value. "One hundred yen."

"That won't even buy cigarettes."

"One hundred and fifty yen. No more."

Koji didn't give a damn about the money. He would have paid to work on it. He'd be spared a few days of boredom.

He carefully tried the machine out, checking its functions. He decided he would first repair the body. He could attach a motor anytime.

"That's the way," Nakayama lauded. "Hang in there and you'll soon be back doing deliveries. Seta's not very accommodating, so unless someone quits or takes a day off, he won't change things around."

Nakayama pulled Koji's cigarette out of his mouth and began smoking it. Swiping one this way had become his new habit. Sometimes he coughed violently. He complained that coughing made his hip ache but didn't quit smoking.

"Seems Hatta's going around bragging again. He told the construction guys that you got your job back because he put in a word for you with the president."

"That bastard's not worth bothering about."

Koji began his struggle with the sewing machine. First, he needed to get its basic structure in his head. If he took it apart without having done that, he'd be lost.

Hatta returned. He was driving one of the store's utility vans rather than a truck.

Koji had just started to take the sewing machine apart. He was dropping small parts and screws into an empty Cup o' Noodles container. Rusted parts needed to be soaked in oil.

"Heard you held on to your job."

Hatta's squashed face distorted into a smile. When he smiled, the lines on his face deepened to a disturbing degree just on the left side.

"I've been promoted to head of the construction team. Here's my card."

Koji looked away from the offered card. Hatta tried to force it into the pocket of Koji's uniform, but Koji brushed the hand away.

"What, you have a problem with me making manager?"

Koji was still looking in the other direction. "Your mouth is what I have a problem with."

"Oh, really? Is that any way for a warehouse guard to talk?"

"Get your filthy face away from me."

Koji felt something whiz almost simultaneously past both ears. Hatta laughed.

"If those had swerved inward, you'd be flat on the ground. Maybe even dead, jailbird warehouse man."

Koji found himself moving toward Hatta. It was neither will nor anger. Something else entirely was spurring just his body.

"Huh, you want to die?"

Hatta took a few steps back. Light on his feet. Koji stepped in. Hatta's eyes shone for an instant, eyes only, in his squashed face. Koji's fist flew toward where the face was. Something crashed against his own chin and the side of his abdomen. Baffling. He was on the ground when he came to. He couldn't breathe; in his pain he banged his fist against the concrete floor. Air seeped out of his mouth. Then he could inhale.

He got up. His feet didn't move the way he wanted. A jab came at his nose, only he didn't see it. A stinging sensation—then tears filled his eyes. Hatta was in a fighter's pose, and his face looked even more squashed. A left, a right. Out of reach. Hatta came closer. Now was the chance. The moment Koji thought so, another one landed on his nose. He tried to retreat, but Hatta charged in quicker. Just when their bodies were about to collide, a punch gouged Koji's stomach.

"What happened? Did you punch him?" It was Nakayama, who had been napping and was now awake. His voice sounded distant.

"Only touched him." Hatta's reply also sounded distant.

He had to be lying flat on his back. He felt nauseated. He'd feel better if he threw up, but he didn't want Hatta to see him like that.

Nakayama tried to pull him up, but Koji brushed him away and stood up on his own.

"Have you forgotten that you used to be a boxer?" Nakayama chided.

"He came at me. It was self-defense. Self-defense."

Koji took three deep breaths. He picked up the Cup o' Noodles container with the sewing machine parts.

"You didn't have to punch him," Nakayama said with genuine anger.

Koji grabbed one of the parts and slammed it into Hatta's face. He let out a yelp and covered his eyes. Koji hurled himself against the man. No punch came—he was squatting on the ground. Lunging at him, Koji kicked, his shoe digging into Hatta's face. It was squashed anyway. Kicking a fallen boxer was a lot easier than dribbling a soccer ball through defenders.

"Please, stop!" Hatta didn't even try to get up. Covering his face with his hands, he rolled around on the ground. Those movements were sluggish.

"Mizui, stop," Nakayama broke in and pleaded.

Koji's shoulders heaved with each breath. When Hatta slowly raised his head to get up, Koji kicked him down again.

"Idiot!" Nakayama yelled. "Get over there, now. Cool your head. If you haven't had enough, then have a go at me."

Koji breathed in a lungful of air. He began to feel queasy again. He went over to the faucet, fell to his knees, and threw up. That made him feel much better.

He turned on the tap and washed his face. The blood felt slimy around his nose. He splashed water on his head. The coldness trickled down his neck, but he didn't care to wipe it off. He practically crawled into the shadow of the warehouse and collapsed on his back.

He noticed a swallow's nest on the iron girder beneath the roof. He'd never seen a swallow in the area and had no idea there was a nest. It looked dirty, like someone had just stuck a clump of mud there. Koji placed a cigarette in his mouth but left it unlit. He thought he'd feel sick again. He shut his eyes.

"Are you two completely nuts?"

Nakayama could bellow all right, but he really had no stomach for violence. Not because of his age—no doubt he'd been that way since he was young.

Koji sat up. His nose had stopped bleeding. "Where's Hatta?"

"He went home. His face was swollen. The guy's no longer a pro."

"Some boxer."

"He got knocked about once and was no good after that. That's why he's afraid of getting hit."

Nakayama swiped the unlit cigarette from Koji's mouth.

"Those drinks you owe me. Can we have them tonight?"

"Are you crazy? Not until payday."

"Got it. I won't hold you to your promise."

"Sorry about it. But you didn't do all that much."

"I'm quitting this job. Tell Seta for me when he gets back."

"Hold on, Mizui. Both sides are to blame in a fight."

"I was thinking of quitting anyway."

"You don't need to just because Hatta's the president's pet."

"That's not it. I'm just fed up. And I'm tired of looking at your old face."

"So you wouldn't quit if I were a pretty girl?" Nakayama gave a little laugh. "You're still a kid. You don't know what it's like to be out of work."

"I do. It means I won't be able to eat."

Nakayama's eyes shone for a moment as he looked at Koji. The gleam wasn't scolding, but rather, almost envious, and melancholy.

"Do as you like. Unlike me, you're young. You'll find work easily."

Koji rummaged in his pockets. There was nothing in them, so he shoved the open pack of Hi Lite cigarettes into the old man's hand.

"Take care of that neuralgia."

"Drop in if you're passing by. You know I'll be here until I can't stand up. You and I got along surprisingly well."

It was true. Saying goodbye to the old man was the only thing Koji felt sad about.

"This is just a suggestion and not a sermon, but say a proper goodbye to Seta. Whether you like him or not, you were in his care. Don't leave like you're running away. That's true not just here, but wherever.

You've got to act decent when you quit."

Koji chewed on that. It would be a drag to see Seta at this stage, but it was old Nakayama's last sermon after all.

"Okay. I'll wait here."

Nakayama gave a little cough.

"You go inside. It's getting cold."

"Treating me like an old fart!"

Nakayama walked away without turning back once.

3

He still had quite a lot of money left.

It was only a little over a week since his last payday. Moreover, he'd spent a few of those days in jail.

He didn't feel like going out to look for work. He hadn't bought any papers or magazines with classifieds, either. Work was something he did to earn money, and as long as he had some, there was simply no need for it. But he was getting tired of lying around in his apartment after two days of it.

When he'd told Seta about quitting, the older man had looked back at him suspiciously.

Seta didn't try to dissuade him. The delivery section had one man too many anyway. He simply said that he'd have the unpaid portion of Koji's wages ready for pick-up. It wouldn't be a large sum.

Koji wasn't even asked why he was quitting. Seta probably assumed it was the boredom of warehouse duty. If he'd asked, Koji would have told him about beating up Hatta. It might have eased his mood.

He followed Nakayama's suggestion, bowing and thanking his boss. Seta looked bewildered for a moment, then stood up in a hurry and nodded many times.

Koji pulled on a sweater, donned his jacket, and stepped out.

The cold wind felt good. It was a wonder he could spend the last two days lying around in his empty apartment. Having thought to survive as long as he could with just the cash he had on him now puzzled him. It wasn't like he had any use for the time he'd have. He was better off not having it in the first place if he had to come up with ways to kill it.

The weirs of the sewage treatment plant came into view. He planned to spend every last bit of money he had. It was seven in the evening, late enough to buy a woman or drinks. It didn't matter how; the point was not to have any extra cash. Humans started to rot if they didn't work.

He saw a phone booth. It gave off a strangely warm light. Koji found himself walking toward it.

There was a young man inside wearing metal-rimmed glasses. His long hair made him look like a student. Koji only caught snatches of the conversation. The fellow was laughing as much as talking; he seemed to be enjoying himself immensely.

A few minutes passed. The young man would glance at Koji but add another coin, showing no sign of hanging up. He had to be talking to a woman. Koji began to feel angry and decided not to budge, no matter what, though his irritation was absurd. There were plenty of phone booths over by the station.

The man inserted another 10-yen coin. Koji gave the booth's duralumin frame a hearty kick. The door shook and rattled. The man, his mouth open, looked at Koji. After a second kick, the man hung up, grabbed the 10-yen coin that fell to the refund slot, and came out.

"How long did you plan to keep me waiting? This phone yours or what?"

The man didn't say anything. He didn't even try to meet Koji's eyes.

The receiver was still warm. After three ring-tones, a familiar voice answered.

"So I hear you're a sixteen-year-old kid."

Makiko remained silent. Light music played in the background. Koji also remained silent for a while.

"I'll be waiting at our coffee shop. Be there at eight."

"I can't. Mom won't let me."

No question the voice was twenty-four-year-old Makiko Endo's. A tired, slightly sinking, calm voice. It betrayed not a hint of alarm at receiving Koji's call.

"You know what happened to me because of you. Don't you think you owe me an apology in person?"

"You're not the only one who got into trouble. I have to go to family court, too."

Koji thought he heard Makiko laugh on the other end.

"Be there at eight. Otherwise, I'll invite myself over to your apartment in Yoyogi Hachiman."

He didn't know Makiko's real name, so he actually had no way of finding her. There had to be plenty of apartment buildings in Yoyogi Hachiman.

This time he certainly heard Makiko laughing at the other end. "Okay. But I can't stay long. Mom's being really strict."

Suddenly, after hanging up, Koji felt hungry. But he didn't have the time to grab dinner first.

Of the two slices of toast he ordered, he managed to finish only one. The coffee was bitter. He chain-smoked.

The clock rounded eight. Ten minutes passed.

He kept wondering if he'd see the Makiko Endo he knew or a sixteen-year-old high school student.

It was neither. Makiko showed up in a red sweater and blue jeans. She came and stood near Koji. Her long, straight hair fell on her shoulders.

She looked like an ordinary young woman.

"You're not wearing makeup?"

Makiko sat down. She sprinkled salt on the leftover toast and bit into it with her white teeth.

"What's the point of tarting myself up for you? You know the truth now."

"Are you really sixteen?"

Makiko gave a little laugh. White teeth. Her lips looked faded in color, but her teeth were the same.

"Chicks are fuckin' scary."

Koji stuck a cigarette in his mouth. Makiko, still munching toast, asked a passing waitress for a coffee. She picked up Koji's half-empty glass of water and drank it. They hadn't yet brought Makiko's water.

"What's your real name?"

"Makiko. Makiko Endo."

"Still playing with me?"

"I'm not playing with you. The woman who's seeing you is called Makiko. Think of it that way."

She had beautiful skin. It was the first time Koji had seen her without makeup. Smooth, without a single pimple on her cheeks or forehead, slightly moist—it was the skin of a grown-up woman. The difference between an adult's and a child's skin was hard to express, but there certainly was one. Koji was beginning to feel oddly domineered.

"Why did you tell the police that you don't know me?"

"How could I? My mom and my school would have found out about us."

"Is that the only reason?"

"That, and I hated you. I wanted you to suffer," she said casually, reaching for Koji's cigarette.

Her remark didn't immediately register. Makiko exhaled.

Koji stared at the smoke as if it held some meaning. "Hate? Me?" He waved away the smoke wafting to his face. "What did I do?"

"You toyed with me. Remorselessly."

"Toyed?"

Koji thought she was joking. But her expression didn't change.

It was ridiculous. There was no reason for her to hate him. Surely they had both enjoyed themselves. No, more—they'd been crazy. He knew she had felt the same.

"Don't give me that crap. Whenever I asked if we could get a room, you came along without a word."

"Right, let me put it another way. You were a man. I hated you because you were a man."

"What the hell's that supposed to mean?"

"I really don't know myself."

Makiko's coffee arrived. She dropped in two lumps of sugar and stirred with her spoon.

Koji's cigarette was now short enough to singe his fingertips. He tossed it into the ashtray.

"Why did you want to see me again?" Makiko asked, sipping her coffee.

Because he'd stepped out of his apartment. Because there was a phone booth when he did. Because a guy in it seemed to be having a good time.

"Because you love me?" she asked.

Their eyes met.

Koji stood up and grabbed her wrist. He didn't want troublesome talk or to berate her about what was done. All he wanted was to make love to her.

They went to their usual hotel. Makiko seemed slightly hesitant, and that wasn't usual.

Once in the hotel room, Koji grabbed her by the hair and pressed his lips against hers.

"Don't rush."

She said that like an older sister, though she was only sixteen. Koji's movements became charged with growing ire. He roughly pulled up her sweater, under which was a white blouse.

"So you were toying with me after all," Makiko said, less accusing him than muttering to herself.

That's right, you're a toy. That or a prostitute who does it for free. Koji's hands moved even more roughly.

"I'm going," Makiko said, suddenly stiffening. She started buttoning up her half-open blouse. "Mom's supposed to call me at ten."

"You've got to be joking."

Koji grabbed Makiko's arm, pulled her closer, and embraced her tightly from behind. He felt a sharp pain on the back of his hand. She was digging her nails into him.

A savage lust welled in Koji, and he grabbed her hair. Makiko screamed. He ripped the buttons off her blouse. It tore at the shoulder.

"Let go—I said let me go!"

He threw her onto the bed. When she tried to get up, he shoved her down again.

The craze set in after that.

Koji took a hot shower. He kept showering until his skin stung.

He was calm now, but his passion wasn't exhausted. In fact it was more vehement, and taking a shower was an effort to quell it. Caring and hate mingled in a peculiar residue at the bottom of his heart.

Makiko sat cross-legged on the bed. She swept up the hair falling onto her forehead and turned a dazed look at Koji. Her mind seemed to be elsewhere.

Koji reached out to touch her face. She lowered her head slightly but didn't try to evade his hand. Her left cheek was red. When Koji tried to hold her close, she pushed his hands away.

"What is it? Are you angry?" He put his hands on her shoulders again.

"Wait. Something isn't right."

"What isn't?"

"I don't know, but something isn't. It wasn't like usual."

"Stop talking nonsense."

Koji got on top of her. Her hands, pushing against him, signaled clear resistance.

That threw him into a rage.

It was just as earlier. She dug her nails into his chest; their bodies were apart for a second, then became entangled again, and tumbled off the bed. Koji mounted her and pressed both her hands down on the carpet. Makiko desperately shook her head, less resisting than afraid of something.

My lovemaking scares her. Koji felt another surge of savage lust.

She became unbelievably still. Only, her eyes were screwed tightly shut, as if she were experiencing acute pain. She was shutting them so tight that lines appeared on her eyelids, the corners of her eyes, and between her brows. The lines were both deep and long.

Koji pressed his cheek to hers as he kept moving his hips. A whimper. It didn't sound like her familiar voice, but some other woman's. He raised his head and looked down at her. The lines on her face were still there, etched even deeper. Koji wondered for a moment if something under her back was hurting her. Then Makiko's arms, which had been motionless on the carpet, wrapped tightly around his back.

With a cry of *No!* her body stiffened like a rod. Lifted up by her arched hips Koji's upper body wobbled twice, then a third time. Then Makiko's body relaxed and grew elusively soft and all Koji could sense was the occasional spasm.

He stayed still for a while.

A slight pressure came from Makiko's hands on his back. She repeated this. He didn't feel calm this time. When he saw drops seeping out of her eyes and trickling down toward her ears, that was the end. His body no longer felt like his own. The wavering in his head spread to the rest of his body. He shut his eyes tight.

Makiko lay on her side in a fetal position with her back to him. Her shoulders twitched now and then. She was sobbing convulsively, though Koji didn't understand why. But something had changed—definitely, both in her and in him.

He tenderly placed a hand on her shoulder. Makiko grasped it and, bringing it to her mouth, bit it over and over. The pain was pleasant.

He'd take whatever she gave. As a man, he'd embrace her fully.

He buried his nose in her long hair. It smelled like sunshine. He inhaled it deep into his chest.

"Don't you need to go home?"

"How kind of you to ask."

"I'm just worried your mother will get angry and we won't get to see each other again."

"I'll call her from here. I'll tell her I'm staying at a friend's place tonight and that I'll go to school direct."

Makiko turned around to face Koji. She wasn't crying anymore.

"Mom has a bar in Shinjuku. By now she'll be so drunk she won't give a damn what I do."

Makiko's fingertips touched Koji's lips. He stroked her hair.

"Are you still angry?" she asked.

"About what?"

"That I didn't confirm your alibi to the detective."

"I suppose." He'd forgotten about that—to his own bafflement.

He reached for a cigarette, exhaled smoke. Makiko took the cigarette from him, inhaled once, and stuck it back between his lips.

"I'd be furious," he said, "if I hadn't been told you're a kid who's only sixteen."

"Don't call me a kid."

"Are you really sixteen?"

"I'll be seventeen in three days. My birthday's the third of December."

Koji put out his cigarette. Makiko buried her face in his chest.

"You've been with all sorts of men, haven't you?" A bitter taste spread in his mouth the moment he uttered those words.

"I won't see any other men."

Something about those words also bothered Koji. He sat up. What mattered for Makiko and him was how they proceeded from now.

"Let's go out," he said.

When he looked into her face, there were tears in her eyes again. He saw that his words had hurt her as well.

"I want to spend the night with you. Stay with me all night."

"In that case"—kindness now enveloped everything—"let's go to my place. It's a mess, but better than here. In terms of mood."

4

Koji looked for Makiko. The supermarket at dusk was a crowded place.

He was covered in cold sweat. In his pocket were lip balm, chewing gum, and a chocolate bar.

He caught sight of her from behind. She was carrying a supermarket basket full of food.

He started to chase her but knocked a small child to the floor with his knee. As he helped the wailing child to his feet, he lost sight of her.

His sweating didn't stop, just growing worse. He wanted a cigarette, and he wanted out of the place as soon as possible.

Someone tapped his shoulder. He turned around to see Makiko, smiling. The basket had been replaced by a shopping bag.

"Let's go," Koji said, making for the exit, but Makiko called for him to stop. A second plastic shopping bag lay at her feet.

They walked side by side to Koji's apartment, each carrying one bag. Despite the urge, Koji didn't dare look back.

The bags were properly sealed with the supermarket's tape. Koji checked his watch—half an hour since they'd entered the store. Thanks to the fresh air, his sweating was beginning to subside.

"How the hell did you manage that?" he asked, throwing the contents of his pockets onto the apartment floor. Makiko had a look and laughed. She couldn't stop laughing.

No question who'd scored the better spoils: out of Makiko's bags emerged meat, vegetables, ready-made foods, milk, wine, bread, eggs, and even clothing for Koji in the right size. Koji's lip balm, chewing gum, and chocolate bar looked as pathetic as offerings at a clearance sale.

"Never again," Koji said as he sprawled out on the floor and lit a cigarette.

"You're hopeless," Makiko said. "I'll just go and stock up by myself from now on."

It was the second time they'd gone to stock up. This excursion had made Koji sweat more heavily than the first. It was bound to be worse the next time.

They did stock up, but without paying—in other words, they were shoplifting. Makiko seemed to feel no guilt. She enjoyed it like it was a game, and that was indeed what it was for her. She had money. Her mother gave her a generous allowance, and her wallet always contained at least a couple of 10,000-yen bills.

Makiko had been coming to Koji's apartment for a week. She'd come every day except Sunday.

Each morning she arrived wearing her school uniform. Koji would still be asleep. Makiko changed into ordinary clothes, made breakfast, and woke him up.

Various objects began to fill Koji's apartment before he even noticed. Pots and pans, plates, teacups, dishwashing liquid and sponges, cleaning rags, and a low table so small that there was only space for a few plates—Makiko had brought all of them. Through these things, the apartment began to feel lived in in a way it never had before.

It wasn't bad, Koji thought, to have a woman take care of him. While Makiko played house, Koji lounged around and watched her. She was no longer an enigma. She was a girl acting her age. That pleased him.

"Why did you go out alone last night?" he asked.

"If I stayed in this room, I'd have seen the ghost. It's really scary."

"Ghost?"

"The ghost of a man. They're usually female, aren't they?" Makiko asked, smiling.

Their conversations didn't hold any deep meaning. It was usually when they were out on walks that they talked that way. In the apartment, they hardly exchanged a word. They just embraced, naked, devouring each other's body without ever tiring of it. The shape of Makiko's fingernails and toenails, the down around her nape, the indentation of her collarbone, the sparse hair in her armpits—no matter how many times Koji saw them it seemed like the first time, so fresh they looked. If he touched them, they could break. Yet he found himself sinking his teeth into her. Those stretches of time were as curiously serene as they were intense.

It's just like a dream. It's ending soon. Many times Koji thought so. Then they would go for a walk. He would breathe the fresh air and put his arm around Makiko's shoulders as if to make sure she was there. She would smile and rub her head against him like a cat. Her slight shoulders were always where he could touch them.

Once Makiko started coming over, Koji once again thought to survive just on the cash he had. He'd no longer have any trouble with the time he'd have on his hands. Food, they had enough of, from Makiko's shoplifting sprees. His money didn't dwindle all that much.

Only, the feeling did linger that he was being supported by a woman's thievery.

He had to find a job. When he was alone, that thought always came to him. Makiko was at his place during the day, so it had to be night work. Bartending, waiting tables. Construction work on subways and roads also took place at night. He felt confident he could handle heavy labor.

But the truth was that he needed a more stable job. Though maybe not just yet, one day he wanted to live with Makiko. They'd need to move into a nicer apartment and have proper furniture. He mustn't let Makiko want for anything.

In a year, Koji would turn twenty-two. Makiko would be eighteen. Nothing would be odd about them living together.

At night, when he was alone, Koji fantasized about a life with Makiko. Not just the two of them—they had a son as well. Koji was working for a firm that dealt with appliances, and in the evening he'd return to their apartment. The family of three went to the public baths with washbasins under their arms, and there they slowly washed away all the fatigue of the day. It was Koji's job to wash the child in the men's bath. They'd meet up with Makiko at the entrance, go home, and surround the table to dine. On weekends, the zoo or an amusement park. A summer holiday by the sea would be a fine thing. He might not be able to afford a boat, but he'd certainly tell his son about how he had once dreamt of buying one.

His imagination expanded endlessly. At times he got so carried away he never went to sleep.

The man appeared on a Saturday.

Makiko came at the usual time. Koji was propping himself on his elbows and gazing at her from the futon as she changed.

When there was a knock on the door, she'd just pulled on a sweater, over which she normally wore an apron. "Who could it be?" she wondered aloud, apron in hand.

He hadn't the faintest. Maybe it was the guy next door; he'd come over once to borrow a screwdriver.

Koji got up and went to the door in his pajamas.

A man around thirty, in a black trench coat, was standing outside. Koji didn't recognize him. Although the man had neatly parted hair and was clean-shaven, his wearing an ascot instead of a necktie gave him the air of something other than a gainful employee.

His intrusive glare was far from pleasant. Apart from being tall and lean, and the bluish tinge that remained where he'd shaved, he didn't have any salient characteristics.

"Who the hell are you?"

The man removed his hand from his pocket, and Koji instantly braced himself. An odd vibe. But that soon vanished, and the man grinned, showing ugly, nicotine-stained teeth. He looked quite a bit older than he had at first.

"Mr. Watanabe!" Makiko let out in surprise.

"You know him?" Koji asked, turning around.

She was giving the man a stern look. "Mom asked you to follow me, didn't she?"

"You seem to be having fun playing newlyweds. I can hardly believe my eyes," Watanabe said, stroking his smooth chin as he looked around. The veins on his thin hand stood out, blue.

Koji felt cold standing there in his pajamas. He pulled up his collar and shuffled his feet.

"I don't want you meddling. This is none of your business," Makiko said.

"I'm afraid it is my business. Your mom was worried and sent me, so you could say I'm her stand-in."

"Her stand-in? Give me a break."

"Then let's say I'm standing in for your father." The man grinned again, then laughed.

Makiko looked aside. Koji had no idea what their relationship might be. He remained silent because the man had mentioned Makiko's mother. Makiko had been skipping school to be with him, so it made sense that her mother would be worried.

"You're Koji Mizui, aren't you?" Watanabe said, turning his eyes to him.

"What's it to you if I am?"

"I heard you were in jail. If you're mad then it's not without reason, but I hope you're not using that to coerce her."

"I come here because I want to," Makiko chimed in.

"Don't you think you've gone a bit too far? Telling the school your mother's ill. Yesterday, one of your lady teachers came by to see how she was doing. Your mom's pretty mad about the embarrassment."

"Embarrassment my ass! Why so prim? Don't fucking make me laugh!"

When Makiko took on a shrewish tone all of a sudden, Koji looked at her, astounded. Watanabe was smiling uneasily. Makiko threw her apron at him. For a moment Koji thought she might even attack him, but she didn't make any further move and just stood breathing heavily.

"Anyway, let's go home. Your mom's probably up waiting for you."

"No."

Makiko went to squat under the sink in the corner of the apartment.

She looked just like a little kid throwing a tantrum. Watanabe seemed at a loss as to what to do but tried again, his tone gentle but insistent. Makiko shook her head.

"She's told you she doesn't want to go."

Koji had been wondering how to respond, but Makiko's behavior decided it for him. He'd force the guy out physically if necessary. The man was trying to take her away.

"Go back alone. If you won't, I have my methods."

"Shut your face, kid," Watanabe spat, his tone suddenly menacing.

Koji almost lost his nerve for a second. "The fuck did you say?"

"I told you to shut your face. Normally I wouldn't let you get away with it, but I don't want to make trouble for Etsuko. That's why I'm leaving you alone."

"Don't fuck with me. Let's go outside and settle this."

"Stop it!" Makiko cried.

It seemed like she was interceding for Koji's sake, protecting a weaker man. But this opponent wasn't one he needed any protecting from. Watanabe looked pretty feeble.

"You stay out of this," Koji threatened. He tried to grab Watanabe by the lapel, but Makiko hugged him back.

"Come, Etsuko, be a good girl. If not, I'll have to tie a rope around your neck and drag you home."

"Wait outside," Makiko said, still holding back Koji's hands.

Watanabe glanced at Koji, then went outside. The door closed.

"Who is that guy?"

"Mom's boyfriend. Well, one of three, and he's the worst. The other two are patrons, but that man, he takes money from her."

"Why did you stop me? I would have beaten him up."

Makiko released Koji's hands. He couldn't sense if Watanabe was still outside the door.

"He might use a knife. I've seen him with one before."

"Those types turn out to be pussies." When Koji saw Makiko putting on her overcoat, he became a little flustered. "You're really going home?"

"I'd better let Mom know I'm okay. I don't think I can keep coming over like this. Maybe you could come to my place when Mom leaves for work. Call me on Monday night."

Makiko folded her apron.

There was a knock on the door and Watanabe called for "Etsuko." Makiko's real name was Etsuko Mitsuya. Koji knew that by now, but it still seemed as if the voice were calling a complete stranger.

Koji got back into his futon, which only had a trace of warmth left. The long and short of it was that these were family troubles that Koji needed to stay out of. Makiko would surely do a fine job of either fooling her mother or cajoling her into letting them do what they wanted. In fact, if he started going to Makiko's at night, he could find a day job. That wasn't bad at all.

"Eat your breakfast, okay?" Makiko reminded him. "There's ham, bread, and tea."

"Sure. I'll manage."

"Etsuko!" the voice came again.

"Do you have enough cash?"

"Yeah." He did still have some money left.

"Hang on to this."

Makiko stuck a single 10,000-yen note under the ashtray. The call of *Etsuko!* was now clearly tinged with irritation.

She threw herself on Koji. She pressed her lips against his and stuck her tongue deep into his mouth. They stayed like that for a while.

Drawing her face away, she said: "See you."

Makiko's saliva remained in his mouth. For a long while, Koji rolled it around on his tongue, then swallowed.

Chapter Three

1

No matter how many times he called, nobody answered.

The pharmacy near his apartment took in its pay phone and closed shop at half past eight.

He walked to Nippori Station and made another call.

Then he took the Yamanote Line to Shibuya. He entered the coffee shop where he and Makiko used to meet. The coffee was totally flavorless.

They kicked him out at eleven.

He walked down Dogenzaka and turned into an alley. A hooker sidled up to him. He pushed her away, but she was persistent and wouldn't let go of the hem of his jacket. He must have looked desperate for a woman. He gave her a kick in the thighs and heard her swearing at his back.

He entered a bar. He was thirsty. That was the sole reason he went in, but two hostesses promptly came and sat on either side of him. Save for the 10,000-yen note that Makiko had left with him, Koji emptied all his cash onto the table. Twenty-eight thousand yen. The women began fawning on him. His mind was on the pink telephone by the entrance.

He didn't get home until after two.

The radio was on in the neighbor's apartment. Usually it didn't bother Koji, but tonight it did. He banged on the wall a few times with his fist. He heard the neighbor exclaim *What?* from the other side. Koji shouted back to tone it down. The guy lowered the volume, but Koji could still hear the grating music.

The tune came from the apartment to the left. Koji had never heard so much as a squeak from the apartment on the right, whose resident was an old woman who seemed well over seventy. He had run into her several times in front of the common bathroom, but that was about it. Just once, when she'd left her door ajar, he'd glimpsed her glued to the television, earphones on. That had been during the height of summer.

He drank some whiskey. As his body warmed up, he began to calm down.

His unseemly behavior started to seem comical. He was acting like a man who had been dumped by his woman. Makiko wouldn't just leave him. Something must have happened—that was why he couldn't get in touch with her. He knew where she lived in Yoyogi Hachiman, which women's high school she attended, and even the name of her homeroom teacher. If he wanted to see Makiko, he could do so at any time.

At some point, he fell asleep.

He woke up just after nine. He gulped down bread along with some tea for breakfast.

He was broke; he'd been foolish enough to drink at a bar the night before. He had no intention of spending Makiko's 10,000 yen. He just needed to find work.

Leaving his room, he bought a newspaper at the station, sat on a platform bench, and glanced through the classifieds. He focused on the ones for temporary staff and day laborers. He needed cash now, and he spotted some leads.

It had been fifteen days since he'd quit work. Today was the thirteenth of December. Only fifteen days. It seemed so long ago that he'd beaten up Hatta.

He called just before eight in the evening.

Makiko picked up after only two rings. Koji felt relieved. Tenderness for her coursed through him.

"I called several times yesterday," he said.

"I wasn't home."

"Did something bad happen?"

"No, nothing like that."

Her tone was distant. She was always like that on the phone. She always had the voice of an adult.

Koji heard a gunshot and a woman's scream. It seemed to be coming from her TV set.

"I went to the employment office and decided on a job. Just stupid grunt work, but it pays 4,000 yen a day. I think I'll give it a shot for a while."

"Sounds tough," she said, as if she couldn't care less.

Koji wanted to tell her he was doing it for her but stifled the urge. Working for her sake was only natural. He loved her. He'd earn money, give it to her, and all would be well.

"Has your mom calmed down a little?"

"She doesn't really care what I do. It's only because she was warned by the police and my school that she's started to give me a hard time."

Another gunshot.

"I'm sitting in our coffee shop. Can I come over to your place?"

"I guess."

"Is it a bad time?"

"No, it's okay."

She didn't sound particularly pleased. Koji began to feel annoyed at her unresponsiveness. He wanted to see her as soon as possible.

"Okay, I'm heading over now. I should be there in about thirty minutes," he said and hung up.

It was a small apartment building five stories high. It took Koji a while to find it. It was almost nine.

He pushed open a heavy glass door and entered a sizable hallway. There didn't seem to be a superintendent. The elevator door was open.

The nameplate outside Makiko's apartment just gave a surname: Mitsuya. Both the walls and the ceiling were white, making the place feel like a hospital.

It was that lean man Watanabe who answered the door.

He gave a slight smile when he saw Koji and glanced back into the recesses of the apartment. The door was barely open, just enough for

Watanabe to stick his head out, so Koji couldn't see Makiko.

No doubt she had sounded so distant on the phone due to Watanabe's presence. Her mother must have asked him to keep her under watch.

"Sort it out between yourselves." It was Makiko.

Koji grasped the doorknob and opened the door wide. She stood diagonally behind Watanabe. She was wearing a blue dressing gown and what seemed like pajamas underneath.

Her expression didn't change upon seeing Koji.

"What the hell's going on?" he asked both and neither of them.

"Why don't we go outside and talk?" Watanabe suggested.

"I didn't come to talk to you. I came to see Makiko."

"Nobody named Makiko lives here."

"You know I'm talking about Etsuko."

"Sort it out between yourselves, all right?" Makiko said again.

Watanabe put his hand on Koji's shoulder, applying some force, as if to push him out.

"Are you okay with this?" Koji asked Makiko.

He brushed Watanabe's hand away, but he didn't want to stir things up. The man was her mother's lover.

"Just talk to him, okay? I don't care either way."

A gunshot sounded from the rear of the apartment. Apparently the television was still on.

I don't care either way—Koji took this as permission to beat the guy up and get on her mother's bad side for good. That would certainly speed things up.

He took a few steps back and waited for the man to come out. Closing the door behind him, Watanabe grinned.

"You're pretty good," he conceded.

While they waited for the elevator to come up, Watanabe kept looking at Koji and laughing. Koji remained silent. He remembered Makiko's warning that the man might shiv him.

"She's come back a woman. Impressive. Her mother being what she is, no wonder she's got it, too."

"What the hell's that supposed to mean?"

The elevator door opened. Watanabe entered first.

"That girl will be quite something. Almost frightening to antici-
pate."

Watanabe laughed again. Makiko had been alone with him in the
apartment. Koji's flesh began to crawl. His blood seemed to sink along
with his body.

"You piece of shit—"

Koji tried to grab Watanabe's shirt but the man brushed off his
hand.

"Etsuko told us to sort it out between ourselves. Let's discuss this
calmly. We'll decide whose woman she is."

A rage beyond words welled up in Koji. He couldn't tell whether
it was directed at Makiko or at Watanabe. All the muscles in his body
were trembling. The elevator halted and the door opened.

"Calm down. If we're going to brawl, let's do it after we've talked."

Whatever the man meant to say, Koji wouldn't forgive him. It
didn't make a difference if he was offering to cede her. She was Koji's
woman first. No, she still was his. He didn't need Watanabe to cede
her.

"Let's calm down a little and have a drink."

"No need to drag things out. Take us someplace where nobody's
around."

"Just hear me out first, all right?"

They left the apartment building and walked on the pavement for
a while.

"There's a place ahead where I go a lot," remarked Watanabe.

He led Koji into a dark, narrow street.

It was a residential area. Tall walls lined both sides of the street.
There was one streetlight ahead but no sign of a place to drink.

When Koji was about to ask where it was, a kick from behind landed on his waist and he stumbled forward.

The blood rushed to his head. From his awkward position he turned
toward Watanabe and lunged at him. Something swished through the
air. Koji felt a heavy lash on his shoulder. The pain wrapped around
to his back, and he fell to his knees. It wasn't a rod. Rather, something
as supple as a whip, but with dreadful mass. Again the wind wailed in
the dark. He swayed backward. Something like a bird's feather brushed

his cheek. Then a third whoosh. From his upper left arm down to his back, he felt such pain he could hardly breathe. He lay prostrate on the road as if he'd been yanked down. *Pisses me off.* Before the thought came he'd rolled over. The swish landed near his face. A dull, heavy sound against the road. What the hell was it? At any rate, he had to get up. A direct hit from that thing and he was dead. His back bumped against something—a large plastic bucket filled with garbage. He knocked it over, rolled it towards Watanabe, and managed to stand up. They were near some dumpster with a host of plastic buckets. Koji lifted one above his head and threw it at his opponent. Garbage scattered everywhere.

"Want to fight dirty, asshole?" Koji shouted, picking up another bucket.

He didn't have time to throw it. Watanabe had closed in. Koji leapt back and barely evaded the swish. He felt that feather-like sensation along the back of his hand again. Now from the side. He dodged that one, but it came back slicing and he couldn't quite evade it then. From his side, from his back, the pain emanated through him. He couldn't breathe, but he didn't collapse. What he'd clamped to his side was holding him up: the swishing thing, some rope, and not even a very thick one. *How could such a thing*—but he didn't have time to think, as they both began to tug at it. The next moment, Watanabe's shoe burrowed into Koji's belly. Koji sank to his knees, and he let go of the rope. It dug in from his shoulder to his back, then into his chest. His arm. His back again. Soon he couldn't tell what position he was in or where he was being hit. Was it really a rope? He could only cradle his head. He began to lose consciousness.

Watanabe's shoe was kicking him lightly around the hips. *I'm lying on my back.* The man's yellow leather attire dully reflected the streetlight. Koji couldn't see the man's face. *I'll kill you,* he failed to vocalize. The receding footsteps, he could somehow hear clearly. *Bastard,* he failed again to utter. He couldn't move, and he couldn't even feel any pain.

On his back, thinking nothing, he looked at the sky for a long time. *Sort it out between yourselves.* Makiko's voice, right by his ear, grew stronger, then weaker. *I don't care either way.*

"What a fool I am." At last his voice had returned.

He stood up, but he wouldn't be able to walk for long. He put his hand on a wall to support himself and shuffled along.

No broken bones. If his bones were broken, he'd be nauseated or breaking out in a cold sweat. It was like that when he'd broken his collarbone. If he rested somewhere for a while, he'd be mobile soon enough.

He came across a perfect park for that. He crawled into some shrubs and lay on the ground. He didn't feel the cold.

2

It started to get brighter at last just before seven.

Koji crawled out of the shrubs. His body was cold and stiff.

When he moved his arms, he felt shots of pain all over his body. He tried broader movements—a second time, then a third. It got a little better. He tried his legs in the same way, and he could turn his waist fairly easily. The problem remained his arms. He had tried to protect his head with them. Watanabe had aimed for his head.

His left cheekbone hurt when he touched it. The skin was broken, and the flesh too seemed to have ripped. He had no idea at what point his face had been hit. All he recalled was that sensation like the brush of a bird's feather.

His jacket was torn in three places. He clicked his tongue in irritation, took out a crumpled cigarette, and lit it.

In his pocket were several 100-yen coins and Makiko's 10,000-yen bill. He straightened the bill, plucked it by its edge, and set it afire with a match. The flame spread, and soon the 10,000-yen note was too hot to hold. In no time it became a square of ash on the ground.

Work started at 9 a.m.

After the bulldozer leveled the ground, the roller packed it solid. They were building a road. Koji simply had to dig holes two-and-a-half feet in both diameter and depth at fifteen-feet intervals along both sides. They were for the cherry trees for the central park of a new public housing development.

Now and then the site manager came to measure the holes. He would count the number Koji had dug and make a face. Koji didn't care. It was the best he could do in his state.

He'd lean his weight against the shovel. When he lifted, pain shot through his arms. The soil was like clay and stuck tenaciously to the metal. It was tiring to stay crouched over as the hole grew deeper.

Farther down, the color of the soil changed, as well as its odor. Water oozed out and pooled at the bottom, and Koji's sweat dripped into the puddle. His hand became damp—another blister had popped. He heard a whoosh and the wrapping pain came back. *Sort it out between yourselves, all right? I don't care either way,* Makiko's voice still hummed. He slammed the shovel deeper into the hole. A fat worm sliced in half emerged from the newly turned earth and writhed around. Cherry tree saplings, their roots covered in straw, were delivered one after another, filling the holes Koji had dug.

His father had been fond of cherry trees. From when they first bloomed to when they scattered in a floral blizzard, he'd go flower-gazing every day and come home drunk. He'd lost all interest in them after Koji's mother had died, which was somewhat strange, since as a couple they'd never seemed close even to the eyes of child. The way his father changed after the passing almost seemed like a lie.

The sun felt strong for winter. When its rays dimmed, he heard a mother calling for her child.

He only got two 1,000-yen bills for his work.

"I thought I was getting 4,000 yen," he protested.

"You've got to be kidding. You haven't even done half a man's work," the site manager rebuffed, returning his wallet into his brown stomach band and looking away.

At least he'd earned 2,000 yen.

He woke up once in the morning, drank a glass of water, and went back to sleep.

He wasn't really awake until evening. He was starving and ate three Cups o' Noodles, and now there were none left under the sink.

He was still in some pain, but it had dulled into something vague as though a haze had settled over it. The scab on his cheekbone had

74

dried and hardened. When he took off his clothes, there were purple bruises all over his body. Those areas were still swollen and slightly warm to the touch.

He pulled out an old jacket from his closet. It had three cigarette burns and a broken zipper, but it was better than a torn one.

When he leaned over to put on his socks, he felt a sharp pain in his back. It was actually pleasant, only hurting that much.

It was past eight.

Makiko answered the phone with her usual simple *Yes*. It was a handy word that covered callers for both "Endo" and "Mitsuya."

Koji stayed silent for a while, trying to get a sense of the room on the other end. He couldn't hear the TV set or any music.

"Is Watanabe there?"

"Oh, it's you."

"Get Watanabe on the phone."

"So you don't want to talk to me?"

"What the hell's that supposed to mean?"

"Aren't you calling because you want to see me?"

"Are you kidding me?"

"Why would I be?"

"Get me Watanabe."

"He's in the shower."

"I'll call again in ten minutes." Koji tried to hang up.

"Wait."

"What?"

"Watanabe was making love to me until just now."

"So?"

"Can you tell I'm in tears?"

Koji hung up.

He started walking toward the station. There were more and more people around him. The ten minutes passed quickly.

He got inside a phone booth in front of the station.

"Yes." It was Makiko again.

"Hand the phone to Watanabe."

Makiko paused and didn't say anything.

"He's there, isn't he?"

"He is."

The traffic on the station-front street was loud, but Koji could vaguely hear Makiko talking to Watanabe.

"You haven't had enough?" Watanabe sounded slightly drunk.

"We're not done with our discussion."

"As I see it, we are. I could have helped myself to one of your fingers, you know."

"You fought dirty. That was a sneak attack."

"So you want to have it out with me again?"

"I'm in no shape for that. You left me in a bad way. I just wanted you to know that I'm heading for Shinjuku right now."

"What's it to me?"

"I'm going to Makiko's mother's bar. I believe it's called Lulu."

Watanabe fell silent. Koji could faintly hear his breathing.

"I wonder what she'd say if she knew you were sleeping with her daughter."

"So you think you're threatening me?"

"I'm just telling you I'm going to get a drink in Shinjuku."

"Go ahead, then." Watanabe laughed. He didn't say another word, and Koji also remained silent.

The man wasn't hanging up. Mother and daughter were being weighed on his mental scale, it seemed. Koji waited. Three minutes passed, and the warning sounded.

"Hey," Watanabe said.

Koji inserted another 10-yen coin.

"What do you want? To get back together with Etsuko?"

"Money. I won't be able to work for a while with these injuries. Call it medical costs."

"How much?"

"Twenty thousand yen. You need to bring it to me right away."

He heard Watanabe talking to Makiko. *He wants twenty thou, for medical costs, he says.*

"Just this once. Ask again and I'll blow your head off."

"I'll be waiting for you in Ueno Park. Back entrance of the art museum."

"Why Ueno?"

"I think I'll have a drink in Ueno instead of Shinjuku. If you're not there in an hour, I'm heading over to Shinjuku."

Koji gave a brief description of the location.

The warning sounded again, but Koji didn't insert another coin. Watanabe began saying something when the line was cut off.

It had started drizzling, and the park looked abandoned. All Koji could see were a few couples embracing and getting wet on benches. It was warmer than it would have been on a clear night.

An hour passed. Koji was standing under an evergreen whose branches spread wide. The rain was beginning to fall harder. The brick-colored museum looked blackish in the night.

He heard a long drawn-out cry that sounded like a woman shrieking. On the other side of the road from the museum was a zoo, with an aviary right along the wall.

Koji heard footsteps—trotting. Beneath the streetlight where slender threads of rain were clearly visible, a dark human shape emerged.

"You're late."

It had been ten minutes more than an hour, and it was almost ten. Watanabe's huffs turned white in the air.

"Traffic was bad on the highway 'cause of the rain."

It was hard to make out Watanabe's expression with the streetlight at his back. Koji could see that he'd turned up the collar of his black trench coat and that he had his hands in his pockets. Perhaps he was holding that rope.

"You'll get your stinking 20,000 yen. But don't think for a second that you threatened me into this."

"Then why are you coughing it up?"

"You're the one who brought up medical costs. You not only had your woman taken away, you got beaten up. I feel bad for your sorry ass."

Watanabe pulled two 10,000-yen notes out of his pocket and fluttered them as if offering alms. Koji snatched them and shoved them into his jacket pocket.

"Don't think you can pull this stunt again."

"Right."

Koji took a step toward Watanabe. The rain was falling hard now. The raindrops trickling down from his hair collected above his eyebrows.

Watanabe made to turn away. Koji kicked out aiming at his lower stomach. With a groan Watanabe doubled over, holding his belly.

"We're even now."

"Dammit. Ain't cute."

Watanabe stood back up but didn't attack right away. One hand was in his coat pocket. Koji took a couple of steps back to open some distance.

"Working me over like that, you ought to have gone ahead and at least broken a bone or two. Then you wouldn't be here tonight to get your own bones snapped."

"I thought I'd broken a few. Looks like you're tougher than I thought. I shouldn't have let you off so easy. Didn't want to kill you."

The rope slithered out of Watanabe's coat like a living thing. It was indeed a thin rope, but with three bulbous fixtures at one end.

Watanabe leapt. He was too far away. Koji easily dodged the first blow. The next howl was coming, and Koji didn't take his eyes off the rope. Distance. He had to stay either glued to the man or a few paces away. One step was the danger zone. The rope was short. When it scythed sideways it would always snap back. He had to be careful about moving in close.

He dashed. All his muscles screamed with pain. The rope chased him and hit the concrete ground with a dull thud. Koji sidestepped and dashed again. Here there was room, not at all like that narrow alley. His pursuer was slow on his feet. Koji halted and faced him. Watanabe's body stretched up; the rope came whipping down. The moment it sounded against the concrete, Koji lunged with all the force he had in him. Their bodies tangled and fell together. Watanabe tried to leap up, but Koji, clinging to his waist, shoved. Watanabe was supine. Koji clambered onto him, his eyes focused on the hand holding the rope. A fist struck up and got him in the nose. For a moment everything went red, his nose stung, and tears rose to his eyes. But he hadn't let go of Watanabe's right wrist that he'd clasped with both hands. Now Koji was underneath, and now on top. He grabbed Watanabe's little finger on the hand holding the rope and yanked it back as hard as he could. There was a dull snap as of a living tree, but he didn't hear it so much as feel it in his palm. Watanabe emitted a low groan. The rope lay on the street like a dead snake. When Watanabe's fist came at him, he ducked.

They stood up at the same time. Maintaining a low stance, Watanabe clutched the little finger of his right hand. They glared at each other for a while. Koji couldn't move right away—his head swooned as if someone had yanked his hair from behind. The previous beating was taking its toll; his body hadn't completely recovered. But he couldn't have waited, not one minute, not one second. Watanabe's breathing was labored as well.

Koji took a step forward. So did his opponent, whose foot came flying at Koji's stomach. Koji's fist was a split-second faster and slammed into Watanabe's chin. Koji himself reeled from the impact, but Watanabe fell like a stick onto his back. Rolling over and lifting his upper body, he went for the rope on the ground, but Koji pinned it down with one foot and, with his other, kicked up at Watanabe's stomach. For a second Watanabe seemed to float in midair, then fell back to the ground, where he lay face down. With the tip of his shoe Koji flicked the rope away behind him. Watanabe rolled over. The rope was out of his reach.

Koji was panting. *We can only ever "sort things out" with our bare hands.* He tried to say this out loud, but his voice didn't oblige. He felt dizzy again and didn't have the strength to deliver another kick as Watanabe got up.

There was some distance between them. Watanabe slowly undid the buttons of his trench coat, one by one, and was waiting for a chance to attack. Koji drew near only to find a black curtain fall over his eyes; Watanabe had thrown the trench coat at him. As soon as Koji swept away the curtain, Watanabe head-butted him in the chest. Koji fell to the ground clutching Watanabe's head. They grappled and rolled. They got back up.

"Wait," Watanabe said, out of breath. Koji's shoulders were also heaving. "If it's money you want, I can give you more."

Koji shook his head. *You think it's money I want?* But his voice still failed him.

"I'm sorry about Etsuko. I'm surrendering her to you."

Shut the fuck up! A silent scream. The water trickling down his forehead went into his eye.

Koji stepped closer. Watanabe turned around and headed into the shrubbery along the zoo wall, and Koji went after him. He felt something strike his thigh. Watanabe was swinging at him with a log. Koji rolled out onto the street, and the log came after him. When he tried to stand, a sharp pain shot through his thigh. The log came booming down, but Koji managed to roll away and dodge it. It broke with a wet snap, having been rotten. Watanabe lost his balance, and Koji went for his feet, bringing the man tumbling on top of him. Their positions switched. Watanabe's fist struck up from below, while Koji straddled him and grabbed his hair. Putting his full weight into it Koji slammed the back of Watanabe's skull against the street surface. There was a sickening sound. Koji repeated this a second, then a third time. A dark stain spread on the wet surface.

Koji rolled off. He lay face down, then rolled over and lay flat on his back. He was panting so hard he couldn't lie still. Steam was spewing from his mouth. He felt faint, like he was collapsing to the ground, but realized he was already supine.

He heard a low moan and got up. Watanabe was trying to stand, but propping himself up on his elbows and lifting his head and shoulders was all he could manage.

"Nobody does this to me," Watanabe said, shaking his head, "and gets away with it." Blood flowed from near his ear toward his cheek.

Koji, unsteady on his feet, picked up the rope. It was a thin rope, about two feet long, and what had looked like bulbs weren't knots, in fact, but balls. The rope had been splayed and something like lead buried into it, giving just the tip a significant mass. He swung it. *Whoosh!* He then swung it into Watanabe, who was on all fours. A cry, like a bird's—just like the zoo bird he had heard earlier. Watanabe was laid flat; then, his back arched. Koji swung down again, and the slicing sound sent a pleasant jolt through his own body. Watanabe's scream was louder, longer. With his body still arched, he slowly rolled over so that his stomach faced up. Koji lashed into him twice in a row on his stomach.

Instead of screaming, Watanabe emitted a choking sound that couldn't be called a voice. He merely writhed on the ground. Then he turned on his side, back curved like a shrimp, and slowly straightened his arm to raise himself up. Koji braced his own unsteady feet. Aiming for the face, he whipped the rope sideways. A sickening sensation, as if he'd pulverized bone—and the very moment he felt the rope's tip get caught in the man's face, Watanabe's body sailed through the air. Koji, too, fell to his butt from the impact. He couldn't stand up. Sitting there, Koji gazed at Watanabe, who looked like he'd dived headlong into the street. When he was sure that the man wasn't about to move, he slumped back spread-eagled.

For a while, his mind was blank. The rain felt good against his face. It was steadily becoming easier to breathe. At last a thought formed: *I've won.* The man had been a coward, who wouldn't fight with his bare hands, but he, Koji, had won.

In the distance he heard an animal growl. The cry of a nocturnal beast. Koji got up. He did not look again in Watanabe's direction.

3

Makiko came over to his place.

Koji was still in his futon. It was nine in the morning. She seemed to have run all the way from the station and couldn't speak when she arrived.

At first Koji had the illusion that he and Makiko were still together. It took a moment for a black rage to well up in him.

He got up.

"Run away, please!" Makiko said, grabbing at his chest.

Koji brushed her hands away. He wondered if Watanabe was on his way to take revenge for last night. But why would she warn him?

"Run away with me, please," Makiko begged. She was still out of breath and panting.

"Get out," Koji said, shoving her away. She hit her back against the sliding door of his closet, then grabbed his pajamas again.

"You have to run away."

"Shut the fuck up. Get out of here."

Koji shoved her once more. Makiko fell onto the futon, then clung to Koji's legs.

"Don't you know? Watanabe died."

Koji's hair stood on end, and he went pale. *That can't be.* No words came out.

"I'm sure the police will find you. That detective from the other day came to my place. The one called Kuroki."

The cop who'd been cutting his nails. The one who hadn't said a word, who'd just sat there facing him.

"Let's run away together," Makiko urged again.

It had to be a lie; he wasn't going to be fooled. The blood started to rush back to his head. "You came all the way to tell me your man's dead?"

"Watanabe wasn't my man. You are. Only you."

"Watanabe's woman, you are. You told us to sort it out ourselves because you didn't care either way. Then you ended up being his."

Koji was stifling his anger. Makiko shook her head violently. She continued clinging to his legs. "You killed Watanabe. You killed him for my sake."

That settled it: she was lying to lure him again to some weird place.

"I'm in love with you. I always thought of you when I was in Watanabe's arms."

"Why did you let him fuck you? Why did you say you didn't care either way?"

"A man makes a woman his no matter how she feels about it. Isn't that right? Just like you two fought it out. If you'd walked away with your tail between your legs, I'd have been his. But you killed him—you killed him for me."

"Stop this. Just go home. Go home and go to school. It's not Sunday."

Tears welled up in Makiko's eyes, but Koji wasn't swayed.

"You mean to run away alone."

"I'm not gonna run away. I'm not running anywhere. I'm leaving now to find work. The straight and narrow. I'm done with a woman like you."

"You still have time. The police don't know that you met Watanabe last night in Ueno Park. I'm the only one who knows."

"So?"

"So I can run away with you. The police might never figure it out."

"Run away together and, what, live by shoplifting? You think I'm that big of a fool?"

"Please don't run away alone. You didn't kill him alone. We did it together."

Something in him snapped. He kicked Makiko, flooring her. She came back up, her hair a mess. He punched her. Hard. Her nose began to bleed.

"Get out. You'll stain my futon." As she stood up he grabbed her by the hair and shoved her out of his room.

"Koji!" Banging on the door, Makiko started screaming his name.

Now he felt less angry than spooked. He slipped out of his pajamas and quickly put on his clothes.

He opened the door and stepped outside. When she came clinging onto him, he dealt her a few blows. Dashing off, he didn't look back to see how she was.

He didn't remain unaffected by what she had told him.

He immediately bought a newspaper at the kiosk in front of the station. He didn't see any articles about Watanabe. But then, it had happened only the night before.

The train was pretty empty. Koji glanced through the classifieds. Somehow he couldn't concentrate.

No rush. There were lots of jobs out there. Classifieds filled two entire pages of the paper. If he didn't find something suitable in this paper, he'd buy another one. There were even magazines with nothing but job ads.

There were two 10,000-yen notes in his pocket. It was the money Watanabe had brought for so-called medical costs. He didn't want the money sitting in his pocket forever.

He began wondering what he should spend it on. The more trivial, the better.

He got off at Shinbashi. He walked along streets festooned with

Christmas lights. When he saw a "50% Off" poster he considered buying some clothes. Walking around in something he'd bought with Watanabe's money, though, didn't cut it. Another model ship kit? No, it would take too long to make. Best just to eat something good with the money. He searched for a restaurant, but they were all covered with Christmas decorations, and he balked.

He ended up buying two boxes of fried chicken and a sandwich. It only cost 1,800 yen. His pocket actually became heavier.

The streets were packed. There wasn't a single spot where he could sit down and eat. He passed by several Santa Clauses. He opened one box of fried chicken and ate as he walked, throwing the bones on the pavement. If there were stray dogs he'd have gifted them, but all he saw were people. The more he walked, the more crowded his surroundings became—he was now in the heart of Ginza.

He stopped at a traffic light. He dropped the empty box and flattened it with his foot. The crowd began to move. He caught a glimpse of evergreens and found himself moving in their direction.

The park was also full of people. There were couples embracing on benches even though it was still daytime. He took the gently curving road from the fountain, through a thicket, and reached a lawn of dried grass, where he sat down.

A few pigeons fluttered down and approached. Thanks to the humans who scattered food for them, they had no trouble surviving in the heart of the city. He looked for a stone. When he couldn't find any, he pretended to throw one. The pigeons spread their wings a bit but realized that nothing was flying their way and slowly started approaching him again.

Koji lay on his back. When he did, the city suddenly seemed very distant. Even the sound of footsteps crunching gravel on the path not far from his head seemed to be coming from beyond a wall. He gazed for a while at the thick, looming clouds. No matter how thick they loomed, clouds had gradations, and they moved.

But learning this didn't decrease the cash in his pocket.

It occurred to him that someone to talk to wouldn't hurt. Treating that person was indeed one way to spend the money. There were a disgusting number of people around but not one he could talk to. He recalled in turn the faces of people he knew.

After a few, Numata's popped up.

It didn't even irk him anymore. Numata, too, had just wanted somebody to talk to. That had to be it.

He sensed something moving at his feet—a pigeon, probably. He'd tired of gazing at clouds and had closed his eyes. Did the pigeon mistake him for food? How funny. He'd stay motionless until it actually started pecking at him.

He recalled a rite called a sky burial where corpses were exposed to birds of prey. The belief was that when the birds soared, the dead ascended to heaven. He learned this from his high school Japanese teacher who once wasted an entire class talking about various funeral rites involving not only birds, but wind, water, and more.

The topic of the class had been a poem about crabs: A child who lives near a swamp sinks his dead parents in the swamp. The crabs in the swamp eat the parents' corpses. The child catches the crabs, plump from feasting on his parents, takes them to market, and sells them. The child's parents and their parents before them have sold crabs, too. That was roughly how the poem went.

The last line read: *There are also people who eat crabs.* The teacher singled out Koji and asked him what he thought it meant. Lost for an answer, Koji said crabs were considered delicious. He still clearly remembered the look of scorn on his teacher's gaunt, abnormally sallow face.

The poem was too difficult. How was he supposed to know what it meant? Yet, oddly enough, the poem had stayed with him. If that teacher had taken the trouble to explain it, Koji wouldn't have treated Japanese class as his lunch break. He might even have developed a taste for poetry.

When Koji was a senior, the teacher died from an overdose of potent asthma medication. He was only in his thirties. Koji ended up disliking not only poetry, but all books.

Something touched his trousers. Was it starting to peck in earnest? Koji didn't move. He even held his breath. It touched again. It wasn't a pigeon—more like a caress. Koji raised his head.

"Oh, you're alive."

He saw a boy of about four or five. He had to be goofing off, to touch at all. A real corpse would have scared him.

Koji got up and gestured to the child to come closer. At least he'd have someone to talk to.

The child bashfully looked down. He wore a gray-and-black checkered coat and blue trousers and even had on an off-yellow tie—so to speak his Sunday best, except for his blue canvas sneakers, which were dirty, faded, and torn.

Koji didn't like children. He didn't know how to deal with them when they followed him around. Normally he would have coarsened his voice to shoo away the kid.

There was no apparent guardian in sight. Koji held out the remaining box of fried chicken and made clicking sounds with his tongue as if he were calling to a dog.

The boy pulled a little chocolate box out of his own pocket and showed it to Koji.

"Fried chicken," Koji said. "I'll trade you one for a piece of chocolate." He opened the box and a nice aroma wafted out. The boy took a couple of steps closer and pointed, not at the box but at Koji's face.

"You're hurt."

Koji still had a dried scab on his cheek. It would be a while before it came off. When he smiled, just that side of his face pulled taut.

"A bad guy hit me. It hurt a lot."

Koji took one of the bony pieces of chicken and bit into it. The boy peered into the box.

Grease glistened around the boy's mouth as he kept sucking on the bone after all the flesh was gone. When Koji offered him another piece, the boy took out the chocolate box from his pocket as if in exchange.

"Help yourself to as much as you like. And I've also got a sandwich," Koji said.

The boy did seem hungry, but he had a modest, almost obsequious manner. Koji forced the chicken into the boy's hands. Bewildered, the boy laughed.

"Come on, eat like a man!"

Still no sign of any kind of guardian. Maybe the kid was lost.

A pigeon approached his feet. He threw a bone at it. The astonished

86

pigeon darted up but soon came fluttering down and pecked at the bone a few times.

"What's your name, kid?"

"Hiroshi," he replied through a mouthful of food.

"You look pretty sharp in that tie. How old are you?"

"Five."

He was the same age as Koji's nephew. When Koji had left Nagano, the child had only been able to utter a few words. His niece had just been a baby then. Koji had yet to meet the youngest.

The chicken and the sandwich were soon gone. The little boy had eaten more than half of the food.

"Isn't there anybody with you?"

The boy shook his head in an exaggerated way as if he'd been asked a naughty question.

"You came with your mom or dad or some other grown-up, didn't you?"

The boy looked down. He lightly shook his head.

"You must be lost. Let's look for your folks together."

The boy shook his head again.

"Can't you do anything besides shake your head? You can recite your address, can't you?"

The boy fell silent. Koji sensed an odd determination.

"Shall I take you to a cop—I mean, a policeman?"

"No," Hiroshi answered clearly.

"What's your plan?"

"I'll stay here."

"Is someone coming to get you?"

The boy shook his head again. This was starting to be a drag. The boy was just lost.

"See you around."

Koji stood up and took a few steps. When he looked back, the boy was staring at him. Koji waved, but the boy didn't respond—he just kept staring.

"You want to stay with me?"

The boy looked at the ground, then straight at Koji with obstinate eyes.

"Come on, then."

Koji started walking. They didn't even hold hands, but the boy followed close behind. It was as though Koji had found a puppy. He'd play at it for a while; sooner or later, the kid would offer up his address. If he didn't, he simply needed to be taken to a police box.

"Want to go to an amusement park?"

The money was still heavy in his pocket. The boy remained silent. Koji just kept walking.

4

Koji came back with milk, hamburgers, and potato salad.

His pocket now had only a few 1,000-yen bills and was considerably lighter. Hiroshi hadn't enjoyed the amusement park all that much. Koji had had to force him to get on the rides. Only on the go-kart had the kid's eyes lit up a little. If he'd been having fun, Koji would have cleaned out his pocket.

The child sat in a daze, perhaps tired, on Koji's apartment floor. It was six in the evening. Koji unrolled a futon in the corner of the room. He placed the hamburgers and potato salad on the table.

No matter how many times Koji asked him, Hiroshi refused to give his address. It wasn't that he didn't know it—he just didn't want to tell. His face betrayed his determination. He didn't want to go to the police box, either. The puppy Koji had found was clinging to him. There was nothing to do but kick it away. His leg had twitched a number of times. It was only on a whim that he'd brought it back to the apartment. The kid could do as he pleased. Koji didn't care.

"Don't tell me you ran away from home."

Hiroshi didn't answer. He looked as if he were trying to figure out where to start on his super-sized burger. Koji handed him a Tetra Pak of milk and made himself a whiskey-and-water.

He opened the evening paper.

He hadn't forgotten to buy one, the matter still on his mind. When he saw the small photo in the city news section he felt as if he'd been doused in cold water. No mistake, it was Watanabe.

The article was substantial. Tatsuo Watanabe, age thirty-three. Real-estate agent. Found beaten to death near the art museum in Ueno Park. Estimated time of death: 11 p.m., December 15th.

Watanabe had belonged to the Kansai-based Shoyukai syndicate. Police were investigating a rival gang called the Tatsumigumi.

Koji read the article again and again.

He felt doomed. He finished his glass and gulped down another half straight. Yet he couldn't get drunk.

He looked at the newspaper again. The print seemed far away. He was reading but couldn't seem to grasp anything he read. He closed his eyes. He could recite the thing, and it was easier to understand that way.

They'd fairly decided it was a gang lynching. There was no mention of *Koji Mizui* nor any bit about a man fitting his description near the scene.

He wasn't under suspicion, Koji thought. No, he didn't even kill the man. There was no way anyone would die from just that much. Watanabe had beaten him twice as badly with that rope. After a night's sleep in the park, Koji had even managed to go to work the next day.

He'd left Watanabe lying there. Somebody had pummeled the guy some more and finished him off. After all, the paper was explicit about a lynching. Given the sort of man Watanabe was, a lot of people must have wanted him dead.

Koji tried to open his eyes.

He couldn't. It was as if something were pressing down on them.

Suddenly, the feel of striking Watanabe with the rope was vivid in his palm. That last blow to the face—for a moment it had seemed as if Watanabe's head had caught on the rope's tip, then he'd gone flying. A sickening sensation.

He still couldn't open his eyes. He rolled on his side. Would Maki-ko say anything? Fine, let her if she wanted. A woman who'd lied once, the police wouldn't believe so easily.

He'd thrown the rope in a drainage ditch. He'd realized while walking that he was still clutching it. Though he hadn't meant to hide it, it would be lying at the bottom, under murky water. Those three balls of lead embedded in the rope's tip had been quite heavy.

He heard a strange voice.

At last he opened his eyes. The voice was coming from within his apartment.

Koji remembered that Hiroshi was there. The kid had gotten into the futon by himself. He'd folded his trousers, coat, and shirt and placed them neatly on the floor by his pillow.

Hiroshi's shoulders were shaking as if he were having convulsions. He seemed to be sobbing.

"You need to pee?" On hearing Koji's voice, Hiroshi stopped crying. "You want your mom?"

Hiroshi didn't move. The child was under the cover, but Koji could tell his body was tensing up.

"Tell me what's wrong."

He glanced at the clock. It was 8:30. He'd been still with his eyes closed for over two hours, probably without saying a word to Hiroshi.

"Is it because I wasn't paying attention to you? Is that why you're crying?"

He crawled over to the futon and put his hand on Hiroshi's shoulder. The child began sobbing again. The small shoulder under Koji's hand was doing the talking.

"Stop crying, idiot!" Koji yelled, surprising himself.

Hiroshi's shoulder twitched for a moment, tensed, and grew still.

"Face me," Koji commanded. He flipped up the hem of his shirt and wiped Hiroshi's wet face. "You've got nothing to worry about. I'll take care of you. If you don't want to go home, stay here as long as you like. When you feel like going home, I'll take you." He gave Hiroshi's head a light tap with his fist.

He didn't know why Hiroshi had been in tears. But the kid wasn't crying anymore. After ten minutes, he heard the regular breathing of sleep.

Koji gazed for a while at the child's sleeping face. He reached for the hamburger on the table. That heaviness had lifted, and he was hungry.

He wasn't the sort who bore that sort of heaviness for long. He'd soon find it insufferable. It was as if the skin on some part of him always burst. The heavy air would escape from that opening, and in its place a dry, light breeze would blow into his body. It was too easy an attitude to be called optimism but was something close to that.

If the police came, he would deal with it then. No point worrying whether Makiko might tattle.

Koji bit into the hamburger. It had gone cold, and a greasy after-taste remained on his tongue.

When there was a knock on the door, Koji was getting into his pajamas. He thought for a moment that it might be Makiko. Then he had a different, unpleasant hunch.

"Who is it?"

His fingers trembled slightly as he did up his buttons.

"Makimura from K Police Station."

A jolt ran through his body like an electric current and then vanished. His mind was clear. He was ready for anything.

He opened the door. He saw Beanpole and the detective called Kuroki. It was Kuroki who took the first step in.

"We saw your light as we were passing," he said.

Koji thought he would immediately be handcuffed, but the detectives were both smiling. They didn't shove any warrants in his face, either.

"You have a guest?" Kuroki asked, noticing the futon.

"My nephew. I have to take care of him for a while. We went to the amusement park today and he's exhausted." The nephew bit was the first thing that popped into his head.

"Your older brother's kid, then."

Koji nodded. He'd been asked about his family when he'd been arrested.

"We heard you quit your job. How are you getting by?"

"Just doing what needs to be done."

It didn't look as if they were going to arrest him right away. Koji chose his words carefully. These guys cast traps with their chatter—he learned that lesson well enough the last time.

"You look like you've been hurt," Kuroki remarked.

"Had a little accident."

"What kind of work are you doing?"

"Day labor. I haven't worked for the past four, five days."

"So how do you make ends meet?"

"Savings. You guys should know that."

Beanpole laughed. Kuroki gazed at Koji, then looked anew at the futon. Koji waited for Watanabe's name to come up, but it didn't.

"Actually, there was something we wanted to tell you. Numata tried to commit suicide in jail. He was found in time."

Genuinely surprised, Koji didn't know what to say.

Kuroki continued, "You already heard most of this from Makimura, but the manager of Lucky, Yoshikawa, and the bartender, Matsuda, were in it together. The robbery was staged. But Numata didn't do as he was told. He clobbered Yoshikawa with a bag full of stones, then struggled with Matsuda, who was waiting to pick up the money. It must have been afterwards that he showed up here. The money was in Matsuda's possession."

"Why did Numata try to kill himself?"

"Dunno. But we managed to save his life. He's on a hospital bed now."

"You talked to him?"

"Yes."

"Did he say why he implicated me?"

"No. We just thought you should know because we caused you grief and because he's your friend."

"We're not friends or anything anymore." He was talking too much. Best to keep mum with these guys.

"As I said, we were just passing by." Kuroki glanced around the apartment. "Cute kid, huh?"

Koji turned around for a moment to look at Hiroshi. He was fast asleep with his mouth open and cheeks flushed.

"Sorry to bother you," Kuroki said.

When the door closed, Koji took a few deep breaths. His body was cold with sweat.

5

The two detectives returned to their car.

"She wasn't there," Makimura said. Kuroki, arms folded, was in the passenger seat. "Why didn't you ask him about her?"

Kuroki motioned for Makumura to get going. The car started moving.

"Does something about Mizui bother you, sir?"

"The one who bothers me is Etsuko Mitsuya."

"Then you should have asked him."

"The kid looked on the verge of waking up."

"Then why talk about Numata when you didn't need to?"

When they turned at the sewage treatment plant, the road got wider.

It had been Kuroki who had kept watch on Koji Mizui's apartment and arrested Hajime Numata. The circumstances had made the robbery at Lucky look like an inside job from the start. Numata had quickly become a prime suspect. He was the only bartender with no alibi and whose whereabouts were unclear.

Numata's circle of acquaintances was small. He was close to Matsuda, the senior bartender, and two former classmates besides Mizui. One of those classmates lived with a woman, while the other lived in a company dorm for single men. The only places left where Numata might show up were Matsuda's or Mizui's.

Kuroki chose Mizui without hesitation. By that point he'd already considered the possibility that Numata, Matsuda, and Yoshikawa were accomplices. Matsuda and Yoshikawa had done time together. Matsuda was also a homosexual who had been picking up runaway boys from Ueno Station for ten years.

Matsuda had forced Numata to become his lover. While Numata didn't display much emotion when confessing to his crime, he bawled like a baby when questioned about his relationship with Matsuda. The shame had been unbearable. Worse, he hadn't been able to resist. The frustration had caused Numata to explode and turn a staged robbery into a real one.

Numata never gave a clear reason why he'd named Mizui as an accomplice. When told of Mizui's arrest, he just smiled glumly. The weak preying on the weak—that was how Kuroki saw it.

There had been something about the look in Mizui's eyes that had reminded Kuroki of someone: a known juvenile delinquent they'd arrested for sexual assault. The victim, a 22-year-old woman, had immediately picked him out from the line-up. There was no other evidence.

For thirteen days the young man insisted he hadn't done it. Then they found a perv, who confessed within a day of questioning.

If that had been all, Kuroki would have forgotten the case.

Three days after being cleared and released, the youth attacked a policeman and stole his gun. It was Kuroki that pursued him to Chiba, shot him in the leg, and arrested him. The youth glared at Kuroki as he handcuffed him, then spat in his face. That had been five years ago.

The look in Koji Mizui's eyes had reminded him of the youth's.

More headlights were coming from the opposite direction. Kuroki lit one of his Short Peace cigarettes.

"I thought investigation headquarters was handling this one. I don't see why we have to drive around late at night."

"You can get off the case if you want."

"No, I'm with you. I owe you one after I botched it with Mizui's alibi."

Although the investigation headquarters for the murder of Tatsuo Watanabe was officially based at K Police Station, it had been placed under Metropolitan Police's Criminal Investigation Section Four. In other words, the force was treating the case as an instance of gang warfare.

Watanabe was part of a vanguard to expand the Kansai-based Shoyukai gang's presence in the capital. Since arriving five years ago, he had become well-known in those circles. The real-estate agency was a front for his actual work, black-market financing. It involved low-interest loans to the sex industry and the like, so there had been no cases. But without a doubt, Shoyukai money was permeating the Tokyo underworld through Watanabe. When Shoyukai expanded to Tokyo in earnest as an organization, the money would come into use.

Section Four must have sniffed out the gang's plans to establish itself in Tokyo. The Watanabe case presented a perfect opportunity to deliver the Shoyukai a rude blow. Although K Police Station's Criminal Investigation Section One had already started looking into the Watanabe killing as a standard murder case, Section Four from Metropolitan Police HQ had more or less commandeered the investigation and designated it as gang warfare-related. Kuroki suspected that the point wasn't to catch the killer but to use the episode of violence to put the syndicate in its place.

But it was a far stretch to declare this a gang war. True, the body was found not far from Tatsumigumi territory, but the method seemed too blatant to be their handiwork. They were the weaker organization, so it made no sense for them to provoke the Shoyukai.

"Mr. Yabe says it was probably a Shoyukai inside job. Kill off Watanabe and make it look like Tatsumigumi did it. Makes a good pretext for a war."

"That's how you'd have to rationalize it if you're wedded to the idea that it's gang-related."

"It appears that you think that's not the case."

"Beats me."

Shoyukai still needed Watanabe. He had been born in Tokyo and had a lot of contacts. As far as the police knew, he'd never run afoul of the gang leadership. Why would they off him just like that? There were lots of other ways to incite a gang war. Nobody would remember what started the war anyway once the blood started to flow.

"So what do you think is the real story?"

"Beats me."

"That again."

"There are two kinds of detectives, Makimura. Those who can't see, and those who won't. Yabe is the kind who won't. I'm the kind who can't. It scares me that I can't, so I sniff around in all sorts of places."

"I'm also the kind who can't," Makimura said, laughing.

Kuroki stubbed out his cigarette in the ashtray.

"But why are you still so focused on Etsuko Mitsuya? Watanabe may have been her mother's lover, but I don't see what Etsuko has to do with anything."

A background check on Watanabe had revealed that he had two women in his life. One was a bar hostess in Ginza. The other was Etsuko's mother, Kinuyo. It seemed he had sponged off of both women while leaving the gang's money untouched. He may have been a louse, but he was straight in his own way.

Watanabe's movements of the day before were pretty clear. In the morning he'd been at home in his apartment in Setagaya Ward. In the afternoon, he'd dropped by two bars in Tachikawa to see the owners. From there it seemed he had gone directly to Kinuyo Mitsuya's apartment in Yoyogi Hachiman. A witness confirmed seeing Watanabe's blue Nissan Skyline parked from 5 p.m. to a little past 8:30 p.m. near Kinuyo's home. Given the time line, Watanabe must have gone directly from Yoyogi Hachiman to Ueno Park.

What bothered Kuroki was that Kinuyo Mitsuya had been out of the house from around 3 p.m. Watanabe and Etsuko Mitsuya had been alone together for over three hours in that apartment.

The mother claimed she'd asked Watanabe to keep an eye on her daughter. Her lover had just been murdered, yet she was opening up her bar as if nothing had happened.

When Kuroki visited the apartment that morning, it was Etsuko who answered the door. She looked nervous, and Kuroki knew he was the cause. He was the one who'd had Makimura tail her. When Etsuko had been brought in for a minor offense, he was the one who had interrogated her and forced her to confirm Mizui's alibi.

Something about her said she wasn't just another difficult delinquent.

When a witness report came in that Watanabe's car had been parked near the apartment until nearly 9 p.m., Kuroki decided to go over there once more. Etsuko wasn't home. Kuroki dropped by again at 8 p.m., but she still hadn't returned.

Then Koji Mizui's face had popped into Kuroki's head.

"Tomorrow, I want you to really look into Etsuko Mitsuya. Especially what she's been up to these past ten days."

"I guess Section Four will deal with the gang warfare angle. I'd sure get a kick out of cracking the case before they do."

"I'm not competing with Section Four. It's just that I can't read Etsuko Mitsuya, and that makes me anxious."

"It's not like you to confide in me like this, sir. You can count on me. I'll find where she is, too."

"Chief's gonna frown on this."

"He looks like he was born with a frown anyway," Makimura joked.

It was only eight months since Makimura had been assigned to K Police Station, CIS One. He was a young detective, only twenty-four.

He still believed in going by the book—or rather, he had yet to handle a case that forced him to question it. An investigation to figure out the likes of Etsuko Mitsuya wasn't exactly by the book.

"Etsuko Mitsuya may be bothering you, but she can't be the perp, can she? What's her deal?"

"That'll become clear once we've checked her out. That's how detectives resolve their nagging doubts."

"So there are detectives who won't see and detectives who can't see. What about the ones who can and will see? Do they become legends?"

"They never join the force."

"Okay. What do we do with Mizui?"

"Leave him alone unless Etsuko visits him. He's probably still mad about being falsely arrested. It certainly took a toll on him."

Makimura fell silent. The first mistake was hard for any young detective. Furthermore, he'd been taken in by a 16-year-old girl.

They drew closer to the police station.

"Are Shoyukai and Tatsumigumi getting into a shooting war?"

"Beats me. Section Four's movements are fanning the flames on both sides, though."

Whatever the truth, a flicker would set off a chain reaction. That was what Section Four wanted. A gang war would force sleeper Shoyukai elements in Tokyo to come out into the open.

Kuroki had heard that troops were gathering at both gangs' offices since the morning. At K Police Station too, the lights were still on and a great many bodies were rushing in and out.

Chapter Four

1

When he opened the door, he could sense somebody moving in the darkness.

Under the fluorescent light, he saw Hiroshi's small figure, knees pulled up to his chest, in the corner.

He hadn't expected him to be there. Looking up at the darkened window from the street, he'd harbored a slight hope that Hiroshi would still be around, and he'd sneered at himself for it. He'd climbed up the stairs sneering with each step.

When he had left that morning, he'd given Hiroshi a 1,000-yen note, telling him to use it if necessary. Koji had also left a can of juice and bread and had not locked the door. Still, this was a kid. Kids didn't just stay quietly in an apartment. If Hiroshi had gone off somewhere and hadn't come back, well, that was okay.

Hiroshi was wearing his coat. There was neither a stove nor a *kotatsu* foot warmer in the apartment. It was as cold in the room as it was outside, the only difference being that there was no wind.

Hiroshi looked up at Koji without a word.

"At least turn the light on, huh?" Only after saying this did Koji realize that the string on the fluorescent light was too short for Hiroshi to reach.

The bread was gone and the juice can was empty. Koji took the can, crushed it, and threw it into the paper trash bag. Hiroshi remained silent, looking at Koji.

He was not a talkative child, but that morning, shortly after waking up, he and Koji had talked for a while in the futon. What's your favorite food? Cake. Anything you want? A radio-controlled car. I know a lot of monster names. Dinosaurs, too. Don't you have a TV? About such things Hiroshi was willing, in stops and starts, to speak, but when Koji asked him what his last name was, where he lived, or what his parents did, the child immediately clammed up.

Koji placed a hand on Hiroshi's head. "Did you go and play outside?"

Hiroshi gave the smallest of nods. His small fingers pointed to the stairs outside the door.

"You were playing on the stairs?"

"Yes."

"By yourself?"

Hiroshi nodded. Looks like he's used to being alone, Koji thought. He ruffled the child's hair a couple of times. Hiroshi's expression didn't change.

Koji took out of his pocket a little toy car he'd bought at the kiosk in front of the station. Hiroshi finally smiled. Koji had intended to buy a radio-controlled toy car, but it cost twice his daily wage.

"You must be hungry. Let's go and get something to eat. Before that, though, we're going to go to a public bath, get clean, and change our underwear. That's some dirty shirt you've got on. I'll buy you a new one on the way."

Hiroshi clung for dear life to his blue Volkswagen toy.

"I'll get you a radio-controlled car, too."

"Really?"

"Not right now, though. When I've worked for a while and saved some money."

"When?"

"I dunno. But it's a promise. So stay here until then."

"Okay, I will."

"Will you be okay on your own like today?"

"Yes."

Hiroshi placed his toy car on the table and observed it from the side.

"I'd like a Porsche for the radio-controlled one," the boy said.

"They have them at the department store."

Koji took the newspapers out from his jacket pocket and threw them in the corner of the room. He prepared for the bath with towels and soap.

He'd bought two different morning and evening papers. The morning editions carried articles and photos of riot police outside the home of the Tatsumigumi boss. The evening edition articles were short, didn't mention Watanabe, and merely summarized the conflict between the two gangs.

Koji felt that Watanabe's death was receding away from him. Yet someday, he also thought, the police would come for him. He had no desire to run away. If he had indeed killed the man, then he should be punished for it. Only, he wanted to continue his present life for a little while. Makiko wouldn't talk. She hadn't so far.

What worried him were those detectives from yesterday, but they hadn't mentioned Watanabe. They hadn't even asked him about anything related to the case. If they came by again and thrust a warrant for his arrest in his face, he'd be docile and let himself be handcuffed. If he went on the run, they would eventually arrest him, like Numata. It wasn't his style to put up futile resistance.

But could he really do it? Calmly offer up his wrists?

Finding work hadn't been difficult. The work itself wasn't easy, but all he needed to do was put his body to the yoke.

He'd gone to the Sanya district at eight in the morning. He unconsciously avoided the Public Employment Office and mingled with laborers gathering in front of an early-morning cafeteria. They shared stories about which sites were dangerous, which ones had difficult managers, and so on. Koji wasn't feeling choosy and simply followed the first coordinator who approached him.

A minibus took him to a construction site for ready-built houses.

He took orders from the scaffolding foreman and did basic construction work, digging holes, laying gravel, and laying down the primary layer of concrete. He threw himself into the work, and before he knew it, it was evening. Pickaxe or shovel in hand, he'd struggled with chunks of concrete and coarse soil mixed with scrap iron, and his mind had been blank. No thoughts of Watanabe and Makiko, nor of

Hiroshi who might be waiting alone in the apartment, had invaded his consciousness.

"Let's go to the bath," Koji said cheerfully, waving his towel around.

Hiroshi didn't let go of his toy car. He took it with him.

Koji crawled into the futon with Hiroshi. They went to sleep cuddled up together.

Through Hiroshi's newly purchased underwear, the warmth of his tiny body, so different from a woman's, radiated into Koji's arms. He'd given Hiroshi a good scrubbing that left him smelling lightly of soap.

Koji fell asleep immediately. He woke up in the middle of the night and found he couldn't go back to sleep.

Thoughts rambled in his mind until morning: the newspaper articles, Makiko, work, Numata's suicide attempt. Suddenly, Koji felt the need to look at the papers again. He'd read the article on Watanabe so many times that he knew it by heart. It was something else.

Koji crawled out of the futon and quietly switched on the light. He reread the papers from one end to the other. There was no mention of Hiroshi's name or any photo of him. No article about a kidnapped child, either.

He didn't understand why. Hiroshi was a missing child. Surely the family must be beside itself with worry, imagining the worst.

Koji felt cold. He got into the futon again. Hiroshi rolled over.

Koji couldn't think of anything else now. The faces of Hiroshi's family—faces he didn't know—kept appearing then vanishing in his mind like some kind of nightmare. How could a child's disappearance not even be in the paper? He had no way of finding out.

He thought he remembered hearing once that the media didn't immediately report kidnappings. But no, Hiroshi hadn't been kidnapped. He was here of his own free will.

A newspaper delivery bicycle passed. He could see that it was getting lighter outside the window.

He got up, threw on some clothes, and put on the kettle. He told himself it was pointless to worry. He had to work. If he didn't earn 5,000 yen today, they wouldn't be able to eat, and he wouldn't be able to buy Hiroshi a radio-controlled car.

The boy woke up.

He could dress and undress himself. He was a low-maintenance kid.

"We're having ramen for breakfast," Koji said.

Hiroshi nodded. Koji had already bought the boy's lunch of bread and juice the night before.

"Turn on the light when it gets dark."

He had added more string to the one on the fluorescent light. That way Hiroshi could reach it.

Koji imagined walking home in the evening and seeing the light in his window. He could get used to that. Just knowing someone was waiting warmed the heart.

"Say 'Takao Mizui,'" Koji ordered.

He'd told Hiroshi to say this if someone asked his name. It was Koji's nephew's name. Hiroshi repeated the name: *Takao Mizui, Takao Mizui.*

"That's enough," Koji said.

Hiroshi laughed.

Koji left for work. It was a clear, sunny day.

It was Monday now.

Koji had relaxed a bit because he'd landed two consecutive days of work. He waited fifteen minutes for the usual coordinator. The laborers went off somewhere one by one.

After half an hour, Koji finally realized he hadn't been picked.

There was a strong wind but the weather was still holding. Koji looked up at the sky. Rotten luck, he thought. He was responsible for a kid.

Those who hadn't been picked hung around, getting some sun. There was nothing to be done. Twice Koji went up and down the crowded street, but nobody called out to him.

He found a closed lunchbox place and sat down on its steps. He had two 1,000-yen bills in his pocket. He smoked a cigarette. He stuck another one in his mouth but stood up without lighting it. If he failed to get a job the next day too, he wouldn't even be able to buy Hiroshi lunch.

He walked around town again. He didn't think he'd find work that way, but he just couldn't keep still.

"Didn't get picked?"

A man in a very rumpled coat emerged from what looked like the back entrance of a flophouse. Koji almost bumped into him. The man gazed blearily at him for a while.

"Want to come with me? I know a way you can make some good money."

He was thin and short, with an unhealthy complexion. The impression was that of a shriveled old man, but it was hard to tell his true age. Something like curtain fabric was tied around his neck. He was obviously an out-of-work laborer, not a work coordinator.

"You won't earn a thing wandering around here."

"How much does this work pay?" Koji couldn't help asking.

"One thousand five hundred yen, lunch included."

"How can anyone work for money like that?"

"It's only for half an hour. All you have to do is lie down."

"Sounds fishy to me."

"You sell what you have to sell. Men can't sell their bodies like women, but we can sell what flows in our bodies."

He seemed to be referring to blood. Koji felt somewhat surprised that he could sell his blood for money. He had donated blood before, when he'd been working at his first job at the parts factory and a colleague had needed blood for a lung operation. The man's family thanked Koji but didn't pay him anything. After the operation, the colleague quit his job and never returned to the factory.

"Must be a rookie if you don't know the squeeze. You ought to experience it. It's like insurance when you're out of work."

The man laughed. All his front teeth were rotten and had turned purple.

Koji and the man got on the subway.

"You read the white-collar ones, eh?" the man said, tugging a newspaper out of Koji's jacket pocket. There was nothing in it about Watanabe. Nothing about Hiroshi, either.

Getting there didn't even take ten minutes.

They went to the waiting room on the second floor of a seedy old building. Three other laborers were already there, hunched over on benches.

Koji wrote a false name and address on the form. When it was his turn to have his photo taken, he hesitated. He didn't want photos of himself circulating.

"Don't worry about it," his companion assured. "It's just that there are guys who try to register twice under different names."

Koji glanced at the man's card. It showed his age as thirty-two. Could a man age that badly by giving his blood too often? In no way did he look below forty.

The man went ahead into the blood-collection room.

Koji, meanwhile, had a sample drawn. "That's good blood, you're type O," the young nurse said.

There were about ten beds in the collection room. Koji lay down on the bed next to his companion, who kept opening and closing his palm.

"You're young. The blood comes out thick and fast. I'm jealous," the man muttered, only his face turned towards Koji. The blood flowing through the vinyl tube was oddly murky and reddish-black. "It's unbearable, lying like this with the blood being squeezed out of you. Makes you feel like you're being sucked dry by a leech. Some people get better with medicine made from this blood. Some people spend what they earn from selling blood to drown in booze and die. It's true there are two classes: the bloodsuckers and the bloodsucked."

The sunlight outside the window was dazzling. Koji shut his eyes. He felt like yawning.

Afterwards they switched to a glucose drip. Eventually the nurse came back carrying reddish-black liquid. It seemed they simply extracted the needed components and returned the rest back into the body. It was creepy. Koji asked her to just throw it away, but the nurse silently completed her task.

"I'll wait over there," his companion said. He wearily raised himself from the bed and pressed his finger over where the needle had gone in.

Koji finished quickly, too.

The man was waiting for him. He offered a hot Cup o' Noodles—

it had to be the free lunch. It was better than nothing.

"I'll be off," the man said. He put on his coat. His retreating figure looked exhausted and really like an old man's.

Koji smoked two cigarettes. He couldn't wait any longer.

"What about my money?" he asked the nurse.

"You and Mr. Okubo were paid together," she replied. *First time here and already trying to double dip?* her tone seemed to imply.

Koji rushed outside. All he saw was the light, too bright for December, reflecting back off the pavement.

Koji returned to the town.

He sat down in the sun and smoked a cigarette. A laborer, reeking of alcohol, asked him if he wanted to come gambling.

"I've had enough," Koji said.

It was already past noon. A haze that filled the air weakened the sunlight.

Koji looked at his watch, but it wasn't because he was worried about the time. There was no way he'd find work today. His watch was about the only thing he could pawn.

He still had 2,000 yen. If he really needed it, there was always the 310,000 yen in savings. He wouldn't dream of spending it on himself, but he didn't mind using it if it meant Hiroshi wouldn't suffer.

He drowsed. When it got cold, he woke up. The sun was setting.

He stood up and did a few knee-bends. He rather liked the idea of going home early and playing with Hiroshi.

On the other side of the street, he saw a man in a black coat. It was him. Koji resolved to claim the money he'd earned, with interest.

The man stopped in front of a sake vending machine. Koji was about to approach him when four laborers crossed the street in the vending machine's direction.

He needed to wait. He didn't want the men to interfere. Maybe the guy had some influence in this town. The man turned around to face the laborers.

The air tensed. In a flash, the man leapt at one of the laborers and struck him with his elbow. But the laborers moved fast, too. One grabbed the man's legs, the other two went for his arms. The man's

106

body sank. The laborer who had been felled by the elbow jab got up and dealt a kick. The man took the hit. He threw his sake bottle at one of the other laborers, but since he was off balance, it just made a smashing sound against the street. His head locked by one of the laborers, he was thrown to the ground and kicked in the stomach. He curled up on the street. They grabbed him by the hair and made him face up. Vomited blood trickled down his chin. His face was pale, his shoulders were heaving, and his expression was blank. One of the laborers held his arms. There was the glint of metal. For a moment, Koji's legs buckled. A sound—the sound of a man's freedom being taken away from him. The handcuffs glinted silver again.

Koji began to run. Terror pursued him from behind. He couldn't see a thing; just that silver light flashed through his head. No, he couldn't stand having those things clamped around his wrists. No way. He could barely think until he left the town.

When he did, he was in another. He chose alleys where there weren't many people and kept running. Nothing was coming after him. Knowing it didn't make his feet stop.

He got his breath back in a public men's room in a park. He began to calm down. He began to see how ridiculous he'd been, panicking and running like nuts.

Koji didn't even know where he was. The sun had set, and it was getting dark.

2

A black shadow emerged from beneath the stairs.

"Are you Mizui?"

The man's figure remained black even in the streetlight. He wore a gleaming black leather racing suit, a black helmet, and sunglasses. Guessing from his voice, he was young. Only his breath was white.

Koji flicked away his cigarette.

"We've got your nephew. How about you come to Ueno Park to get him?"

Koji stole a glance at his apartment on the second floor. The light wasn't on in the window. "Son of a—"

Blood rushed to his head. The man took a nimble step back.

"Don't you care what happens to him? He's hungry and crying. You know the place. Right where you killed Watanabe. Etsuko Mitsuya asked me to tell you." The man stepped further back. "And I've told you now."

A sudden glare of lights made Koji cover his eyes with his arm. There was a roar. A wind with mass brushed past. A big motorcycle.

Koji ran up the stairs. In his empty apartment, there was no sign of Hiroshi. Unfinished lunch bread, an unopened can of juice, and the blue toy Volkswagen lay there. He could easily picture the way Hiroshi had been snatched.

Makiko had abducted Hiroshi. Moreover, she was telling him to come to the place where he'd killed Watanabe. Before he could fathom why, rage coursed through his body.

Koji grabbed the kitchen knife. It was Western-style and somewhat larger than a fruit knife. One of the things Makiko had brought over.

He was sure she wouldn't be waiting for him alone. Men would be there, too, perhaps from Watanabe's gang. Koji wasn't afraid. No matter how many they were, he would get back Hiroshi.

It was almost eight.

He sped to Ueno Park in a taxi. Once there, he ran to the pathway behind the art museum. His breath was white.

He saw no one on the road along the zoo. He could hear birdcalls.

He regained his breath and began walking slowly.

Suddenly, light appeared ahead. A car with its lights angled up. Vehicles were prohibited on this road, but it started to approach him. A large car, almost as wide as the road. Did the driver plan to hit him? Koji threw a glance toward the shrubbery along the zoo wall and gauged the distance. Four steps. Could he leap into it? The dark shook with engine roars, but the oncoming lights weren't picking up speed. It wasn't a car, but two motorcycles. A gush and tremors swept by Koji on both sides.

Getting off the motorcycles, two men walked over. They were dressed identically in black racing suits. Koji felt the knife beneath his jacket.

"I want the kid back."

One of the men gestured with his chin. When Koji turned around, he glimpsed the shadows of people. It was a group of three with a child in the middle, like a family.

The small shadow detached itself from the others. It came running toward Koji.

Glistening with tears, Hiroshi's cheeks seemed to shine in the streetlight. He clung to Koji's trousers.

"It was a real pain trying to cheer him up. He just kept crying." The male voice was unpleasant, high and cracking.

Koji asked Hiroshi in a hush if he was all right. The boy nodded.

Three men stood surrounding them. Behind a man in a white trench coat stood Makiko. She was wearing jeans, and her long hair fell on the shoulders of a red duffle coat. A pair of gleaming eyes like a lynx's gazed at Koji.

Their eyes met. For a moment, something seemed to leap into Koji's mind, as if he'd been spoken to in words that didn't take that form. Only for that moment, his hatred vanished.

Koji turned his eyes toward the man in the white trench coat. He was the oldest of the three men. The other two were tall but looked like boys.

Did she want to watch these men beat him to death? Was that behind her not telling the police? But why?

He took another look at Makiko. Their eyes met again. There were flames in her eyes, he didn't know what for. He felt as if he'd catch fire. *Makiko,* he almost uttered her name. He looked away.

He didn't understand this woman. There was nothing about her that he understood.

"Thought I'd settle the score on Watanabe bro. Sorry about taking the kid. It was here, wasn't it, that you killed him? Bro must have let down his guard against an amateur," Trench Coat said in his high voice.

One of the guys in black leather clinked metal against metal. He held a chain over three feet long.

"I'm afraid you'll have to die the same way. Otherwise I won't be able to face the gang."

Trench Coat's voice had become more shrill. He sounded oddly flippant, and he talked too much. He lacked menace. Koji thought to himself that he was calm if he could sense all this.

He crouched down and told Hiroshi to wait for him under the light. The boy only gripped Koji's trousers more tightly. Koji unclenched the small fingers one by one. He told Hiroshi to go and not move from the spot and gave his shoulders a little push. Hiroshi began to walk, looking back a couple of times.

"Don't worry, we won't hurt the kid. We're not even insisting that you die. If you want to live, a finger will do. Then you turn yourself in. Confess to killing Watanabe bro. You've only got two choices: get beaten to death here, or lose a finger and spend some time inside."

"Liar!" Makiko suddenly cried. "You told me you'd kill him!"

"Shut the fuck up."

Trench Coat shook off Makiko, who'd clung to his back.

"Normally we'd have to take your life. But you're an amateur. And if you turn yourself in, the public will see how high-handed the cops have been. This is in exchange for your life. I can't give you time to think. Make up your mind here and now."

Koji took a step toward Trench Coat, who hurriedly pulled a dagger out from his pocket. Its sheath dropped to the ground with a curiously dry clank.

"Have you ever killed anyone?" Koji asked, taking another step.

"What's that supposed to mean?"

"I'm asking you if you've ever killed anyone."

"Are you trying to fuck with me?"

"Well, I have. Right here, too. I killed your pretentious fuck of a bro." Koji took another step closer. He didn't find the dagger frightening.

"You bastard!"

Trench Coat brandished his dagger but retreated a couple of steps. Instead of stabbing, he was waving it around. From behind Koji came a yell, and a lash sounded against the street. The chain seemed thick and heavy; it didn't hold the wind-slicing menace of Watanabe's rope. The guy was being wielded by his weapon, and dodging it would be no challenge. Unable to brace himself, each time he swung the chain, his shadow bobbed and danced.

"Get at him from both sides," Trench Coat ordered.

When the chain landed again, Koji held it down with his foot, grabbed it with both hands, and swung it around hard. With Koji as the center, one of the black leathers described a circle playing tug-of-war. The other one jumped on Koji's back. Koji fell to his knees and let go of the chain. He sank down his upper body, lifted up the man on his back, and dropped him from his shoulders. A blade flashed. With hardly a pause Koji went face down on the ground and rolled a few times. When a black shadow holding a chain loomed over him, Koji instinctively reached for his kitchen knife. He readied it next to his hip and stood up. Two bodies collided.

A sound like the leaking of compressed air came out of the man's mouth. Koji heard it right by his ear. The body weighed down heavily on him. There had been almost no resistance, but the knife was in the guy right up to its hilt. No matter how hard Koji pulled he couldn't pry it loose. It was as if some other creature in the guy's body had decided to hold on to it. Koji shoved aside the slumping body. It collapsed silently to the ground.

He heard a cry from behind. The knife handle stuck out of the black leather covering the fallen guy's chest, like a small, erect penis.

Koji bellowed. He grabbed the guy's chain and flung it around like a madman. Trench Coat cried out in panic. The other one fled into the shrubbery. Koji beat the chain against the ground and chased after Trench Coat. Under a tree stood Makiko. She was looking intently at him. Their eyes met.

In a second Koji was himself again. He threw the chain at Trench Coat, but it didn't fly far, falling to the ground with a clank.

He turned his back to Makiko and started running. Hiroshi, standing under the streetlight, was sobbing as he reached out both hands. Koji picked him up under one arm and kept running. He wasn't being pursued, and he wasn't trying to flee. He simply ran.

He'd had enough. He didn't want any more violence.

He cursed and swore as he ran. He didn't know if he was cursing at himself or Makiko and those men. Words just came pouring out of his mouth.

His legs caught in each other. His lungs felt as if they would burst.

He tumbled into the shrubs amid some trees. Hiroshi's face looked taut with terror. Koji couldn't speak at first. He lay on his back, panting.

Hiroshi stretched out his hand and touched Koji's shoulder.

"I'm okay," Koji assured, raising his torso. "I'm fine, so don't cry. Remember, I don't like cry-babies."

But Hiroshi wasn't crying. He was worried about Koji's shoulder. Koji didn't think he was injured. Nothing hurt.

With his left hand he touched the area around his shoulder and felt something moist and sticky. Blood. But not his.

Was the man he'd stabbed dead? No matter how hard Koji had pulled, the knife hadn't come out. He had to be dead. A certainty that he hadn't felt when he'd whipped Watanabe was palpable in his hands. Had to be the sensation of killing a person.

He removed his jacket.

There were bloodstains, though faint, on his sweater as well. He turned it inside out and wore it like that. His sweating had begun to subside, and it felt cold sitting there without a jacket. His teeth were chattering.

"Okay, take a look," he said to Hiroshi, who seemed limp. "Would I look funny walking down the street like this?"

"I don't know. It's so dark."

Koji examined his appearance one more time in the darkness. "Let's go and see someone I know. You're going to spend the night there."

"They won't come, too?"

"We're going somewhere they don't know."

Hiroshi held Koji's hand. It looked as if they had reached the edge of the park; cars could be heard passing nearby. It was cold, and Koji was shivering. He'd rolled up the bloodstained jacket and tucked it under his arm. He couldn't see any suitable place to throw it away.

"They're the bad ones, right?" Hiroshi asked as they walked, looking up at Koji.

"Did they say anything to you?"

"They said you killed someone."

"You didn't take them seriously, did you?"

Hiroshi shook his head vehemently. "They said they were going to kill you. I got scared and cried."

"They can't kill me, not them. Those guys are scum who can't do anything on their own."

Had Hiroshi not seen him stab that guy? Yes, he had. He must have seen everything. Perhaps, even then, he didn't comprehend the scene.

"You gotta be cold. Keep your other hand in your pocket."

The hand that was in Koji's was cold, too, but regaining heat. He wasn't warming the child's hand up so much as they were warming each other's.

Koji kept banging on the sliding glass door. It was quite some time before a light came on and he heard Nakayama's lazy voice.

"Ha, Mizui," the old man said.

He was wearing pajamas with brown stripes. Tugging the collars together against the cold, he looked at the boy who was standing next to Koji.

"I need to ask you a favor," Koji said. "Can you look after this kid? Just for tonight."

The old man shivered. He looked back and forth at Koji and Hiroshi.

"He's my nephew. My brother's eldest. He came to stay with me, but I can't have him over at my place at the moment."

"Well, come in. It's too cold to talk out here."

The old man folded his futon in two and shoved it to a corner and lit the kerosene stove.

Koji felt relieved that Nakayama wasn't drunk. They wouldn't even have been able to talk otherwise.

"Come here, kiddo," Nakayama said. "I'll bet it was cold outside. You're chilled to the bone."

Having picked up Hiroshi and put him on his lap, Nakayama glanced at Koji's shoulder. It was clear under the light that the stain on the sweater was blood.

"What's your name, son?"

"Takao Mizui," Hiroshi recited without hesitation.

Koji saw the electric massage chair still there, in a corner. "We're both starving. Can we order some takeout?"

"Not at this hour. There's some eggs, broth, and vegetables in the fridge. Throw some rice in and make a gruel or something. I planned on making some for dinner but didn't have the appetite."

"Are you sick?"

"Nah, just a bit of trouble with my stomach. Besides, I'm not always hungry like you young guys."

Koji opened the refrigerator.

Nakayama mumbled by Hiroshi's ear, and the boy gave monosyllabic answers. Koji stood waiting for the gruel in the saucepan to start bubbling.

"This boy looks like he's about to fall asleep. His head's all wobbly."

When Koji brought the hot gruel, Hiroshi's eyes popped open. The child tried to eat it right away, but Nakayama took the bowl away and blew on it repeatedly to cool it.

"What are you up to these days?" he asked.

"Day labor."

"Making enough?"

"So long as the weather's good and there's work."

The hot gruel warmed his gut. Hiroshi, sitting on Nakayama's cross-legged laps, worked his chopsticks intently. The old man stroked the child's head a couple of times.

"The guy who replaced you got into a big accident just a few days ago."

"Huh, what kind?"

"It was on a highway. He crashed into the car in front, then got bashed in from behind. Quite a mess. It had just rained. He's in a hospital right now."

"Who was in the truck with him?"

"Hatta. Yonekura had left, too, after arguing with Kawashima, so the bastard was working in delivery."

"Why? I thought he'd been promoted to manager."

"He went whining to the president, saying you'd beaten him up. The president got mad—not for complaining to him but for letting an amateur like you trounce him. See, he was proud of Hatta like you'd be proud of a fighting dog."

"A fighting dog, eh?"

All was quiet in the warehouse. Koji wondered if the swallow's nest was still there. It seemed like a long time since he'd quit the company, but it had only been a little over two weeks.

Hiroshi spilled some of the gruel onto Nakayama's lap.

"Don't worry about it," the old man bade Koji, who moved to stand up. "The kid's sleepy. Look, his eyelids are sealing shut."

Koji downed the rest of the gruel. His stomach was full, and his body had warmed up.

"Lay out the futon for him," Nakayama said.

Koji spread the futon that had been placed in a corner, carried Hiroshi over, and laid him down. The child mumbled something unintelligible, already half asleep.

"He's not your nephew, is he? Where did you find him?"

"He's my nephew. I'm asking you to take care of my nephew. Believe it please."

Nakayama took a bottle of whiskey from the shelf. His movements were rickety, like those of a disabled geriatric. Perhaps the cold spell had worsened his neuralgia.

"You've really changed, Mizui. And it hasn't even been a month."

"You've changed, too. You've aged all of a sudden."

"That's not what. You're giving off the smell of a beast. It's the smell I hate the most. If you weren't with the boy, I'd have turned you away."

Nakayama poured just one glass of whiskey. Koji reached out for it and said, "Don't tell me you've gone on the wagon."

"I don't want to drink with a guy who gives off your smell. Makes me want to puke."

The smell of a beast. The words pricked his feelings like a thorn, all the more because they came from old man Nakamura.

The whiskey felt bitter in Koji's belly, full with gruel.

"I've been holding on to some money. The remainder of your pay. The receipt's inside so sign your name and do a thumbprint."

The envelope that the old man handed over contained 13,000 yen. It was salvation. Koji had paid for a taxi and was down to two 100-yen coins.

He pushed 3,000 yen into Nakayama's hand.

"To shut me up?"

"For putting up the kid. I'll come and pick him up tomorrow morning."

When Koji stood up, Nakayama pointed to the work outfit on a hanger on the wall and said, "Put that on first."

<h1 style="text-align:center">3</h1>

It was an unusually quiet night.

The year's end always saw a slew of minor incidents, yet nothing had happened so far tonight.

Like on any night shift, Kuroki had a thick volume of Japanese history opened on his desk. He had started with ancient times and was entering the Edo Period.

When the phone rang, he was reading about the background of the revolts that marked the beginning of the end for reformer Okitsugu Tanuma.

A corpse had been dropped at an emergency hospital's entrance. Kuroki clicked his tongue and stood up. It immediately reminded him of infighting among extremist factions. If so, the killer would be hard to find. After a wild goose chase, all they'd have to show for it would be yet another file for Public Security.

It was already past ten.

Two police cars had already arrived at the hospital, which was near Ueno Park.

The victim was wearing a black leather racing suit. He'd been stabbed once in the chest. The position of the wound indicated that he'd died almost instantly.

Perhaps it was a fight between biker gangs, Kuroki revised his opinion. That would make it easier to find the killer. Biker gangs weren't as impenetrable as the extremists.

Officers from K Station's CIS One who'd received the emergency duty call were beginning to show up. In any event, this was a murder.

The first task was identifying the victim and locating the crime scene. Police cars were already searching for witnesses who might have seen the vehicle used to transport the body.

Kuroki called his station's Juvenile and Traffic Sections; the victim appeared to be a minor. His attire indicated that he owned a motorcycle rather than a car.

Within the hour, the victim's identity was clear. Ten minutes later the crime scene was too. A patrolling policeman had found the victim's abandoned motorcycle.

Officers from the Watanabe case headquarters came in droves to the hospital. Kuroki was released from having to work on this year-end murder.

When he returned to K Police Station, he found Makimura waiting for him.

"I think novels are more interesting," the young detective said, glancing at the history book still open on Kuroki's desk.

History books were the more interesting. They were based solely on facts; that was what made them interesting. Facts were the only thing Kuroki cared for.

He closed the book. His hobby would have to wait.

"Funny, it happened at the same spot where Watanabe was murdered."

"What's more, the victim was a punk in Watanabe's circle," Makimura agreed. "Investigation HQ must be thrilled. For four days they had that calm before the storm—troops gathering at both the Shoyukai and Tatsumigumi offices, but nothing happening."

Section Four had done right to couple the Watanabe killing with Shoyukai's efforts to establish a presence in Tokyo. When troops were summoned to the Tatsumigumi office, a surprising number also began to gather at the Tokyo office of Shoyukai when it was supposed not to be operating in the metropolitan area. These movements deepened each gang's doubts about the other.

Tatsumigumi had sought support from its umbrella organization to double its numbers. In response, Shoyukai also doubled its numbers. The Kansai gang posed an eerie threat; its sleeper elements in the capital were slowly coming to light but were not yet fully visible. Their presence was certainly far more extensive than originally suspected. But it couldn't be in Shoyukai's interest to get into a conflict at this stage. Its infiltration of the capital would become manifest and needlessly put other organizations on guard.

As for Tatsumigumi, even with backup from its umbrella organization, a serious war with Shoyukai was a hopeless proposition.

No, a gang war didn't make sense. It was even stranger that one of Watanabe's punks should be murdered in the same spot.

"Question is, what's Shoyukai's next move," Kuroki said.

"The guys from headquarters should be coming back soon. I heard Mr. Yabe is concentrating on Shoyukai at the moment."

Yabe was the only detective from K Police Station CIS One who was part of the special investigation headquarters. He knew a thing or two about organized crime.

"I'll ask Mr. Yabe what's going on, though he probably won't have time if the showdown's about to begin."

This time of year there were more arsons and robberies than at any other. Both Kuroki and Makimura had been swamped with such cases over the past several days. They would solve a case only to find another on their plate.

They found time in between them to check on Etsuko Mitsuya.

She'd gone missing. Yet it seemed unlikely that anything had happened to her. She'd shown up once at her mother's bar in Shinjuku, on a Saturday night.

Her mother Kinuyo had asked them not to waste time on her daughter, who was just "like that." Her daughter had only shown up to get her allowance.

Koji Mizui and Etsuko Mitsuya had gotten back together. Though not clear from exactly when, it was probably a few days after Mizui quit the company. Around that time, Etsuko had been granted a long-term absence from school on the pretext that her mother was ill.

Etsuko had shown up every morning at Mizui's place in her school uniform. The old woman next door remarked that they'd been like newlyweds.

On Friday the ninth, Kinuyo was informed by Etsuko's school that her daughter had requested long-term leave. The next day, Kinuyo sent her lover, Watanabe, to tail Etsuko to Mizui's and bring her home.

Kuroki's focus was the period from the tenth, when Etsuko had been brought home, to the fifteenth, the day of Watanabe's murder.

He and Makimura had done a thorough job looking into mother and daughter for that span. Makimura had sniffed around Kinuyo, while Kuroki had done the same for Etsuko.

Kinuyo had gone on a little overnight trip to Yugawara with an elderly patron from Sunday the eleventh to the twelfth. Once back, she'd gone directly to her bar without returning to her apartment. Etsuko and Watanabe had also gone out, but it wasn't clear where they'd gone or when they'd returned. Three witnesses attested to seeing Makiko driving off with Watanabe in his blue Nissan Skyline.

Etsuko started back at school on Tuesday the thirteenth. The daily routines of mother and daughter seemed more or less back to normal. Etsuko would leave for school in the morning and return in the late afternoon. Almost immediately after that, Kinuyo would leave for her bar and then return at around two or three in the morning. That routine lasted until the fifteenth.

Kuroki was bothered by the fact that Watanabe's car had been parked in front of Kinuyo's building three days in a row, from the thirteenth to the fifteenth—moreover, only for a few hours each time, and at night, when Kinuyo was out working. There were multiple witnesses, including an employee of a local restaurant who had delivered two servings of tempura *donburi* to the apartment.

Had there been something between Etsuko and Watanabe? If so, it meant Mizui's woman had been stolen by Watanabe.

Only today, in the afternoon, Kuroki learned that a woman resembling Etsuko had visited Mizui the morning after the murder. Kuroki was in the area for another case but dropped in on the old woman next door to talk to her again. It seemed that Mizui and Etsuko had had a violent quarrel. Mizui rushed out, while Etsuko stayed outside the door crying for a full hour. While the old woman's memory seemed to be unreliable, as did her vision and hearing, she had no shortage of curiosity.

Mizui wasn't in his apartment. Only his nephew Takao was there, playing with a toy car. When Kuroki asked him if he was home alone, the little boy nodded.

"Why did Mizui get back with Etsuko?" Makimura wondered

aloud. "She'd already burned him once with that false statement of hers."

"It's not just those two. A lot of what goes on between men and women is a mystery." Kuroki placed his history book in its box, then put it away in a drawer. He didn't feel like reading anymore tonight.

"Care for a game of *shogi*?" Makimura offered. There was nobody else in the squad room this late at night.

"We might be at a dead end. Why don't you go home?"

"I'll stay here until Mr. Yabe gets back."

Kuroki almost never talked to Yabe. They weren't on particularly bad terms, but they didn't get along well.

"That incident tonight is definitely in our corner, don't you think? Gang wars aren't for rubbing out punks. Section Four is really bulldozing its way through this one."

"The point is to catch the killer. It doesn't matter who does."

Section Four was getting results. One more push, and it might get a handle on Shoyukai's power base in Tokyo.

Yabe returned.

He looked exhausted and grouchy. A stakeout at night couldn't be easy on a man who was pushing on fifty.

Makimura ushered Yabe to a conference room and took him some hot coffee. Kuroki waited at his own desk. Twenty minutes later, Makimura returned alone.

"Where's Yabe?"

"He's going home. He said Shoyukai members have been starting to scatter since this morning."

"And the Tatsumigumi?"

"The same, though there's no sign that they've made peace."

"That's strange."

Shoyukai needed to settle scores for the Watanabe murder. It was how they did things in that world. If both gangs were laying down arms, it could mean only one thing: Watanabe hadn't died in a conflict, and both sides had come to know it.

"Have you ever heard of Shibasaki? Watanabe's 'younger brother.'"

"Nope. I barely even knew anything about Watanabe. Just his

120

face."

"Shibasaki's soft, but he's good on a motorcycle, and he's been trying to subsume biker gangs. Tonight's victim also used to belong to one. Seems Shibasaki brought him in and he caught Watanabe's attention."

"So?"

"It looks like Shibasaki's living with Etsuko Mitsuya. But he's not at his place now."

"What does that mean?"

"I don't think Mr. Yabe knows, either. But if someone was going to make a move for Watanabe's sake, it was likely to be a younger brother like Shibasaki. I guess investigation headquarters also had their sights on him. Mr. Yabe just happened to recognize Etsuko's face."

"I'm surprised he told you."

"He said it was about time."

"I see. I guess if the gang members are dispersing, then there's nothing more for headquarters to do."

In his mind, Kuroki added new facts to the old ones.

On the morning of the sixteenth, Mizui and Etsuko had fought. Immediately afterwards, Etsuko became an item with Shibasaki, a gang brother to Watanabe. That was what it meant.

Etsuko Mitsuya was getting even harder to figure out.

There was something like a compass needle in Kuroki's head. As facts accumulated, it would begin to oscillate and eventually point in one direction.

At the moment, the needle was moving only slightly. There weren't enough facts. Yet, the trembling needle pointed at a blurry image of a face that came and went.

Tomorrow was his customary day off after a night shift.

He'd check Koji Mizui out. In the main Etsuko's behavior had to do with him. That was a fact.

4

The light was on in the window. Koji didn't remember if he'd turned it off when he'd rushed out.

Trying to warm his hands by breathing on them, he looked at his window for a while from a distance. There was no sign of human movement in the light.

The door was unlocked.

The apartment was exactly the way it had been when he'd dashed out. He could hear the radio in his neighbor's apartment as usual.

He kicked the bread packaging lying on the floor. Then he lifted a double-sized bottle of Suntory Red to his lips and drank. Some of the liquid dribbled down his neck.

He thought about what he needed to do.

First, he stripped naked. He changed all his clothing, including his underwear. He was covered with goose bumps. For a moment he recalled how he'd changed soiled clothing like this before, then immediately realized it was a trick of the mind. It was Numata who'd done the changing, not him.

He stuck his mouth to the tap and drank. Then he sat down on the tatami floor and lit a cigarette. He smoked many more. Before the ashtray could become full, his pack was empty.

He put Hiroshi's underwear in a paper bag, along with soap, towels, and toothbrushes. There was nothing else to bring.

He plucked one of the longer cigarette butts from the ashtray, stretched it out, and lit it. Its taste irritated his throat.

The thought of money suddenly entered his mind. He pulled the empty whiskey bottle from the closet and removed the lid. He turned the bottle upside down and shook it repeatedly, but not one of the 10,000-yen bills fell out.

He smashed the bottle on the sink. The savage sound seemed to linger forever in the calm of the night.

After counting his thirty-one 10,000-yen notes, he squeezed them into his trouser pocket.

He walked around his apartment, using his foot to scoop up the clothes lying on the floor and pushing them into a single pile. He didn't feel like doing anything more with them.

He was about to leave the apartment when he noticed the blue toy Volkswagen on the floor. Without removing his shoes he went back in and threw the toy car into the paper bag.

He was halfway down the stairs when he turned back again. He couldn't leave his clothes in his apartment. They had blood on them.

He didn't hail a cab. He needed his own car.

He walked, peering into the parked cars. He couldn't find any with keys left in the ignition. He circled the sewage treatment plant and walked to the bank of the Sumida River, without luck.

He put some stones in the plastic bag that had his clothes. He knotted the mouth and threw the bag into the river. It hit the water with a smack. He became worried about whether it had really sunk; it was too dark to see the surface of the water very well.

He walked along the river for about half an hour. He was only wearing a thin sweater over his undershirt, so he felt quite chilly despite walking fast.

The embankment ahead of him suddenly lit up. A car was coming in from a side road. It drove slowly for about a hundred feet along the river then stopped.

Two silhouettes emerged, a man and a woman, the woman apparently very drunk.

Koji sneaked forward. He began crawling once he was about thirty feet away. The woman was vomiting loudly. She then staggered away and climbed onto the embankment; beneath the streetlight, a red coat was walking the tightrope. The man followed her and held her. She lay down on the embankment.

Koji swiftly opened the car door and got in. The indoor light went on for just a moment. He reached for the ignition.

The astonished face of a middle-aged man appeared in the glare of the headlights and receded.

It was warm inside the car. It even smelled of perfume. It was a domestic mid-size car, nothing that would stand out. There was plenty of gas in the tank, too.

With his hands on the wheel, he was beginning to relax. He could go wherever he wanted. He felt as though he'd sprouted wings.

He was careful not to drive too fast. He soon found himself on a road he knew well. It would take less than ten minutes to the warehouse.

He turned onto a side street. He decided to wait a while. He didn't want to startle the old man out of his slumber or wake up Hiroshi.

He parked on a concrete gutter lid near a factory wall. There were no houses around, and the only sound was the faint humming of machinery from the factory. He wanted to smoke a cigarette. He turned on the light inside the car and rummaged in the black handbag on the passenger seat. There was a wallet, cosmetics, a schedule book, keys, a six-pack of condoms, and a pack of Seven Star cigarettes, along with a disposable lighter. He threw the handbag out of the window with its contents, keeping only the cigarettes and lighter.

There was a brown coat in the back seat. Koji smoked two cigarettes, covered himself with the coat, and reclined the seat.

He couldn't sleep. But he kept his eyes shut. He refused to worry. There were a lot of matters he couldn't solve no matter how much thought he gave to them. Once in a while he consulted his watch.

It was now 5 a.m. It was still dark out and as silent as midnight.

He stepped outside and urinated. Steam rose as if he'd spilled boiling water. He rushed back into the car, lit a cigarette, and turned on the engine.

Faint light seeped out of the window.

The old man's face showed right away to the rumble of a car. He was slightly drunk, but not enough to make him incoherent.

"You're awfully early," he said.

The room stove made the place almost hot. Hiroshi was wrapped in a blanket, asleep.

"Were you drinking to the kid's sleeping face? I thought you had stomach problems."

"Don't talk so loud. The boy will wake up."

"I need to wake him. I'm taking him."

The old man put a finger to his lips with a *shh!* He peered at Hiroshi's face. "How did you get that car?" he inquired.

"Borrowed it off a friend."

"What friend?"

"Stop asking weird questions. It's none of your business, is it?"

"I'm just worried that you're about to do something you shouldn't— or maybe you've done it already—and are on the run."

124

"So what if I am?"

"What's done is done. All I'm saying is don't drag the boy into it."

"You're very concerned about my nephew."

"Anything wrong with that?"

"Nope. Strange, that's all."

Nakayama let out a small cough. Koji stuck a cigarette in his mouth. Hiroshi shifted slightly and stuck his hand outside the blanket. It was a small, dirty hand, with grimy, overgrown nails.

"A good kid," the old man said. "He woke up in the middle of the night looking for you. When I told him you'd be back soon, he nodded and went back to sleep. He trusts you completely."

"Of course he does. I'm his uncle and he's my nephew."

"You really think I believe that bullshit?"

"Believe what you like."

Koji was about to shake Hiroshi awake when Nakayama grabbed his hand and stopped him. "Mizui, why don't you leave the kid with me? Not forever, just until you sort out your mess. Look, I'm not asking for money. I'll feed him three square meals a day."

Nakayama was not letting go of Koji's hand. Koji was astounded to see tears falling from the old man's eyes and instinctively looked down as if he'd seen something he shouldn't. Then the old man let go, wiping his runny nose with his fingers a couple of times, the lines on his face deepening in an embarrassed smile.

"Guess I'm a bit drunk."

The old man poured some whiskey into a cup and added hot water. Koji took the cup away from him. "Not a good idea. You're going to work soon."

The old man sniffled again.

It was still dark outside. It was that time of year when the break of day came at its latest. Koji shook Hiroshi's shoulders.

The boy rolled over, rubbed his eyes with his hand, and squinted as if the light was too bright for him. When he spotted Koji's face, his own relaxed just a little.

"Come on. We're off."

Hiroshi nodded and got up. Nakayama helped the child into his coat. The old man snatched last night's 3,000 yen from the low table and pushed it into Koji's hand.

"I told you it was for his bunking for the night."

"It's not for you. Think of it as an allowance for the kid."

When Koji tried to force the money back, the old man brushed his hand away. Hiroshi yawned and sat down on the futon.

The old man could get, though not downright ugly, nasty when it came to money. He'd been the sort to make a fuss about one measly cigarette. Three thousand yen was something he'd be on about on his deathbed.

"You saying I can't even give the kid an allowance?"

Though his tone was angry, the old man sounded sad more than anything. Koji bowed his head slightly in thanks.

"Bring him here if it gets to be too much. I'll think of him as your nephew and look after him."

Koji carried Hiroshi on his back and went outside. When he collapsed the passenger seat and laid Hiroshi upon it, the child soon started dozing off again.

"Where will you go?" Nakayama asked, having stepped out to send them off.

"I'm taking him back to Nagano. My older brother is waiting."

It was a hasty lie. After he'd said it, Koji thought it might not be such a bad idea. He didn't have anywhere to go anyway. He bid Nakayama adieu and got inside the car.

It was bright now. There were more cars on the road, especially from the other direction.

"I lost my car," Hiroshi mumbled.

"Look in the bag. I brought it for you."

There was the rustle of Hiroshi opening the paper bag. "It's true!"

"You ain't seen nothin' yet. I'll get you a radio-controlled Porsche."

"When?"

"Soon. When we find a toy store that's open."

Hiroshi raised his body and looked outside the window. They were on a highway. No way he'd spot any toy store.

"Hang on a bit. Once we're off the highway, we'll go buy it."

Hiroshi stuck his hand in his trouser pocket and pulled out 3,000 yen. It wasn't Nakayama's 3,000 yen, which was in Koji's pocket. Hiroshi said it was money Koji had given him. The boy must have held on to the 1,000-yen notes Koji had left before going to work.

"Were you saving up to buy a radio-controlled car?"

The boy nodded and asked, "Where are we going?"

If they continued on, they would reach Yokohama. Around the time they got to Yokohama, places to grab breakfast as well as toy stores would be open.

"Be a good boy for just a little more. That old man who took care of you gave me 3,000 yen to keep for you. Put it together and you have 6,000 yen. I'll chip in, too. We'll be able to buy any radio-controlled car you like."

Koji wondered why Nakayama had wept. He'd never seen the old man in tears.

In the rear-view mirror, he saw a police car. It was gaining ground. Koji's back broke out in sweat. Could it be coming for him? He almost stepped on the gas to go faster but managed to restrain himself. It was now right behind him. Then next to him. Nothing happened. He breathed a sigh of relief as its rear sped away.

"Once we buy the radio-controlled car and get breakfast, why don't we take another spin and go check out the sea? I grew up in the mountains, so I've never seen the ocean in winter."

There was no answer. When Koji cast a sideward glance, Hiroshi was sunk deep into his seat, head lolled to the side, fast asleep.

5

Kuroki got off at Mikawajima and headed for Koji Mizui's apartment.

He bought a chocolate bar on the way, a present for Mizui's little nephew, Takao.

It was a clear day. Three little boys were playing where he'd parked that time he'd lain in wait for Hajime Numata. Takao wasn't among them.

He climbed the stairs and stood in front of the door.

An odd smell, though just a whiff, assailed his nose. Kuroki turned the knob. The door was unlocked.

It was the smell of gas. There, sitting in that smell, was Etsuko Mitsuya.

The gas was not that thick yet. It seemed that quite a lot was leaking outside through gaps. Making sure not to touch the light switch, he turned off the gas and opened the window. A cold breeze blew through the apartment.

He tried to lead Etsuko Mitsuya outside, but she sat rooted to the spot. Blood was oozing from her wrist, and she held a piece of glass between the fingertips of her right hand.

Kuroki wrenched the glass away and bandaged her wrist with a handkerchief. She had not cut an artery. Blood loss was minimal.

"It's better if you go outside," Kuroki said.

Etsuko shook her head. There was no need to drag her out. He could hardly smell the gas now. The wind blowing from the window through the door had cleared most of it from the small apartment.

Etsuko was dressed casually in a red sweater and jeans. Even after Kuroki removed his coat and put it over her shoulders, her blank expression didn't change.

Mizui wasn't there. No sign of his nephew, Takao, either. There was half-eaten bread, a can of juice, and an ashtray full of cigarette butts; fragments of glass from a broken whiskey bottle lay scattered on the draining board. Etsuko had tried to slash her wrist with one of the pieces. On the red label were six tallies of five plus one more stroke. No money.

He opened the closet to find futon, just a few clothes, and about a dozen model ships. He left the closet open. Gas concentrated in unlikely places. Closets and attics denoted lingering danger. Better not try to smoke, either.

"I had all sorts of questions for you. Had to search for you a bit. Sounds like you were at Shibasaki's place."

Etsuko was slumped down on the floor, both her knees drawn to her chest, and didn't move. Her long hair hid half her face, and she stayed almost expressionless.

Kuroki decided on a somewhat rough measure. Grabbing Etsuko's right hand—the one which was not hurt—he placed a glass shard against it. He pressed down. The skin broke and blood oozed out to the size of the thicker end of a guiding needle. Etsuko remained expressionless. Kuroki put his lips to the blood and sucked.

Etsuko tried to pull her hand back, but Kuroki didn't let go.

"That's sleazy for a cop."

"I could also beat you or throw you into a cell for a few days. But I didn't think that would get you to talk."

"I've got nothing to say to a cop."

Etsuko turned away. She glanced at the blood on her right wrist, made as if to lick it, then seemed to decide against it. She casually pressed the wound against her jeans.

"Why did you come here?" Kuroki asked.

"To die."

Kuroki gave a wry smile. "Why did you want to die in here?"

"Because it's Koji's place. I can still smell him here."

"I'm asking you why you tried to kill yourself."

"Because Koji is going to die too."

Something like a premonition flashed through Kuroki's mind, but it quickly faded. "Couldn't get him to die with you, huh? Instead you tried to die with the shell of the man."

"Shell?"

"This place. Mizui isn't coming back, is he?"

"But Koji will die."

The premonition began to assume a clearer shape. Etsuko was convinced that Koji Mizui would die. Kuroki didn't doubt that. "So you're going to kill Mizui?"

"Yes."

Suddenly Etsuko laughed. Her eyes gleamed like a cat's.

It was cold. The wind from the window was too strong.

"Koji is mine. Once he's dead, he'll be mine forever."

Kuroki picked up a can of juice from the floor and opened it— grape juice. "Want some?" he asked.

Etsuko shook her head. Kuroki sipped the juice. He pulled the chocolate bar out of his pocket and broke it up without removing the wrapper.

"Does Mizui hate you?"

"Koji doesn't understand the first thing about me. That's why he tries to run away. He didn't even try to understand."

"I think any man would be hard pressed to understand you."

"I loved him. It was first love. For both of us. That doesn't happen often."

"There are lots of men and women who are in love with each other."

"You don't understand a thing."

"Some things, I do. You made a mistake. You slept with Watanabe."

"So what? I just wanted to know what a man my mom even paid to sleep with would be like. He wasn't all that much. Besides, I didn't sleep with him. He raped me."

"Is that how."

"What is?"

"Is sleeping with someone so simple?"

"With Koji it wasn't."

"Why not?"

"Because it's Koji. Because Koji is in love with me and I'm in love with Koji."

Kuroki put a piece of chocolate in his mouth.

He was beginning to see the path the case took, clearly, like it was some movie he'd seen once. A nasty case.

But he still couldn't figure out this woman Etsuko.

"Want a piece of chocolate?"

He needed to take her to the station and formally question her, but he didn't feel like getting up right away. Etsuko reached out for the chocolate. With a crisp sound, she bit. The girl had white teeth.

"Did Mizui fight with Watanabe over you?"

"Yes. Twice. I knew he would win me back from that bastard and he did."

"Twice, huh?"

When Kuroki had come here with Makimura on Friday night, there had been a terrible wound on Mizui's face. Mizui had explained it away as an accident. The gash looked fairly recent but had already formed a scab. Watanabe had only been killed the night before so it was hard to imagine that the wound had been inflicted then.

Kuroki put another piece of chocolate in his mouth. He needed a stiff drink.

Out of the blue he remembered something Makimura had reported about Etsuko's mother, Kinuyo. She'd given birth to Etsuko at age twenty and at twenty-four moved from Akita Prefecture to Tokyo. She'd been arrested twice for prostitution. There had been no gang involvement; she'd simply been picking up clients and taking them back to her place.

Kinuyo had found customers at an *oden* stew stall. Makimura had found the daughter, Etsuko, at such a stall when he'd been hunting for Mizui's alibi. He had brought her in for smoking cigarettes, a banal pretext, and conducted a banal questioning. Etsuko must have grown up watching her mother sell her body for money. She'd been playing at being a prostitute at open-air stalls.

It was eleven years ago that Kinuyo had opened her first bar in Shinjuku.

"Is Shibasaki after Mizui?"

"It's not like that."

"You think he can catch up, don't you?"

"Who knows?"

"You do. That's why you tried to kill yourself."

Etsuko fell silent. Kuroki put another piece of chocolate in his mouth.

"Shall we go?" he said.

Makimura came bounding out of the car parked in front of the sewage treatment plant. He was with another detective called Fuse who had joined the force in the same year.

"What's the deal, sir?"

Kuroki seated Etsuko in the rear. Fuse, who'd been in the front passenger seat, went back to sit beside her.

"Mizui and Watanabe fought over the girl. Watanabe got killed, so one of his juniors, namely Shibasaki, came into the picture. We're talking about last night. Mizui killed again. Shibasaki is after him this very moment."

"You're sure about that?"

"Aren't both Shoyukai and Tatsumigumi dispersing? It's because they found out that Watanabe hadn't died in a gang conflict. That girl was the only one who knew. Watanabe must have been in the apartment with her when Mizui visited the place. The girl told Shibasaki and naturally he reported it to Shoyukai."

"So she told you everything?"

"Nope. She won't, no matter how much we question her. But it's the truth."

"You're going to bring her in on what charge?"

"Doesn't matter. Even underage smoking would do. She also needs to be on suicide watch."

"Is that really the whole story?"

"On the surface."

Kuroki hailed a passing cab.

"Find out what Shibasaki's up to. Let Juvenile or some other section question the girl. We no longer have to hold back on account of Section Four. Thanks to them, Mizui's killed a second guy."

Kuroki got into the cab. It was ready to roll away, but he told the driver to wait.

"There's something that bothers me," Kuroki said. "Call Mizui's family in Nagano. Find out whether his older brother really left his kid with him."

"Where are you off to, sir?"

"I can only think of one place right now. I'll check it out, after which I'll be back at the station."

Kuroki gave the taxi driver directions.

It was 10 a.m. A bit too late.

The trucks had already left. There was just one old man getting some sun.

He saw Kuroki but didn't come over.

"You've got a customer, Gramps."

"You must be from the police, sir. The gentlemen who came over last time didn't call me 'Gramps.'"

"Ah. Sorry."

"Is it about Mizui?"

"So he came here?"

"Last night in the middle of the night. He rushed out leaving a kid with me and came back early in the morning in a car. He wasn't even here ten minutes. Haven't heard from him since."

"Did he say anything?"

"Something about taking the kid to Nagano. I wonder, though."

Kuroki took down the car model and what Mizui and the child had been wearing. If they'd left early in the morning, they might be quite far by now. Had they escaped? He wondered if it was too late.

"About an hour ago two young bikers came here, eyes all blood-shot. They asked the same questions. You police are a step behind, you know. Though I guess for you guys it's a walk in the park to look up a number plate so maybe it's a dead heat."

The old man seemed to know what kind of predicament Mizui was in. He knew but wasn't protecting him.

"I know what you're thinking, sir."

"Why did you talk?"

"It's a bet. Can that bastard Mizui pull it off or no?"

"And what's your stake?"

"My life. If Mizui gets away, then I'll pay the hospital a visit sure that I won't die."

"You've got something wrong with you?"

The old man thumped his chest. "Cancer. The damned thing seems to have spread to my hip. I'm in so much pain I can't walk."

Nakayama gave a loud gargle and spat into a tissue. The phlegm was dark red, like strawberry jam.

"Everything down to the last detail is the same as my older brother, who died six years ago."

"You could just be neurotic."

Yet Kuroki knew that cancer could spread to the lumbar region. His own father had died of that kind of cancer. By the time the hip pain set in, the cancer in the stomach was so large that it could be felt from outside.

"I nursed my brother at the end. I know much more about this illness than your run-of-the-mill doctor."

"Do you know what Mizui has done?"

"I don't really care."

"What if he doesn't get away?"

"Then I'll stay here, getting drunk. It'll swing one way or the other by the end of the year."

Kuroki stuck one of his Short Peace cigarettes in his mouth. The old man reached out for one.

"Any family?"

"Kind of have one, kind of don't."

"This is a tough game, Gramps."

"So it's 'Gramps' again?"

Kuroki used the warehouse phone to request a check on cars stolen the night before.

"Who's that little boy?" the old man asked from behind as Kuroki stood up to leave.

"He's no nephew."

"That bastard Mizui was really taking care of him. The kid was attached to him, too. They were like brothers."

"Brothers, huh?"

Kuroki flung down his cigarette and stubbed it out with his foot.

Chapter Five

1

The engine revved.

Though not enough to be called a roar, the speeding Porsche was quite loud. Hiroshi screamed in delight.

"Right turn, dummy," Koji chided and grabbed the remote control from Hiroshi. The Porsche came whizzing back.

This toy was a little on the classy side for a child. There had been cheaper, slower cars. But Koji had bought the big one because Hiroshi's abject reluctance had annoyed him. The boy could read numbers but didn't quite understand how many zeros meant how much. He nevertheless seemed to assume that the big one was expensive.

"Start practicing with the remote. Don't go too fast from the get-go."

They were in a park near the harbor.

Koji was wearing new black jeans. He'd gotten them in the same department store as the radio-controlled car. He'd also bought shoes and gloves for Hiroshi, as well as identical blue scarves for the two of them. The scarf was just the right size for Koji, but on Hiroshi it was too long even after going around his neck twice.

For about an hour, Koji let Hiroshi practice with the toy car in the park. The boy got better. When Koji stood legs apart, he could guide the car slowly through them.

"Okay, that's enough."

Koji consulted his watch. It was time for the pleasure boat to leave for a trip around the harbor.

A middle-aged woman taking a walk pointed at the toy Hiroshi held hugging to his chest. "Nice car," she said. Hiroshi laughed bashfully.

Koji realized that perhaps they looked like father and son or brothers. It was not a bad feeling. He regretted not having bought matching clothes as well as scarves.

The pleasure boat left the pier.

The smell of the sea became stronger. A thin mist enveloped the harbor, somewhat obscuring the cranes in the shipyard and the breakwater in the distance.

A blond youth smiled and waved from a moored green cargo ship. Koji muttered some jealous words. The word "seafaring" had a nice ring at the moment.

"Kid, be a sailor when you grow up."

Hiroshi, however, was more interested in the toy car in his arms than the ship.

The desperate urge to run away was gone. He'd already run and had arrived here. Near or far didn't change the fact that he'd run.

He didn't want to think about what was past. Nothing could come from finished business. Watanabe died. Koji stabbed one of his subordinates. That was all there was to it. Only the sensations of striking with a rope and stabbing with a kitchen knife remained, in the palms of his hands.

He had no desire to persuade himself with words that he'd struck and stabbed for a reason. If the opponent ended up dead, then he was a killer. He couldn't complain about being pursued. If he didn't want to be caught, he'd run. If he didn't feel comfortable with today, he'd take a shortcut and dash toward tomorrow.

"Can you buy me new batteries?"

Hiroshi was holding Koji's hand. The child was worried about not having spare batteries. I'll buy you a dozen, a couple dozen batteries, Koji thought. *Don't worry about silly things.*

The pleasure boat was approaching the edge of the long pier. Three tugboats with red masts were moored there.

"Hiroshi, you don't want to go back to your mother?"

This was something he needed to ask sooner or later. Hiroshi's eyes, gazing up at Koji, had a glint of fear like a frightened little animal's.

"If you want to go home, you can say so, you know. Don't worry about me. I'll take you there."

"Mom isn't around anymore."

"Not around? You just got lost in the park, right?"

"But she isn't. That's what she said. She won't be around anymore."

"Where did she say she would go?"

"I don't know. But she said we couldn't see each other anymore."

"Your mother said she couldn't see you anymore?"

"Yes."

She abandoned you, Koji almost said but stifled the words. Hiroshi probably understood that much anyway. The child never spoke of his mother.

It would be more convenient for Koji if Hiroshi were indeed abandoned. Nobody would look for him. Koji didn't have to give him back. A mother who'd abandoned her child and disappeared was one that Hiroshi would soon forget.

"Hey." Koji placed a hand on Hiroshi's head. This kid is mine, he thought. It filled him with a strange emotion akin to joy, but totally unlike feeling that Makiko was his. The kid was his like some part of him. "You'll be with me, always. Hear me? Always."

Hiroshi was looking up at him. Koji roughly tussled the boy's head.

After gazing at containers being piled onto cargo ships at the Honmoku pier, they headed for Negishi, where they had lunch.

Hiroshi was still fiddling with his radio-controlled car. Koji had bought him as many batteries as the boy could carry. While Koji drove, Hiroshi incessantly asked questions. He wanted to know the names of the various parts of the car. Koji painstakingly responded to each question. No matter how many times he did, eventually the child asked it again.

Four motorcycles were behind them. Koji only noticed just before Otsubama.

He'd planned to go to Zushi. He'd once seen boats on the sea out there. Now it was winter so he didn't know if he'd see boats, but there was a beach and he wanted to see waves lapping against the shore.

Koji drove faster, but the motorcycles held the distance. When he dropped speed, it was the same. He tried both many times.

They were following him. No doubt about that.

It's them. Buddies of the guy I stabbed.

He didn't know how they'd found him. It was as if they'd welled out of the ground. At any rate, he had to get away.

Top gear. He stepped on the accelerator. Fifty, fifty-five, sixty, sixty-five miles per hour. Visibility narrowed. He could only see a little bit of what was in front of him. He clenched the wheel and stuck out his neck.

It was insane to drive on a regular road at that speed. A car coming from the other direction blasted its horn and dodged him. It seemed to veer onto the pavement, but Koji couldn't see very well.

He couldn't get rid of them, he realized after racing for a while. He dropped speed. It would be stupid to get the police on his tail to boot. Moreover, the motorcycles merely pursued and didn't attempt to catch up. They kept a steady distance as if they were measuring it out.

Koji began to calm down.

Before he knew it, he'd passed the road into Zushi and was heading for Yokosuka.

Had the bikes been pursuing him from the start? That seemed to be the only explanation. He'd never run into them on such a road. Why had they revealed themselves now? Maybe it was because so far he'd been driving in places crowded with both people and cars. He'd only gotten off in town. Perhaps they'd wanted to accost him but couldn't.

In other words, they were about to make a move now. He glanced at the rear-view mirror. The distance to the motorcycles, despite the vehicles in between, still remained constant.

He drove into the Yokosuka city center.

Parking the car in a crowded place, he gauged the movement of the bikers. They drew a little closer than they had been on the road and parked as well.

"They tailed me," Koji muttered.

Hiroshi had long noticed that something was wrong; he held the radio-controlled car close and looked tense. His voice quavered a bit when he asked, "You aren't going to the police?"

"I can't go to the police. I have my reasons."

"Is it because you had that fight in the park?" Hiroshi probably knew everything that happened there. He knew but hadn't said anything until now.

"Anyway, I can't go to the police."

He was sure the gang wouldn't hold back for long. They'd shown themselves. He didn't give a shit about himself, but he was worried about Hiroshi.

Koji emptied his trouser pocket of all his cash. He didn't want to be mulling things over. Saying goodbye was never pleasant.

"You go to the police. If you tell the policeman everything, he'll find a relative or someone who will look after you."

Hiroshi looked up at Koji. His eyes, fixed on Koji's face, gleamed. Koji winced.

"They won't do anything where there are lots of people. Better get off here."

"What about you?"

"I'll just keep driving. I have to go really fast again. I don't want you in the car."

He was talking too much. He should just open the door and throw him out. That would be best for Hiroshi. But Koji's hands wouldn't move. Instead his mouth opened again.

"Fine. You get off here and wait for me. I'll come and get you in an hour or so."

"No!" Hiroshi cried, grabbing Koji's arm. The radio-controlled car fell to the floor. "I'm going with you."

"You dummy."

Koji poked Hiroshi on the head. But his desire to get the child out of the car was dashed surprisingly clean. He had been waiting for Hiroshi to say it. He'd wanted him to say it. A complete scoundrel.

Koji stuck a cigarette in his mouth, took a few puffs, and threw it out of the window. He felt certain about not letting Hiroshi out of the car. He didn't care if he was a scoundrel. They were like father and son, brothers, something more, even. Why shouldn't they stay together?

"Okay." He firmly fastened the seatbelt on Hiroshi's small body.

"Don't cry, all right? Close your eyes and hang on to this." He put the radio-controlled car and batteries into the paper bag containing toiletries and underwear and gave it to Hiroshi. Even with his body firmly fastened, the kid might want to cling to something in a pinch. It'd be dangerous if he grabbed Koji's arm.

He started to drive. In the rear-view mirror, the four motorcycles were moving too. Same distance.

He didn't drive along the coast. Instead, he turned onto a road from the city that went right across Miura Peninsula. He'd once delivered a whole pile of electrical appliances to a company dormitory in a place called Kinugasa. He was familiar with the road, which cut through hills. It was hard to see far ahead. There were not many houses around, either. He might as well make the first move.

The road was now running through woods. He could hardly see any cars. Just one truck ahead. It, too, soon disappeared behind trees.

The motorcycles began to shrink the gap.

Here we go. Koji braced himself.

He took his foot off the gas and slowed down. The distance from the bikes almost immediately closed. Koji waited. They were right on his tail. He stepped on the gas again. They stayed close. Two of them shot out and ran parallel on either side. Their black full-face helmets looked sinister.

"Take that!" Koji shouted.

He turned the wheel sharply to the right and hit the brake. The shock made the car vibrate. It rolled once on the road and sat facing in the original direction. Reverse gear. Two motorcycles lay by the side of the road. One of them had its wheel spinning in the air with a ferocious roar. He rammed that one. He glimpsed a figure tumbling into the woods. The car bounded from the impact. The lights shattered and the front bumper crunched, Koji could tell. Reverse gear. The car was back on the road. A motorcycle that was heading in tried to turn but fell. Its rider jumped up and ran for the trees. Koji's car sent the abandoned bike flying. Then he was off again. He saw someone in the rear-view mirror. The man was not on a motorcycle. A bang sounded from the man's direction, and Koji drove faster. The man vanished from the rear-view mirror.

"It's okay. You can open your eyes now."

Hiroshi lifted his face up from the paper bag. Koji had destroyed two motorcycles. If more came after him, he would do it again. They were on two-wheelers, no match in a collision. But what about that bang? It hadn't sounded like backfiring; the rear would have tilted up in that case, and the sound hadn't been that close. Maybe it was a gun.

"Were you scared?"

"I'm okay," Hiroshi replied, but his voice trembled.

Koji kept an eye on the rear-view mirror. There was no sign of pursuit yet.

He eventually got on a national route, and soon the sea came into view. There were more cars now, and plenty of curves in the road. If they came after him, he wouldn't know until they were right behind.

Koji took a side street to the beach. He parked in the shade of pine trees that blocked the view from the route and got out of the car. He went belly down on the sand and peered at the route. Barely five minutes had passed when there was the roar of a motorcycle. It whizzed along, weaving its way between cars. Just one bike, but with two black-helmeted riders on it. After a while, another one, also with two riders, sped past. Ten minutes later, the two motorcycles came back together. They were looking for him, it was clear.

Koji returned to the car.

"Come out, Hiroshi," he said.

He opened the door, but Hiroshi didn't move. The boy couldn't undo his seatbelt. Koji felt mirth well up, and at last he was able to laugh.

2

The stolen vehicle was promptly identified.

It was a white 1978 Toyota Corona Hardtop Coupe. According to its owner, while he was attending to his drunk passenger, the thief made away with it. The site was a road along the Sumida River not far from Mizui's apartment.

The model and number were relayed throughout the metropolitan area. Although emergency backup watched the main arteries of Tokyo, Kuroki harbored no hope that Mizui was still in the capital.

It was already noon. If Mizui had wanted, he could have gone quite far by now.

Since 10 a.m., Section Four was conducting a coordinated search of the Shoyukai and Tatsumigumi Tokyo offices. The charge—not murder but assembling with weapons—revealed what had been the section's goal from the outset. No big fish appeared to have been snagged. The members had dispersed too soon. Section Four must have gone ahead knowing that their time was nearly up.

Only the killer of two murder cases was left like some forgotten item on a train rack.

There was no warrant for Koji Mizui's arrest. There was no material evidence, and Etsuko Mitsuya hadn't broken her silence. Nor was there proof that Mizui had stolen that car. He was being sought as a crucial witness.

Kuroki didn't move from the squad room. All he could do was wait for leads as to Mizui's whereabouts. He was worried, however, that Shibasaki may have found him.

Makimura entered. He placed a large color photo on Kuroki's desk. "Who are they?"

The picture showed five women and two children. One of the children was the boy who'd been with Mizui. It was already confirmed that Mizui's nephew Takao had not been taken outside the family home in Nagano.

"Hiroshi Suzue," Makimura said. "This photo was taken at a dorm for nightclub workers. The woman at far right is his mother."

She was a delicate, pretty woman. The photo was taken in the summer; both the women and the children were dressed lightly.

"Is there a search request?"

"No. I looked into that first and wasted some time. On the sixteenth of December, at 10 a.m., the mother committed suicide by throwing herself on the tracks at Ginza station on the Hibiya line. She'd quit her nightclub in early December. It was the sort of place that forced her to do kinky stuff, and apparently she'd cry her eyes out when she came back to the dorm. Maybe she couldn't bear it anymore."

The sixteenth was the day after Watanabe's murder. Etsuko Mitsuya had gone to Mizui's apartment that morning.

"Why didn't the kid come up after the suicide?" Kuroki asked.

"He did. But it's a bit complicated. The mother had run away from home with the kid. Since over ten days had elapsed between her quitting and dying, the thinking was that she must have checked in at home at some point to leave her kid. She was alone when she died, and she didn't leave a note. No child was taken into custody in the site's vicinity. They couldn't confirm because the husband, who's heavily in debt, also disappeared. I suppose they concluded that he'd disappeared with the kid."

Kuroki lit a Short Peace.

Makimura picked up the photo and fluttered it. "Can't we get an arrest warrant for kidnapping?"

"Waste of time."

Unless there was a ransom, kidnapping was an offense only upon complaint, and there was no guardian to file one. Hiroshi Suzue was only five years old, so perhaps the requirement could be waived in this case. Yet what was the point of charging Mizui with kidnapping at this point?

"Better than doing nothing."

"We wait. We're bound to get a lead." *If Mizui is alive*, Kuroki kept himself from adding.

Just after 1 p.m., they received a report that a biker gang connected to Shibasaki had blazed through Usui Pass. There had been about ten riders. Biker gangs were supposed to be hibernating this time of year. Going down a national route in those numbers could not but attract attention.

Kuroki stood up and went to the interrogation cell.

Fuse sat facing Etsuko Mitsuya.

She clearly hadn't broken her silence. Yet there was nothing defiant in her manner. More depressed than calm, she exuded an aura beyond her years that wasn't sleazy, either.

The girl, or rather woman, was still in love, Kuroki sensed.

"Hey," he said, changing places with Fuse. That feline gleam was gone from the eyes she turned on him. They were slightly moist, chaste even, and for a moment Kuroki felt himself drawn in and confused.

"You still think Mizui will die?"

A pointless question, he knew that. But he wanted to break her down somewhere, somehow. He wanted to put that feline gleam back in her eyes. Then this woman would go back to being an ordinary woman, or rather, girl. He didn't desire this as a detective. The man in Kuroki ached and screamed to see the woman he didn't see.

"It turned out just as you said. Koji Mizui is dead. Killed."

Etsuko showed no immediate reaction. Then her white skin began to flush from her neck upward toward her cheeks. She closed her eyes. Kuroki suddenly felt enveloped in something voluptuous. While resembling sexual climax, it felt different too. He turned his face away.

"Joke." He lit his cigarette. "Mizui is still on the run."

Etsuko opened her eyes. Her face went pale. That feline sparkle was in her eyes.

"A cop acting and joking like you do?"

Kuroki stood up. "Mizui won't die. I'm going to cuff him."

"Then bring him here. He can fuck me right in front of you," the voice of an overexcited girl hurled at his back.

Makimura was waiting. "Shibasaki's on his way to Nagano, isn't he?"

"We're not sure if Shibasaki is with them."

"Still, at this point it could only be Nagano. Nakayama at the warehouse said so too, right?"

Mizui had picked up the boy from Nakayama around 5 a.m. Just past 9 a.m., two men had visited Nakayama and asked where Mizui had gone. An interval of four hours. It couldn't be ignored; in fact, it was a hopeless gap for those in pursuit.

"It's Nagano, sir."

"We wait."

"For what? For Mizui to get killed?"

Etsuko Mitsuya was convinced that Mizui would die. She had to have some basis for that conviction. It had nothing to do with Nakayama's mention of Nagano.

"You want Mizui to die, don't you?"

"Pipe down. The Nagano Prefectural Police has been informed,

144

hasn't it?"

"That Shibasaki," a voice cut in from beyond the desk. It was Yabe. "He's clever. He lacks balls so he has to use his brain. He was really good at deceiving patrols when he was a biker."

"But—"

"See what he does."

Yabe had been released from special investigative headquarters once Section Four had launched its coordinated search of the gangs' Tokyo offices. He was no longer needed to gather info. He was supposed to be off duty today, and Kuroki hadn't even noticed he was around.

"He's not the type to go riding wild at a time like this." Yabe was talking to Makimura, but his voice was loud enough for Kuroki to hear. "Shibasaki is slated to take on Watanabe's work as a younger brother. But it's not so sweet as stepping into Watanabe's shoes now that the man's dead. He needed to prove himself. And he failed."

"You mean that punk getting killed yesterday?"

"Yeah. Shibasaki's clever, but he's not cut out for the knifing part. He's desperate now, though. It's no longer about whether or not there'll be a Mercedes waiting when he gets out of prison. Worst case, his bosses and peers will force him to take responsibility."

Makimura fell silent.

Yabe was indeed the type of detective who chose not to see. So when he decided to see, he did.

Around 2:30 p.m., a report came in that nine bikers had been apprehended in Ueda City, Nagano Prefecture after a long chase by police cars. Shibasaki wasn't among them. The riders weren't carrying any weapons and had been arrested for violating the Road Traffic Act.

"Was that a red herring just for us?" Makimura muttered.

They found Mizui's car about an hour after the motorcycle affair in Ueda.

"Step on it!" Kuroki urged, lunging into the car.

Makimura needed no telling as he sped off. Kuroki placed the red police light on the roof.

"Looks like they've lost him."

The radio dispatches were frequent.

The car had been spotted in the Kamakura city center by a policeman patrolling on a bicycle. He had confirmed the number plate but had not been able to follow the car.

By the time Kuroki and Makimura reached Kamakura, it was already getting dark. Nearly ten cars from Kanagawa Prefectural Police had been mobilized.

Kuroki enlisted the help of local taxis equipped with radio. Kamakura streets were tortuous. Best have as many eyes on the lookout as possible.

They took the route along the Shonan coast toward Enoshima. It seemed likely that Mizui had headed west, given where the car had been spotted and the subsequent dragnet.

A taxi radioed in that the car was on Route 134 heading toward Chigasaki. It was somewhere near Kugenuma beach. The taxi continued tailing the car and sent updates every few minutes.

It wasn't that far and they caught up soon. A police car was already there ahead of them. They were doing almost seventy miles per hour.

Mizui's car soon became visible too.

"Get out in front of it," Kuroki radioed the police car. To the right were houses, to the left was the coast. Pine trees and then sandy beach beyond. Mizui's car and the police car were now side to side. They drove like that for a while, then the police car pushed forward.

"Corner him into the pine woods, Makimura."

Sandwiched, Mizui's car suddenly veered sharply to the left. It sped through the pine woods and onto the beach.

Tires skidded on dry sand, a futile roar overpowering the sound of the waves.

Makimura leapt out of the car before it had even halted. He was holding a gun. The engine stopped.

"Get out," he shouted.

Two men got out. Neither was Mizui. Kuroki clicked his tongue.

3

The waves sparkled golden. Soon the sun would set. There was a gentle ebb and flow.

"Put on your gloves, Hiroshi. It's getting cold," Koji advised.

Hiroshi pulled out from his pockets the yellow woolen gloves they'd bought that morning at a department store.

Koji was beginning to get the knack of handling the oars. The boat proceeded at a fairly steady pace.

Land was far. He had no desire to get near it again.

He'd approached it once after rowing for an hour. He saw the coast road and a familiar car driving along. It was the one he'd dumped in the pine copse. Two motorcycles were in front of it. Those guys hadn't given up.

After that he'd rowed out and not even gone near the shore.

He'd been rowing now for almost three hours. He wasn't in a rush. He had been for the first ten minutes, but he quickly learned that hurrying didn't make the boat go all that much faster.

His body moved mechanically. At some point, pain and exhaustion had vanished. If he were to shake off pursuit, it was best to keep rowing for as long as possible.

Eventually the sun set.

It got astonishingly dark. He couldn't see Hiroshi's face though it was right near him. All he could see were the lights on land far away.

"Big brother."

"What's up? You scared?"

"I'm fine."

"Ah, just felt like calling out to me, huh? Can't see a thing, can we?"

The boat didn't seem to be advancing at all. The wind was getting stronger. It was a headwind, too.

"Are you cold?"

"I'm fine."

The boy's teeth were chattering. Koji removed his own coat and, fumbling in the dark, threw it over Hiroshi's shoulders. He then wound the two scarves around the child. Koji didn't feel too cold because he was rowing.

"Where's the radio-controlled car?" Hiroshi asked.

"Don't worry. I've got it by my feet."

Koji prodded the paper bag with his foot so that it rustled.

There was the sound of the oars hitting the water and the wail of the wind. It was eerily silent when they didn't talk.

Koji's body kept moving. Another blister burst on his palm. No pain.

"Big brother?"

"I'm here, kid. You can hear the oars creaking, can't you? As long as you can hear that sound, I'm right here."

The dark was thick, heavy. Wave it off as they might, it weighed upon them.

"What day is it?"

"Huh?"

"It's not the nineteenth of December, is it?"

"That was yesterday."

"So it's gone?"

"Yup."

Hiroshi needed to talk, it seemed. He was sitting still, bundled up in Koji's coat. Maybe it was harder to just sit like that than to row.

"What's special about the nineteenth?"

"It's my birthday."

"Ah ha. How old are you now?"

"Six."

"I would have thrown a party for you if you'd told me."

Yesterday had not been that sort of day. Perhaps Hiroshi would remember it as the worst birthday of his entire life. The boy fell silent.

"Let's talk about something," Koji said.

"Okay."

"Bet you look really funny. All cocooned up like a bagworm."

"No one can see me."

The oars slipped on water. This had happened a few times after getting dark, and Koji's body creaked.

"You know, Hiroshi," he resumed. The oars slipped again, sprinkling spray on his head. He raised his upper body and tried to push the oars in deep. "I wanted a boat. Not like this one, though. A big boat with an engine. I saved for it too—310,000 yen. I often thought how great it would feel to just sail away."

"Where would you go?"

"On that boat? Oh, fishing, swimming in the ocean, all that. Have you been to the sea a lot?"

"My house was near the sea."

"Ha, so you grew up by the sea. Me, I grew up in a town in the mountains. I saw the sea for the first time when I was fifteen. I was amazed. I'd seen it on TV and stuff so I knew what the sea was like. Still, I was bowled over. All my friends had been to the sea several times and they'd laugh when I'd say I'd never been. They'd been to the sea on school trips too, not a single one of them had never seen the sea. I wonder why I didn't go on those school trips. I can't remember. Anyway, I didn't go."

"I've never been on a school trip, either."

"Yeah, but you don't go to school yet. Once you start school, there are these things called school trips and they take you to all sorts of places. My family was poor but not so poor that we couldn't pay for these trips. I wonder why I didn't go. I was never ill or anything."

All the talking didn't thin out the darkness. Even talking began to feel like a burden.

"You must be thirsty."

"Yeah."

"And hungry too."

The oars slipped on water again. Before he could notice, his body was leaning forward and the oars wouldn't slice in.

"Hang in there just a little more. I can still row. Let's go as far as we can. Then we'll get off the boat and have something to eat. Something hot sounds good. So hot it almost burns your tongue."

His body kept moving. He felt that the body wasn't his. He could keep rowing forever.

It was just the darkness. So unbearably heavy.

"Damn, it's so dark."

Koji looked up at the sky. There were no clouds and some stars twinkled. One of the oars slipped. It was because he had moved his head. Spray flew, though he couldn't see. He just felt it on his head.

The wind was getting stronger.

"Hiroshi," he voiced so raspily the wind could blow his words away. "Say, 'Yeah.'"

"Yeah," Hiroshi said faintly.

"Once we get off the boat, why don't we head for the mountains? Not just any, but mountains covered with snow. There it won't be as dark as this at night because there's something called snow light. Snow is great, it sucks up sound. And yet it doesn't get dark, not so dark as this."

Wind wailed above his head. The boat rocked.

"Don't fall asleep, Hiroshi."

Was the boat really making any progress, against this wind? At dawn, would they find themselves in the middle of the ocean?

He began to feel anxious. He could as easily be dead: one blow to the head would have made him the victim and Watanabe the murderer when the guy attacked him with that rope. It was a fluke that he was alive.

But he didn't want Hiroshi to suffer. The kid had been through more than enough suffering.

The wind wailed again. Blasts akin to gale winds were assailing them intermittently. All Koji could do was row. Just row, for now.

"Don't fall asleep." He repeated this several times.

Suddenly he felt a cramp in his side. He leaned forward, unable to raise his torso. He couldn't inhale, either. He groaned. Hiroshi said something. I need to answer, Koji thought. Just utter a word. But all he could manage was a groan.

At last he was able to breathe. He gradually began to feel better. He could finally sit up.

"Don't fall asleep."

When he got back to rowing, the oars felt unbelievably heavy. On the second go, they felt somewhat lighter. With the third, he regained his former pace.

His mouth began to move on its own. He was just spouting, but he sought responses from Hiroshi. The responses kept getting shorter.

"Don't fall asleep."

He tried to kick Hiroshi but couldn't lift his leg.

How many hours had he rowed like this? The faraway lights at left seemed to have come closer. He turned around. Light on land. Not just points of them, but diffuse brightness scattering into the sky. Were they close? Were they really city lights?

He rowed harder, or intended to, but his arms' movements didn't change one bit. Something other than will was moving his arms, his body. Though that was exasperating, he also felt certain that his arms would never cease.

The wind blew even harder. It whirled and switched direction above them and violently shook the boat. Quite a lot of seawater had washed into the boat. There was nothing to do but row. It was a sort of gamble. Row and see where they end up.

"It's okay," he said to Hiroshi.

There was no answer.

"I always come through when it counts."

"Okay," Hiroshi mumbled.

More time passed. Five minutes, ten minutes, maybe an hour, two hours. Koji felt like screaming. In the beginning he just screamed like an animal frightened of the dark. Still, it emptied his mind. *Bastard*, the scream turned into a word. *Fuck you, die, go to hell, I'll kill you.* All sorts of curses came tumbling out, not as screams now but as barely voiced whispers. These whispers vanished too, leaving only a mouth that moved. His arms were moving, too. The oars were slowly but surely displacing water.

He thought he heard the horn of a car in the distance. His ears also caught the faint roar of an engine. *Bullshit!* The word didn't come out. He cursed his own ears. They were in the middle of the sea. How could he ever hear a car?

A heavy, dragging impact came from the bottom. The oars caught on something, and the boat stopped moving.

It had run aground in sand. It took a while for Koji to realize what had happened.

"Big brother?"

Hiroshi's voice. Not just his voice. His form was visible.

Koji tried to stand up, but his legs wouldn't move. The oars were stuck to his hands. No matter how hard he tried to disentangle his fingers, they wouldn't let go.

"Dammit." He collapsed on his back. His bones responded with an excruciating snap. "Stay still for a while, Hiroshi."

He could see the sky. The stars were out, but still no moon. Yet, the heaviness of the dark was lifting. *We're near a city,* he tried and whispered. He could hear the lapping of the waves.

He peeled his hands off the oars. It felt like peeling off scabs. He lay down again. He stretched out his arms. He raised his upper body and rolled out of the boat. He didn't fall on water, but wet sand. He wondered if the tide had receded.

He lifted Hiroshi down. The child really did look like some mistletoe.

"Bag," Hiroshi mumbled.

"Of course I wouldn't forget."

The bag was soaked.

It was a beach. The breakwater darkly reared up, and beyond it there seemed to be a road.

They climbed the stairs of the breakwater. Koji's body was swaying. Bright lights from houses broke into view. For the first time he felt that he'd gotten off the boat.

It was past eleven. Lights were on but it was quiet in what seemed like a residential area. While he felt a bit creaky, he could walk. Hiroshi's breath was white.

A sign on a telephone pole indicated where they were. Zaimokuza. Koji felt deflated. He had run, but he hadn't come very far. He'd had the impression that he'd rowed all the way across Sagami Bay. At any rate, he'd surely thrown off his pursuers. He had to provide Hiroshi a hot meal.

A dog barked from the other side of a fence. Koji didn't know the way to downtown. Hiroshi was clearly exhausted. The child had to have a hot meal even if it was instant noodles from a vending machine. When Koji crouched down, his back to the child, Hiroshi wordlessly fell against him. His body was so light.

Towards brightness, to whichever way was brighter, Koji led him.

There was extensive damage to the front of the car, clearly from a collision.

"Where did you find it?" Kuroki asked on the spot.

Both men were injured. One just seemed bruised, but the other's shoulder dangled from a broken collarbone.

Kuroki poked it. The guy groaned.

"Sir," Makimura tried to intervene, but his superior brushed his hand away.

"Out with it. Where did you find the car?"

Kuroki lightly shook the man's shoulder. His face contorted.

"Let's take care of that."

Kuroki showed no mercy. He lifted the guy's arm and moved it backwards and forwards. His groans became screams.

He spoke.

Kuroki lunged back into his car. Makimura followed him.

"You stay."

"But—"

"There's a lot to ask. Has Mizui already been killed? Is he still on the run? Was he with a child? What's up with Shibasaki? Hurry. Go ahead and exercise his right arm. There'll be time to treat it later."

"Yes, sir."

A local police officer joined Kuroki. The car had been found in pine woods about a mile and a half from Chojagasaki, in the direction of Misaki, along Route 134.

"I have a basic idea," the police officer said. It got dark early. Already the sky was suffused with a light wash of ink.

After searching three sites, they found some tire tracks. While they couldn't say for sure that Mizui's car had left them, it was already getting dark. The area was mostly steep slopes dropping into the sea and there were few pine woods to drive a car into.

"There's a beach here," the officer said. Relying on his flashlight, they got out onto the sand.

"And that?"

Lit houses were visible in the distance. It looked to be a village.

"That's Kuruwa. This is the only place on the coast around here that's sandy. The rest is all rock. Used to be a secret beach-going spot, but now it gets quite crowded."

"Let's walk along the beach. I want to ask some questions in Kuruwa."

If Mizui had switched cars, it had to be in some sort of community. That meant he'd walked along these sandy shores. The gang would have seen him if he'd walked down the national route.

Just in front of the village was a boathouse—a roof to shelter vessels and a shed. There were two fishing boats. These refused to budge no matter how much they pushed. It looked like a winch in the pine woods was used to pull them out of the sea.

"Are there small boats here? One you could move alone?"

"I wonder."

The shed door rattled in the wind. The lock was broken.

They looked inside with the flashlight. All they could see were a row of metal barrels.

"Can you get somebody?"

The officer ran off.

Kuroki examined the area around the shed. There were marks on the sand right to the waterline. Deep grooves, as if something had been pulled along.

A few men came running, then spoke at once.

"The boat's gone."

"Oars too. A pair of them, and the oarlocks."

Kuroki met up with Makimura in Hayama.

The consensus was that the farthest Mizui could go in the boat was Hayama. In a head wind, it may have been impossible to go beyond Chojagasaki.

The area precinct was tasked to search along the Hayama coast. Ten o'clock came, then eleven, but the boat wasn't found. Canvassing the locals yielded nothing. After landing, the boat must have been pushed out to sea. They couldn't conclude otherwise.

The precinct arranged for a night's stay at a sailors' inn.

"The one who broke his collarbone," Makimura began after getting into his futon, "was at the crime scene in Ueno Park. There were four of them: him, Shibasaki, Etsuko Mitsuya, and the victim. It seems they abducted the child and summoned Mizui. It got nasty and Mizui knifed one of them, but they couldn't get him there.

"Under orders from Shibasaki, he went to keep watch at Mizui's apartment. Meanwhile, Shibasaki and Etsuko Mitsuya got rid of the body. Mizui returned very late but left again soon, so the guy followed him on his motorbike. He saw Mizui steal the car and pick the kid up from Nakamura. All the while he kept in touch with Shibasaki."

"So the business in Nagano was a diversion, after all."

"Well, it seems Shibasaki assembled his pals to get revenge."

"Three on his side and Mizui trounced them anyway, so he's downright hopeless in a fight. But Shibasaki has a few brain cells. Acting up in Nagano would deflect our attention and provide their whole group with an alibi."

Makimura stubbed out his cigarette and turned off the light at his pillow. Once dark, the crash of the waves seemed closer.

"Sir," Makimura said just when Kuroki thought him asleep, "why do you think Mizui went to Ueno Park? The kid isn't his nephew. Just an abandoned child and a total stranger. Still Mizui put his life on the line."

"Don't ask me. Mizui's still alive. Why don't you ask him?"

"I guess it all began with me botching his alibi check, didn't it?"

"You think so?" Kuroki rolled over. "In that case, don't forget it."

Howling wind accompanied the roar of the waves. Kuroki closed his eyes. Makimura didn't say more.

Just before 7 a.m., they found the boat. Kuroki and Makimura rushed out of the inn without having had breakfast. Even at this early hour, the national route was congested; perhaps many in this region commuted by car. With the red police light up top and siren blasting, the detectives sped.

"Whoa! He went three times farther than we thought."

The boat had been found on the beach in Zaimokuza, Kamakura.

"There was a terrible head wind, supposedly. He rowed all that sea, and in wintertime, by himself?"

"It's not impossible, if you're desperate."

Kuroki lit a Short Peace. His mind was elsewhere. He was thinking about Nakayama, the warehouse caretaker. Perhaps that old man might win his bet. Mizui had shaken off Shibasaki, who'd gotten closer to him than the police, and also fled an unlikely distance in a small boat.

If the old man did win, it wasn't as if the cancer eating away at him would go away. Cancer was cancer. His was a bet with no winnings. Still, the old man would feel like he'd gained something. Not life, not money, but something better.

The detective who'd contacted them was waiting with an officer on the beach in Zaimokuza.

It was certainly the boat Mizui had stolen. It hadn't drifted there, either. There were footprints of an adult and a child.

"They must have come ashore about 11 p.m. last night. That's the time the tide was up here. Since then it's been ebbing."

The detective from the precinct looked young, about Makimura's age. His movements were brisk, and he also seemed to be efficient—the search for the stolen car, keeping the crime scene intact, all of it by the book.

The boat revealed nothing special. Just reddish-black bloodstains on the oar handles. Mizui must have kept rowing with flayed palms.

They started questioning locals. Eleven at night wasn't so late that nobody would be out on the streets. Moreover, Mizui had rowed a great distance against a headwind. He must have been utterly exhausted as well as chilled to the bone.

As a start, they checked restaurants and cafeterias that stayed open late into the night.

Mizui's first steps were tracked unexpectedly soon. He'd gone to a ramen place about a third of a mile inland.

Man and boy had been a curious pair to show up close to midnight, so the proprietor remembered them well. After ordering ramen noodles and *gyoza* dumplings, they fell silent as though completely exhausted. But once they had food in their stomachs, they seemed to gain some energy and started talking.

"They were discussing stuff like whether a car could run on snow," the proprietor said, showing no ill temper in spite of having been roused from his slumber.

"Did they come in a car?"

"No, it seemed like they'd walked. The man was piggybacking the child. At first I thought the boy was asleep, but he was just tired and hungry."

"A car, huh."

"I can't say for sure, but I thought they might be talking about a toy car."

"A toy car?"

"Yes. The child had a big one. 'Radio-controlled,' was it, the ones that move by remote?"

That was the extent of their findings. The tracks vanished there.

"On snow, sir?"

Once full, the next move would have been to leave Kamakura.

"Another stolen car," Kuroki said without much hope. The young detective from the precinct was already looking into it.

Mizui hadn't necessarily stolen one in Kamakura. He'd have had enough time to catch the last train, and he could also have hailed a cab. They investigated all the possibilities, to no avail. Nobody else remembered seeing a man and a child at that hour of the night. Makimura, unable to give up, went as far as Nikaido and Yukinoshita for clues but returned before noon empty-handed.

For over two hours, Kuroki interrogated the two men they'd arrested. A night's sleep seemed to have done them a world of good, however, and they refused to be lured by snares. It would take time.

And Kuroki had none.

It was past 1 p.m. when the precinct received a relevant complaint of theft.

Just before midnight, a car parked with the key still in the ignition had been stolen. A common blue Nissan Sunny.

"The owner's really laid back. He's under the impression that stolen cars get abandoned and found after a few days," informed the same detective who'd reported about the boat in the morning. "He said he went to pick up a friend who'd been drinking and left the car in front of the bar, but I bet he'd been drinking too. That's why he didn't report the theft immediately."

Whatever the reason, they were twelve hours behind. The saving grace was that Mizui wouldn't have been able to drive for long given his extreme exhaustion. He must have stopped somewhere to sleep.

There was no news on Shibasaki and company. In any case, they didn't seem to be here. If they'd headed for Tokyo, then Route 1 via Tozuka or the Yokohama New Road immediately came to mind, but they hadn't been caught in the net set out by the Kanagawa Prefectural Police. It was easy to imagine that an ex-biker gang leader like Shibasaki knew the Shonan area roads by heart.

"Kamakura can be a bitch whenever they go over a mountain," the young local detective apologized as if the ancient capital's convoluted geography were his fault.

So they were back to square one.

There was nothing to do now but to wait at the desk at the station until news came that Mizui's car had been sighted. Yet Shibasaki was on the move. Was waiting really it?

Once again Kuroki interrogated the two arrested men. The one with the broken collarbone was of more interest since he had been following Mizui and reporting to Shibasaki since the day before yesterday.

Fuse arrived from the station to take custody of the two men.

"I think I'll head over to Nagano."

"We've got nothing solid there, sir."

"The car will eventually be found, maybe along with Mizui's body. That'll just sadden my handcuffs."

"You're just going to go there on a hunch? You of all people?"

"Hunches are nothing to scoff at, though I've tried not to rely on them. Anyway, I don't have to explain myself to you."

Since two nights ago, Mizui's behavior had been both spontaneous and erratic. Interrogating the man who'd tailed him didn't yield any impression of a desperate escapade. Mizui had spent half of yesterday relaxing in Yokohama. He'd let the kid play with a radio-controlled car in Yamashita Park and boarded a pleasure boat like it was some school outing. He had only become serious about getting away when he had to, no doubt after four riders assailed him near Kinugasa. Desperation would awaken something in Mizui's soul. Once cornered, something close to the heart showed its face even in the most erratic man.

His hometown, a woman, friends. His behavior could become more predictable.

On snow. The words stuck in Kuroki's mind. Snow linked up with Nagano, where Mizui was from.

"Please take me with you," Makimura implored.

"You do a bit more work grilling those two. There's more there. Besides, the problem with hunches is that when they're off, you get seriously burned. Your staying in Tokyo would be like insurance."

Tracking Mizui down had been left more or less to Kuroki and Makimura. K Police Station's violent crimes investigation section had more cases than it could handle. Moreover, it was the end of the year when crimes of impulse were more frequent. They couldn't assign extra shoes to this case.

"Through the Nagano Prefectural Police, we've got the local precinct on Mizui's family," Makimura reminded.

"I know."

Mizui seeking refuge at his family home in Ueda was unthinkable. That would be too reckless. What Kuroki suspected was that Mizui might subconsciously steer in that direction in his desperation.

On snow. Those words were all that stuck. Hokkaido and Tohoku had snow, too.

5

Koji sped along the highway in the dead of night for four hours.

Sometimes he found himself trying to pull the wheel hard toward him. His body did that, the monotonous motion of rowing having become second nature. While his mind knew he was driving a car, his body took it for a boat.

He needed a break. Every time his eyelids drooped, he pulled at the wheel as if they were oars. The car veered across the partition line or threatened to careen off the road.

He got off the national route. Driving onto a side road, then off it into some woods, he parked.

Hiroshi was curled up asleep in the reclined seat. He must have been really tired; he wasn't moving a muscle.

Koji stepped out and felt the wind, inhaled the cold air. Soon his body began to shiver. Still, his eyelids kept drooping.

He returned to the car and reclined the driver's seat.

He was stroking Makiko's long, silky hair with his palm. She had lowered her face slightly and had placed one hand on his knee, while her other hand toyed with the fingers of his left hand. In the room were a TV set, a stereo, a sideboard, furniture for hosting guests—all of the ordinary type found in any household. Only, there were picture books on the sideboard.

Makiko had painted her nails pearly pink. A faint whiff of perfume came from around the nape of her neck. She was pregnant. The swell of her belly was both mysterious and infinitely precious to him.

They had a visitor. "Ma'am, why won't you let me see him?" the guest pressed Makiko. It was Numata. He kept bugging her to let him in. Koji stepped out.

Smiling upon seeing Koji's face, Numata said hi. He was smartly attired in an indigo three-piece suit. His hair was long.

Out of the blue Koji punched him.

"You're barking up the wrong tree."

Numata didn't argue. He just stood there letting Koji beat him up. Blood came gushing out of his nose and soiled his suit. Damn, Koji thought. Everyone had something they didn't want soiled.

"Let him in," Makiko said in an oddly haughty tone. Somehow she'd already had the baby. "If you don't let him in, I'll kill this kid."

A child cried in Makiko's arms. It was a boy. Hiroshi.

Why? Why do you have to kill our child?

"I mean it. I can do it, you know."

If you have to kill someone, kill me. Don't touch the child. I'll get pissed—if you kill Hiroshi, I'll kill you.

He woke up.

He wiped the sweat from his forehead. It was now bright outside the car. Eight in the morning. Hiroshi was still asleep.

Koji's mind was clear. His eyelids weren't heavy anymore.

Suddenly he smelled Makiko. It was a smell as familiar as the odor of his own body. He saw her white, nude body, and his urge was strong to devour it. There was no grudge, no hatred. Only longing. He wanted to drown in her flesh.

Makiko's eyes were gazing at him. They sparkled a lot, those eyes. He gazed back. He was being drawn in, but his will resisted it. Then, she vanished. Beyond the front window was a morning landscape consisting merely of trees.

He stepped outside and did a stretch. His muscles screamed in agony. Whichever part he moved was shot with excruciating pain. What was going on? For a moment he was confused. He even feared he'd fallen gravely ill. But the pain wasn't deep. He urinated and felt much better by the time he returned to the car.

When he took the wheel, he winced again. The skin of his palms were peeling off, exposing red flesh. That pain only really stung for a moment, too.

Hiroshi woke up.

Koji propped up the car seat for him. Hiroshi peered into the paper bag, confirming that his radio-controlled car was still there, and looked outside.

The intent had been to get away from the national route, but a large trailer that drove past was visible between the trees.

"What's today?" The boy rubbed the window glass with his little hand.

"The twenty-first, of December."

"The nineteenth is over, isn't it?"

"You worried about your birthday?"

"I just want to know if it's over or not."

"It's over." Koji lit a cigarette. "Let's still have a party, though. Just the two of us. We're gonna have to throw a party for Christmas, too." There was no way he could be sure of that. He just felt like saying it, but it did soothe him.

"Are there gonna be candles?"

"Yup, on a cake."

Koji adjusted the car mirror to reflect his own face. It looked like shit. The scabs hadn't come off, either.

"We're leaving, Hiroshi. Go pee first."

Off the boy went. Koji lowered the window and watched his back.

On Usui Pass, there was not as much snow as he'd expected. Just clumps of white on the bamboo leaves along the road.

A nasty vibration shook the car. That was because the chain in the trunk had been wound around the tires. All the cars descending the pass had chains on their tires. It had to be snowing higher up.

There was no sign of pursuit. He'd shaken them off completely.

The question now was where to go. The face of his older brother in Ueda vaguely came to mind. Traversing the pass and driving straight on would get them to Karuizawa, then Komoro, then Ueda.

Somehow he'd ended up on this road.

Yet he had no intention of showing up at his brother's place. How would he explain Hiroshi? What if those guys pursued him there? This wasn't like asking for help in a fight when they were kids. His brother had three children. He was a skilled plasterer. He even supported their father. Involving him in risky business was out of the question. It was wrong.

Still, changing routes wouldn't do at this point. They were already halfway up the pass.

The thinking could wait until they got to Karuizawa. From there, roads probably headed every which way.

His palms hurt every time he turned the wheel at a curve. His arms ached too. It was the same when he changed gears. It felt as though he were driving purely to inflict pain on his body.

He didn't think the police were giving chase. There hadn't been a single indication of that so far. Even then, his heart pounded wildly when a patrol car came his way right after rounding a curve. Nothing happened.

Not a soul was paying attention to his car.

Soon he began to feel weary. They'd eaten a breakfast of bread and juice along the way, so he wasn't that hungry. The fatigue was of a different nature, what they called lethargy. Wanting to give up on everything. Dropping this ridiculous getaway act and lying, spread-eagled, on the road. It was an impulse in whose face he was helpless. All he could do was rub his palms against the wheel and concentrate his nerves on the pain.

At last they cleared the pass. The road was now flat and straight.

"There's snow." Hiroshi had his face against the window.

It must have fallen the night before, leaving a thin blanket and a white landscape. The sight was familiar to Koji from his earliest years. He'd spent long winters in much deeper snow.

He felt less moved, however, than he'd anticipated.

Was it all right to have come this far? To be so near his brother's house? That was all he could think of.

He stopped for gas just before Karuizawa. The staffer at the station who came over in a huddle as if he were freezing barely glanced at Koji's face when he took the keys.

"It's a bit early, but shall we have lunch?"

It was a little past 10:30 a.m. Koji wasn't hungry, but gripping the wheel had become a bother. He also had to figure out where they were going. If he didn't watch out, they'd be in Ueda in no time.

At the first drive-in restaurant they spotted after the gas station, Koji and Hiroshi had hamburgers. The boy had a huge appetite. Somewhere along the way he'd regained his liveliness. It was a little weird. Maybe kids were like that.

As for Koji, it was no good. The lethargy was affecting his thinking. He said to himself, several times, that he didn't give a damn what happened.

"Can I make it go?" Hiroshi placed the radio-controlled car on the floor.

"No. They'll tell you off. Hang on for a while."

"But—"

"You're worried that it's broken, aren't you?"

Hiroshi nodded. Koji took away the remote control, held the car in his other hand, and flicked the switch. There was a whirr as the wheels went round and round.

"See, it's fine."

With a dissatisfied look on his face, Hiroshi put the toy car in the paper bag. "Brother, how far are we going in the car?"

Koji still had no idea. When he tried to think, inconsequential things popped into his head. "Sick of being on the road, huh? We'll be done soon. Let's go somewhere where there's more snow."

Koji couldn't finish his hamburger. Maybe his stomach was acting up. Nausea lurched to the back of his throat.

"Come on, we're off."

He stood up. He still didn't know where they were going.

They went into the city, and it was a nasty place. If it weren't for the snow, the attires of passers-by and the storefronts would have fomented the illusion that they were somewhere in Tokyo.

Best to get through such a city as quickly as possible.

On the main road a traffic light forced a stop.

A family of three, the little boy about Hiroshi's age, crossed in front. They were holding ice skates. Next came a group of women wearing trendy coats and boots and licking ice-cream cones despite the cold.

An idea came.

Wasn't this city the perfect place to hide? Everyone walking the streets was a stranger, nobody knew who anybody was. They weren't even interested. Whoever you were, you didn't stand out. It was like Tokyo.

People in country villages disliked strangers—or rather, didn't easily accept them. Provincials wouldn't mind their own business until they knew what kind of person you were and what you had come to do. Koji himself used to be like that.

Here it was different. The place was overflowing with people. Moreover, those who came here yesterday were gone tomorrow. It was that kind of city. To the handful of locals, all the visitors probably looked alike—same faces, same getups, just another bunch of people throwing money around and then leaving.

The car behind honked. The light had changed. Koji started driving, now paying heed to the number plates of the other cars. Tokyo, Yokohama, Chiba, Shizuoka. Local number plates were in fact the minority.

He drove for a while, then branched off onto a side road. There too, cars were parked chock-a-block to avoid paying for parking.

Putting both hands on the wheel and resting his chin on them, Koji set to thinking.

How might they live inconspicuously in this city? Inns and hostels were out. Camping sites were probably closed during winter.

There were the second houses. This region was best known for its summer retreats. If he searched, he'd find a house that was vacant off-season. If everything went smoothly, they'd be able to live unmolested with a roof over their heads until spring. An isolated summer house without a caretaker or visiting security staff that wasn't near a ski resort or skating rink—if he searched, he'd find one. He just had to keep driving.

He started the car. Now that he had a plan, he suddenly felt vigorous. The bouts of lethargy seemed false now.

He parked in front of a supermarket. First, get plenty of food. If necessary they could sleep in the car for a night or two. As long as they had food, they could cope. Best shop in a large supermarket in a busy street to avoid notice.

Koji pulled out the key and got out, leaving Hiroshi in the car.

6

At 7:20 p.m., Kuroki cleared the Usui Pass.

The Gunma and Nagano Prefectural Police had set up checkpoints along Route 18 and outward. If Mizui had crossed Usui Pass in the morning, however, it was all for nothing. It was after 2 p.m. that Kuroki had requested support.

Snow began to fall on the streets of Karuizawa.

Kuroki raised the collar of his coat and walked down the main street. Even at night there were a lot of people out, couples, families, groups of young women.

He was twelve hours behind Mizui. The gap was all too large for the side giving chase. Still, Mizui must have stopped for sleep somewhere. Above or below Usui Pass, maybe just after getting out of Kamakura. How many hours had Mizui slept? His fatigue would have been extreme.

Snow struck Kuroki's cheeks and he could feel them melting into droplets of water. Even in the dark of night, his breath was white. His coat was thin. His body soon felt the chill, and his freezing fingers refused to move.

Had Shibasaki pinned down Mizui's whereabouts? This time, getting punks on the man's tail must have been a tall order. Shibasaki, too, would be acting on his gut.

The city center shone bright, its lights, glaring to begin with, amplified by the reflecting snow. Discos, boutiques, cafes, restaurants, arcades, bars, nightclubs, supermarkets, this city had everything. And all sorts gathered here. Though not as vibrant as summertime, the liveliness here exceeded some quarters of Tokyo itself.

People hid people, and the same held for cars.

Kuroki paid a visit to the local police station. There were only two detectives in the squad room.

He borrowed a road map of the Karuizawa area. Even a basic grasp of the locale would help. Until he unearthed some clues about where Mizui had been, he couldn't demand further support. He was grateful that they had at least set up checkpoints along Route 18. They might not nab Mizui, but there was a chance they'd get Shibasaki.

"Wasn't the Watanabe murder part of a fracas between organized gangs?" This was a detective called Takao. He was overweight and balding but seemed younger than Kuroki. His red cheeks and nose accentuated his baby face.

"It was judged to be a conflict between gangs. As a result, we lost valuable time. Mizui, a crucial witness, killed another man in the meantime. If we'd pursued his line from the start, maybe he'd only have killed once."

"So the conflict angle was just an excuse to get at the gangs? Didn't seem like such a jerry-rigged job when I read the papers."

"There were two lines of inquiry, the gang conflict and an entirely different one. Yet we only pursued one."

The media emphasized the gang conflict angle. Investigative headquarters had issued statements along those lines, and indeed both Shoyukai and Tatsumigumi had mobilized. It was hardly surprising that a detective in the provinces didn't question the gang war story.

Chatting like this wasn't going to help track Mizui, but Kuroki needed to talk to someone unrelated to the case. He couldn't but talk.

But he managed to check himself there. If he said more, he'd not only be divulging his own missteps but criticizing the force itself.

"Mizui's family home is in Ueda, isn't it?" Takao's tone seemed to encase another question: *Why are you in Karuizawa?*

Kuroki lit one of his Short Peace cigarettes and warmed his hands above the kerosene stove. Takao offered a teacup. Kuroki smiled and waved it away.

"It'll at least keep the cold at bay."

"It's not because I'm on duty. I can't drink at all. Half a cup of beer is enough to give me a headache."

"Has a search been arranged in Ueda?"

Kuroki nodded. Most likely, some detective was keeping an eye on Mizui's family home as well.

Yet, Karuizawa. Wherever Mizui was heading, if he came up Route 18 he must have passed through Karuizawa. The first step was to find traces of Mizui in this city. Moving on without a clue would be pointless.

"Some places aren't accessible by car. Would you like to use our station's jeep?" Takao asked, peering at a map.

"If I need it, yes, I'll ask you."

The jurisdiction of a provincial police station was vast, several times that of Tokyo if the map was anything to go by. Conducting a search here was like trying to grasp a cloud.

Kuroki asked Takao's permission to use the phone.

Makimura was still at the station. Kuroki hung up, instructing him to call back.

"We're grilling them right now. They've come up with some beauties. Seems like Shibasaki has indeed been issued an ultimatum from above. He's also been taken to task by his peers for his recent stumble."

"Both the pursued and the pursuer are desperate, then."

"Could Shoyukai make a move as an organization?"

"Not possible. If they do, they give Section Four another excuse to mess with them. They probably only set Shibasaki's ass on fire."

"Also, it seems that Shibasaki has a gun. An M10, they're saying, but I don't know. Shibasaki couldn't obtain such a gun easily."

"Shoyukai could, though."

"You mean someone from Shoyukai gave it to Shibasaki to put a hole in Mizui?"

The SW Model 10. Dubbed "military and police," it was a .38-caliber revolver with a longish barrel. It was an efficient piece of machinery, one of the most popular guns in America. During training sessions for new recruits, a cutaway of the M10 was used to explain the structure of revolvers.

"Did you get anything on Shibasaki's movements? Still some biker gang types out there, no?"

"Fuse is looking into that. Can you tell me how to contact you, sir?"

"I'll make sure the police here know where I'm staying."

"Does that mean you're going to spend the night in Karuizawa?"

"I've taken to this city."

"They're issuing Mizui's arrest warrant. Not for the Watanabe murder, but for stabbing the punk. Etsuko Mitsuya is still not saying a word, by the way."

"Let that woman be. Just keep an eye on her."

Kuroki hung up.

He tried to return the map to Takao, who told him to keep it. Folding it and tucking it into his coat pocket, Kuroki stepped outside.

It was snowing miserably.

On his shoulders, on his head, sat snow. His body no longer felt the cold.

It was 11 p.m. He'd gleaned nothing from talking to the locals. There was nothing remarkable about the stolen car, a blue Nissan Sunny, but Mizui had a distinguishing characteristic. A scar on his cheek. That scab would still be there. He was with a kid, too.

Kuroki went into a disco. All of a sudden, his body surface felt flush from the heating. No way Mizui would be in a place like this. But the decent places were starting to close, limiting his canvassing options.

He left the disco and went to a cafe that stayed open late. Then a bar, and an arcade, all for nothing.

It was still snowing.

He found himself far from the city center. The snow gave a crunch with each step he took. The city hubbub felt distant.

He made a point of checking the parked cars. Almost half had metropolitan-area number plates. Schools and such were probably already on winter break. Couples were sleeping in some of the cars.

When he got back to the city center, naturally it was less crowded.

He walked around the shuttered shopping district. The walking didn't tire him, nor did coming up empty discourage him. After fifteen years as a detective, he'd gotten this way. What tormented Kuroki were all the shuttered stores and not even spotting a potential witness.

A woman emerged from an alley.

Or rather a girl. She looked only fifteen or sixteen to Kuroki.

"Wanna have some fun?"

He had another look at her. Her cheeks were red, and her teeth chattered from the cold. He replied, "I take it you don't have a place to stay, or the money to."

"I haven't the money. Why else would I not find a room? Come on, spend the night with me. I'll settle for 10,000 yen."

"How old are you?"

"Eighteen."

She was trying to act that age. Kuroki started to walk away. *Please, daddy,* she called out and clutched his arm. Three men emerged from the alley.

"I see. So this was the deal."

"What deal? The fuck you think you're doing to my girl?"

All three of them were still boys. Pompadours, gangly legs, black leather jackets. Kuroki took two steps forward. He grabbed the tallest boy by the collar, put his waist into it, and slammed him onto the snow. The other two stood there dumbfounded. He stamped his shoe on the vacant face of the boy lying on his back. The scream that came was very much a child's. Kuroki waited for a while, but nobody else appeared. No one seemed to be pulling strings.

"Get lost."

The boys ran off.

Kuroki allowed himself a wry smile. The girl had perfect timing. He'd been thinking about Etsuko Mitsuya.

He pulled the map out of his coat pocket and unfolded it, but not in search of a place with potential witnesses. It was to confirm the location of the inn the local station had recommended to him.

Chapter Six

1

These summer houses had to be in the deepest part of Karuizawa.

Moreover, the area was easy to miss. The side road leading up to it was covered in snow and had eluded his notice the first time he'd passed by. Only when he was coming back from a dead end did he find it.

At the dead end, there'd been just a single big summer house. Even though nobody seemed to be around, it was too imposing. The brick chimney, surely for a fireplace, gave the impression that the owner might drop by on a whim even in winter.

He'd been on the verge of giving up, resigned to spending one night in the car. It was already evening and he'd been driving around the retreat areas for three hours. He'd only taken that side road because it seemed like an ideal place to hide the car.

When he climbed up a hillock surrounded by woods, two cosy little houses smiled at him. Beyond them were more hills, with no path leading into them, at least not for vehicles. A perfect cul-de-sac. Thanks to the hill in between, not even the roofs were visible from the wider road.

He chose the building to his right. Its roof was blue. That was the only reason.

There weren't even footprints, let alone tire tracks, around the house. The two houses stood over a hundred and fifty feet apart. Birch trees sparsely dotted the space between them.

"Our house, Hiroshi."

The boy nodded and laughed.

It was unclear if Hiroshi understood what Koji was up to. Carefree, the boy laughed a lot.

Koji removed tools from the car's trunk.

The house was scrupulously locked up. Such thoroughness meant there was no chance anyone would return until summer.

The wooden door had three locks and didn't even budge. There was a sturdy iron grill on the window near the door. Windows without grills had rain shutters that were also firmly locked. Though a two-story house, the concrete base was as thick as a whole floor so it was in fact three stories high. The interior of that concrete seemed to function as a cellar, and the door accessing it was quite a humble piece of work compared to the main entrance.

For a while, Koji fiddled with the front door. He couldn't pick a single lock. Simply getting in would be easy, but he didn't want to break anything. They intended to live here.

He tried the cellar door. When he used the tip of his spanner to release the padlock, it opened easily.

He didn't want to live in a cellar. Still, he might find better tools than a spanner, so he bothered to enter.

There was one drum can. Beer and juice were piled up in units of dozens. Relying on the light coming in from an air vent, Koji burrowed further in. In the back was a concrete partition and a gap wide enough for a person to pass through. The room beyond was not a cellar. All there was on the exposed floor was a motor. It looked like a pump for bringing up ground water.

Something about the light was strange. When he looked up, he saw thin glass plates and light coming through them. There were four plates. Squares had been cut into the floor and fitted with them.

A wooden crate served as a foothold. The square plate lifted up with no resistance.

It was the kitchen. The legs of a table and its matching chairs were visible as well as the white of a refrigerator. A no-brainer. How foolish he'd been to battle with those mean locks on the front door.

He lifted himself with a pull-up and crawled onto the kitchen floor.

He removed his shoes. It wasn't some stranger's home.

It was easy to open the front door from inside.

"Come on in, Hiroshi," he said.

The boy, who was standing by the car, looked up toward him and trotted up the stairs to the front door.

Despite it being winter, the room was heavy with the moldy odor of decay. Koji flung open all the windows and let the cold wind blow through.

A spacious living room and the kitchen made up the first floor. Upstairs were two more rooms. Cloths resembling shrouds covered the chairs, sofa, and table. The house was fully furnished with kitchen utensils, other furniture, and futons.

"I'm thirsty," Hiroshi announced and turned on the kitchen tap. No water came. There was no electricity.

Koji stepped outside to check that the meter was on. It meant a master electrical switch for the house existed somewhere but had been turned off.

Guessing the grid layout from where the cable entered the house, he searched for it. This sort of thing was a piece of cake for him. He soon found a little metal box on the wall between the kitchen and the living room.

He opened the lid, lifted up the lever, and turned on the electricity. A motor whirred lightly. The empty fridge was beginning to function. The tap, which Hiroshi had left on, began burping and spouting air. After a while, water came gushing out. It was cold.

Thanks to the snow it didn't seem that dark, but it was already sundown.

Koji found stoves in the closet upstairs. There were three identical units with the brand name Aladdin Blue Flame. They'd been dismantled for storage and took a bit of work to reassemble, but he did all three, placed one unit in the room on the second floor he'd chosen as the bedroom, and took the other two downstairs.

It would get awfully cold at night. The more stoves, the better. The bath was designed to be heated on kerosene. There was a drum can's worth in the cellar. If the propane gas in the kitchen ran out, the heating stove could be used for cooking, too.

Koji heated the room, prepared hot water for the bath, and sat on the comfortable sofa. He felt relaxed. He'd never once felt as unfettered as this.

A pang of hunger hit him like a flash of memory.

He put a pot on the gas burner to boil some spaghetti. On the other burner, he set a frying pan. Coating it with oil, he cracked in six eggs. They made a hearty, sizzling sound. The fried eggs were soon ready. He chopped some ham to throw into the pan he'd used for the eggs. The aroma of meat cooking was pleasant. Once the spaghetti was done, he dropped it into the pan along with plenty of butter. He added ketchup and mixed it around with the ham.

Worcester sauce, soy sauce, salt, sugar, vinegar, salad oil, sweet cooking sake, they all stood unopened under the kitchen counter.

He piled a basketful of tangerines and washed four sturdy sticks of celery.

On the living room carpet, Hiroshi was busily driving his radio-controlled car. Koji brought up two bottles of beer and some juice from the cellar. They were wonderfully cold. The cellar was a natural fridge.

It was snowing outside. They could eat dinner in a warm room while gazing out at that snow. It was hard to believe.

"Dinner's ready."

Hiroshi rushed over. He looked astonished when he saw what lay on the table. Man and boy sat facing each other. There were four chairs, so this was probably a summer house for a family of four, but that didn't matter. Right now it was their home.

"Yum!" Koji cried after his first mouthful of the spaghetti.

Hiroshi laughed. Soon he had ketchup around his mouth. Koji took a sip of beer. It spread to the tips of his toes. His appetite was whetted, and saliva kept rising in his mouth.

"This is the best. Food never looked so good to me."

Koji downed his beer in one go and stuffed his face with spaghetti at a ferocious pace. As for the celery, he sprinkled some salt and bit into it whole. Hiroshi copied him.

"We've got everything. Last night I didn't dream of finding a house like this one. Our luck is changing, eh?"

Hiroshi was digging into the yolk of his fried egg.

They didn't need anything. Nothing more now.

Koji's belly was full. His heart was full. He lit a cigarette. It burned away with a tiny sizzle. He heard nothing else. The snow erased all other sounds.

It felt like their first bath in a while. In truth, they had gone to a public bath three days ago on Sunday. Too much had happened since then.

Koji carefully washed Hiroshi's body. It really was a small, thin body. Whatever frame a five-year-old boy was supposed to have, at the public bath Hiroshi's had compared poorly to that of other boys his age. Now covered in soap, he was whooping it up. He scooped up suds and rubbed them against Koji's chest. Koji retaliated. Then he held the child still and lathered his hair. He dumped hot water on the boy's head. Hiroshi shook his head like a dog.

Koji grabbed him by the arm and dried his wet hair and face with a towel. The boy's face was flushed red. Yet, his body was pale. Except for his face and hands, his skin was so pale it was almost bluish white, and not a mole, birthmark, or blemish marked it. The shaking of his body, from laughter, traveled through the thin arm in Koji's grip.

"Make sure you eat lots. Otherwise you won't grow. You've got to get big and make sure that you're a match for anyone in a fight. You're a guy, all right?"

With his round face Hiroshi looked a little plump when he was dressed, but actually he was almost pitifully thin. Koji lightly shook the boy's arm. Perhaps taking it as some joke, Hiroshi pulled Koji's ear in response.

It was still snowing outside. It would pile high.

"We have to buy pajamas, don't we? We should get matching ones."

His body was flushed from the hot bath. He could feel the beer. Hiroshi was at it again with his radio-controlled car. He'd become quite good.

"You know, getting too into one thing is a bad habit to pick up."

"Brother, look!" Hiroshi managed to get the car to U-turn when it reached the table.

"You better learn more ways to play," Koji continued. "Like skiing and skating. Kids gotta do those things. Skiing, I can teach you. I wore skis instead of sandals since I was a little brat. I can even show you how to ski in a way no one else knows."

"I don't think the car will run on snow," Hiroshi said, looking up.

Koji gave a wry smile. "Okay, okay. I'll harden some snow and make a racing track for you. It'll be harder than indoors. It'll be a highway of ice."

"Are you really going to make one for me?"

"Yup. But there's a bit of work to do first. Not just me. We both have work to do."

Cleaning, doing the laundry, washing the dishes, and cooking, all that living was now their work. Spending their days comfortable and clean would mean they were being diligent.

Koji went upstairs alone.

He went to the room where he'd laid the futon and lit the stove. Then he went to the other room.

Without turning on the light, he looked outside the window. The light from the snow allowed him to see across to the hills. Nothing moved except for falling snow. It was silent, too. Nobody was watching him from anywhere. *This really is our home,* he tried whispering. His heart swelled.

The rumble of the radio-controlled car was audible from downstairs. Hiroshi was speeding.

Koji went downstairs. His legs felt wobbly; he seemed a bit drunk. He'd never gotten drunk on just one beer.

He took the remote control from Hiroshi and turned off the switch.

"Time for bed. Play again tomorrow."

Hiroshi nodded. He ran to the toilet. He always did so without being told before he went to bed.

Koji woke up around eight o'clock.

He'd slept well. More than long, it was a deep slumber. Moments after slipping into the futon, ten hours had passed without a single dream and it was morning. He couldn't believe right away that he had slept so much.

He felt very good. His mind was clear, too. In this frame of mind, he could solve any problem.

Hiroshi had slept next to him but wasn't there. The radio-controlled car's faint whirr came from the floor below.

Koji got dressed and went downstairs. Hiroshi was wearing his overcoat and lying on the carpet on his stomach to admire his cruising toy from a low angle, enraptured.

"You should have woken me up. Bet you were cold."

Koji lit the two stoves.

The snow from the night before remained piled up. It was completely white outside the windows. The car parked under the front entrance also had mounds of snow on its roof and hood.

"Yikes!" Koji cried when he turned the tap on. The water was so cold it almost seemed bizarre that it wasn't frozen. "You haven't washed your face yet, have you?"

Hiroshi ran around, fleeing from him. Koji grabbed his collar, carried him over to the bathroom, and forced him to wash his face. This was the first time Hiroshi had ever resisted like the child he was. It was more pleasant than seeing him nod quietly whatever he was told.

They had a simple breakfast of bread and eggs.

Then, together, they cleaned the room and washed their underwear in water left over from their bath. During that time, Koji confiscated the radio-controlled car. This was communal living, and Hiroshi naturally had his share of chores. It would be better for the kid that way. When he slacked off, Koji poked his head. There were no other adults around. How the boy turned out was entirely his responsibility, Koji admonished himself, but at that point he had to laugh. He felt like a fool for pondering over it in all earnestness. Still, he didn't intend to alter the setup.

The cleaning and laundry were done in an hour. The dishes were spotless, too.

"Brother, let's go outside." Holding his radio-controlled car, Hiroshi said this as though he were asserting a right. The promise was to let the child race the car on snow.

Koji donned his coat and went outside. The snow was deep enough to come up over his ankles.

"Have to make a racing track first."

He started stamping the snow solid with his feet, about twenty inches wide. Where Koji roughly packed the snow, Hiroshi's small shoes followed, stepping meticulously. Weaving in between the trees, which were sparse around the house, they made a long track. It was bumpy. They brought a crate of beer bottles from the cellar and proceeded to drag it along the track. It became flat. A decent circuit.

Koji tried it out, ginger with the remote. Except for skidding precariously at bends, the car ran all right.

Hiroshi cried out in excitement. On the second lap, Koji drove faster. It was quite a sight. It distracted him, and he got careless. Having launched into soft snow, the car's wheels spun futilely.

"It's pretty hard. The curves are key. Think you can do it?"

"Yes." Hiroshi reached up for the remote control in Koji's hand.

"Go slow at first. Try going faster when you get the hang of it. Pretend you're actually on it, and you won't drive crazy."

"Okay."

Hiroshi's eyes were already glued to the radio-controlled car. The Porsche crawled along the track.

Using a mop from the cellar, Koji wiped the snow off the real car's front window and hood.

"I need to run an errand. You're okay playing here on your own, yeah?"

Hiroshi looked at Koji for a moment. The toy car immediately fell off course, burrowing into snow. "Can you get me batteries?" he asked.

"I will. But promise me you'll go inside if it starts snowing. I'll leave one of the stoves on."

He had to shop for more food. There were some other things he wanted, too.

Although the clouds were thick, the snow's whiteness was dazzling. Remembering the sunglasses in the glove compartment, Koji put them on.

There were still chains on the tires. Last night's snowfall had completely erased yesterday's tire tracks.

He went over the hill and reached the wide path. It was still some distance from a paved road. He kept his eyes open but saw no sign of people in the few summer houses along the way. Not even tire tracks, all the way to the paved road.

Instead of driving into the city, he parked in a nondescript copse at the top of a slope. It was a stolen car. If a policeman questioned him, that would be the end. Best be careful. He didn't plan on coming into the city for a while after this anyway. Sure, it was a pain, but he'd walk the rest.

2

It was a quiet morning.

Gazing out at the snowy woods from the inn's window, Kuroki smoke one cigarette after another.

The serene morning landscape did not reflect his state of mind.

He'd ruminated several times over his own behavior yesterday from when the boat had been found on Zaimokuza beach in the early morning. There was hardly any basis for his conjecture that Mizui was in Karuizawa. It was a dire leap of thought.

Still, he wasn't regretting it. There had only been two options: wait for new leads, or jump on a hunch. The situation didn't permit waiting around.

In the end, the checkpoints hadn't caught Mizui's car. By 2 p.m. yesterday, Mizui's car had cleared Usui Pass—Kuroki could only act on that hypothesis. Whether Mizui had driven through Karuizawa or was still here, he didn't know.

There was no news either of Mizui showing up at his family home in Ueda.

After breakfast, Kuroki first dropped by the local police station. He asked them to halt checks on Route 18. Instead, he requested a search for Mizui's car within this jurisdiction.

He resumed his canvassing using a car. It was in order to cover a larger area than last night. Not only where to go, but whom to talk to was hardly evident. Gas stations, food stores, restaurants and such did merit some focus.

He got no results even after driving around for three hours. There were so many people—twice as many visitors as local residents. Apparently, during the summer, there were ten times as many. It wasn't as bad as that now, but there were still too many people. In a couple of days it would be Christmas Eve, a Saturday to boot. There'd be even more people starting next night.

He ventured as far as hot springs resorts in Hoshino and Shiotsubo. Those places were crowded, too.

It was 1 p.m. when the local police contacted him by radio. There had been two calls from Tokyo.

Kuroshi dashed into a hotel in Hoshino and showed his police I.D. to use their phone.

Fuse answered. "Makimura is heading your way. He's on the express that'll reach Karuizawa around 3 p.m."

"What happened?"

"We've identified Shibasaki's car. We've been grilling his biker gang pals all morning, and they've sung at last. A red Nissan Bluebird, details on model and number plate have been transmitted to the police there. I'm sure they've already launched a search."

"Why are you sure he's heading this way?"

"Yesterday evening, a red Nissan Bluebird got away from a patrol car, near Takasaki. It was handled as an ordinary case of reckless driving, so until we cross-referenced the car with the Gunma Prefectural Police, we didn't know about it. We just missed him."

"Takasaki, huh? He might have crossed Usui Pass overnight."

"One more thing. He could be intercepting our radio dispatches. The fact that he was able to shake off the patrol car is almost proof. Must be a technique from when he was a biker. Apparently Shibasaki's got top-quality radio equipment."

"That means he's listening in on us here, too. Since this morning we've been sending dispatches all over the place about Mizui's car."

"I've informed the local police about that too. Regarding Mizui's and Shibasaki's cars, they shouldn't be using radio anymore. But we only told them a moment ago."

Kuroki now understood why the message from the local police had been oddly vague.

"We were way too late," Fuse admitted.

They had to assume that until just now, Shibasaki had been privy to all radio communication about Mizui's car. Still, it was not all bad. If Shibasaki had been playing tag with a patrol car near Takasaki yesterday, he had been clueless about Mizui's whereabouts. Then, after arriving in Karuizawa, he'd have heard the radio dispatches about Mizui's car.

Shibasaki had to be convinced that Mizui was in Karuizawa, which increased the likelihood that Shibasaki, at least, was here. He was closing the net in on himself.

"Just one car?"

"Yes. But it seems there were two people inside. Some punk who's just a kid of eighteen that Shibasaki's taken under his wings. It's unverified, though."

Kuroki hung up.

He sped to the local police station. Once they got Shibasaki, they wouldn't need to be in such a rush. Only the police would be after Mizui.

He bumped into Takao at the door.

"Ah, good. I was wondering how to get in touch with you, sir."

"Have you found him?"

"No, we've only confirmed that they were here at one point. This fellow Shibasaki and his car, I mean."

An officer on patrol and another one on duty in a police box had confirmed that fact around 10 a.m. It had been a typical biker-gang car, crimson with radial tires, its body extremely low, and as such the officers had bothered to take down its number plate. When word for the search went out, they immediately reported their encounter.

So it was confirmed that Shibasaki had been in Karuizawa. He probably still was, too.

"What's Shibasaki like?" asked Takao.

"Actually, I've never met him. One of our young guys, Makimura, will be here soon. He'll have photos."

"We'll find him soon enough if he's in the city." Takao looked Kuroki in the eye. "Why don't we feed him some bait? He's listening in on our radio dispatches, right?"

"That will require a few patrol cars."

"You can count on our support. No major incidents on our turf at the moment."

Kuroki pulled out the map. He made pencil marks at spots about half a mile from the city center.

"I'll move from here to here. Best if you make it seem like a call from a third party."

Kuroki got into his car. Takao came up to it and said they'd be starting at 2:30 p.m.

Kuroki waited for about ten minutes at the designated spot.

Mizui's car had been found, the radio dispatch announced. No patrol car was in a position to get there right away. Takao was yelling his head off. *Car no. 4! What, twenty minutes? Be there in fifteen minutes. Yes, fifteen!*

Kuroki lit a Short Peace. He puffed through three. A car went by, a Thunderbird full of youngsters.

Takao was still yelling. Ten minutes had passed. Kuroki moved as he'd indicated on the map. There he waited again.

His pack of Short Peace cigarettes dwindled to nothing. His expectations hadn't been high, but he squashed it and clicked his tongue.

Takao's car showed up at 3:30 p.m.

"Was this a futile exercise?"

"I've heard that he's a cautious guy."

"That red car hasn't been sighted in the past hour within a half-mile radius. Three red cars were spotted in the city, but none of them were Shibasaki's."

"Can't be helped. Please send out a dispatch saying we failed to catch Mizui. And that he hasn't left Karuizawa."

"Yes, I know."

They returned, their cars running side by side.

In the squad room awaited Makimura.

"You let him get away?"

"His phantom, yes. In other words, we tried laying a trap."

"Oh. It was so intense, I thought you'd really cornered him."

Kuroki sat down near the stove. Makimura handed Takao photocopied pictures of Mizui and Shibasaki.

"Why did you come?"

"Oh, come on. I thought you'd be overwhelmed on your own."

"I thought I told you to stay in Tokyo as insurance."

"Fuse has taken over that role. Anyway, there's nothing more to investigate in Tokyo."

"How is Etsuko Mitsuya doing?"

"Silent as a clam."

Kuroki stood up.

"Canvassing?"

"Let's split up. We'll start in the center. You haven't got legs just to be standing around. Don't let them idle."

"I know, sir."

Makimura grabbed his coat and followed.

Outside, it had started snowing again.

It was at a tea parlor near the train station.

"Didn't he come in around 11 a.m.?" the woman at the cake stand called to another employee upon looking at the photo of Mizui.

Something in Kuroki that had been going slack tensed up. "He should have been injured here," he said, pointing to his own cheek.

The woman staffer looked unsure. "Now that you mention it, it did look like a scab had just fallen off."

"He was wearing sunglasses, though."

The women remembered him because he'd bought a birthday cake. Due to the time of year, they only had Christmas cakes, but the man had tasked them to write *Happy Birthday* on a slab of chocolate.

"How many candles did you put on it?"

"We didn't put them on. But he asked for six to be packaged with the cake."

Kuroki called Tokyo from the telephone booth in front of the station. Fuse picked up.

"Hiroshi Suzue, that boy with Mizui. Check up his birthday asap."

"Hang on, please."

Kuroki could hear the shuffling of papers. He added a 100-yen coin in the slot.

"December nineteenth. He turned six."

On the night of the nineteenth, a punk had been stabbed in Ueno Park. Mizui had gone there to bring back the abducted Hiroshi Suzue.

They'd been in no state to celebrate. It had stayed that way. They could very well be trying to throw a birthday party three days late.

Kuroki met up with Makimura.

They visited the toy stores in the city one by one.

"Isn't it a bit ridiculous? Throwing a birthday party?"

"They probably couldn't until today. But if they've managed to settle down somewhere…"

"But the women weren't even sure it was him, right?"

Still, this was the first thing resembling a clue. Despite his dismissive tone, Makimura had a different look in his eyes.

They visited four toy stores. According to the women at the tea parlor, the customer had been carrying a toy store box.

The owner of the fifth toy store remembered. Only, he wasn't positive about the face. Two days before Christmas Eve, a toy store was fairly full of people seeking to buy presents.

The man who could've been Mizui had bought a radio-controlled car and a model ship kit.

"Isn't the radio-controlled car a wash? Hiroshi Suzue already has one. He'd end up with two."

"No. It was Mizui."

"You sound so sure."

On Kuroki's mind were the more than dozen model ships in Mizui's closet.

3

With brimming bags of food in each hand, Koji made two round trips between city and car. The city was still thronging with people. It seemed to be even busier than the day before.

There would be more people over the weekend. Saturday was Christmas Eve.

It was on his third round trip as he was carrying a cake, a radio-controlled car, and a model kit.

Glimpsing a red car on a side road through a copse a pretty distance from the city center, Koji halted. The car alone wouldn't have caught his attention, but he thought he recognized the face of the man standing beside it. He looked like the same man who had brought Hiroshi to Ueno Park with Makiko. That time, he was wearing a white trench coat and frantically waving around a knife when Koji had gone for him. That face wasn't to be forgotten.

Was it really him? The guy got into his car.

Koji dashed up the slope. He got into his own car, put his purchases on the back seat, and sat in the driver's seat pondering.

I mistook someone for him, he thought once more, because I'm cowering. Even strangers were starting to look like that guy.

Yet the face of the man by the car was seared into his eyes. True, there was no white trench coat. Instead he'd been looking warm in a leather one. But that was the face, no matter how many times Koji recalled it.

He had better make sure. If he were mistaken, he'd have to worry constantly over an idiotic thing. And if it really was Trench Coat…

Koji descended the slope. He didn't rush.

The car was still parked in the woods. What the hell was the guy up to in such a place?

Koji crouched behind bamboo leaves and waited for the man to leave the car.

He started to feel cold. He waited thirty minutes, but the man did not come out. No way that guy could be in Karuizawa. He absolutely hadn't been tailed. If he had been, then the guy would be near the summer house. He was cowering, indeed, if a total stranger had looked like that guy.

Koji began to calm down a little.

He smoked a cigarette. The car was a decent distance away. The smoke wouldn't be visible—even if it was, why worry?

Still, he didn't consider leaving. If it was a mistake, he wanted to be sure.

There was only one man in the car. It looked like he was listening to the radio. Now and then his head moved. Koji sat himself down on the snow. It was powder snow, and he wouldn't get that wet.

When forty-five minutes had passed, he started to get irritated. He felt like going up to the car and asking what the hell the guy was up to. But he waited. Something was telling him to wait.

Finally the car door opened.

The man got out and peed into a roadside shrub. Koji felt shaken. That profile was definitely him. Then the guy turned in Koji's direction. Clearly, it was him.

Something hot coursed through Koji's body, quickly cooled, and turned into a hard, intransigent lump. It differed from rage or hatred. It resembled fear, but he didn't in the least feel like running away.

Wherever I go, this fellow will show up. Something about me draws him to me. He's like my shadow or something.

Koji yearned to get rid of the shadow. He didn't need a shadow. If it was going to pursue him even when he fled, he'd best get rid of it.

He raised himself and crawled along the road toward the red car. The bamboo leaves he brushed against gave a dry rustle. Snow fell off the leaves.

Standing outside the car, Trench Coat stuck a cigarette in his mouth. With one elbow on the open door, he was looking down at the city. It was hard to tell whether the white smoke coming out of his mouth was from the cigarette or from his breath turning white.

Trench Coat turned around. Koji stood up. He was running. He caught a glimpse of the guy's mouth gaping open in surprise.

Body collided with body. Trench Coat went flying and then rolling on the snow. Koji shouted. He didn't know why, the shout welled from the bottom of his being. He was kicking at the guy's body. Snow flew everywhere. As the kicks came, Trench Coat rolled over a few times, went on all fours, and swiftly took something out of his coat pocket.

It was a gun. For a moment, Koji stood still. There was a tremendous blast, but it was all sound. The bullet zipped off somewhere. Koji found that he'd thrown himself on his opponent. With both hands he twisted the hand with the gun—twisted, with all his might. It fell silently onto the snow. We're even now, he thought. He drew back one of his hands and landed a punch on the chin. The guy's head burrowed into the snow. A weird bounce. Koji's stance faltered. He took one from under.

Their bodies parted. Koji stood up. Trench Coat stood up as well, his shoulders heaving with every breath. Koji stepped in. Something gleamed, reflecting the snow. A knife. Their bodies collided. Just before they did, Koji had grabbed the guy's wrist. Koji was stronger. He bent in the wrist so the knife's tip pointed toward his opponent's stomach. Trench Coat let go of it. Now they were really even.

Repeatedly, Koji slammed his fist into the guy's face. No counterattack came. Trench Coat sank to the ground and rolled on the snow to try to get away. Koji went after him, kicking. He kept kicking.

"Help!" the guy cried.

Koji didn't stop kicking. Trench Coat hunched his back.

"Help." The voice was fainter.

Koji grabbed him by the hair. The guy's upper body was now erect. Koji kicked it again. The sickening groan was clear to hear. I'll stop now, Koji thought. But his legs kept moving on their own. The groaning dwindled until there was nothing. Match over, Koji told himself. His body wasn't persuaded. The guy lay on his back, and Koji's hands went for the neck. His grip tightened. He lifted him up like that, all the way up above his head, like some offering to heaven. A palpable tremor ran through the guy's body. Koji still didn't let go. He clenched his teeth. Blood rose to his head. It felt like all the veins in his body were ready to rupture. He did not let go. He shouted. Shouted several times. His feet wobbled. Damned if he stumbled. He spread his legs apart. The guy's tongue was lolling out of his mouth. His eyes showed white. The pupils had gone somewhere. Koji felt unsteady again. He felt something burst in his head. Then he was lying on his back. The guy's slumped body fell onto him. He shoved away the heavy doll. A deep breath. The sky was spinning.

Hiroshi had built two narrow bypasses on the racing track and was stamping snow in place with his small feet to create some sort of parking area.

It was just past two in the afternoon.

"Brother, look!"

The car went quite fast along the course. It almost got stuck in the snow over the bypasses, which were narrow and hadn't quite hardened yet, but still managed to get through.

Hiroshi looked up at Koji smugly.

"You're pretty good. Looks like you'll be able to race me."

"Race?"

"Yup. I bought another radio-controlled car. I also got loads of extra batteries."

"Really?"

"Help me unload. I bought us hamburgers for lunch too."

He had spent about 40,000 yen, but now there was enough food to see them through New Year's. They also had new underwear and matching sweaters.

Hiroshi began carrying bags of food into the house.

The corpse, Koji had dumped into the red car's trunk and left by a summer house quite far away that looked unused. From the road the car wasn't visible, so unless the house's owner showed up, no one was likely to find it.

A lighter that had fallen, and the knife, he'd thrown into the trunk with the body. He'd meant to do the same with the gun. But the moment he picked it up, a subtle presence suffused his whole body through his palm. It was not a sensation, but clearly a presence, the kind that living things emanated. Brutal yet submissive, rebellious yet considerate, the presence was insinuating. Lying on the snow, it had been a mere object, but as soon as he touched it life dwelled in it. *Please,* it seemed to ask, *don't throw me away.*

Koji tried gripping it several times. Each time, the presence grew stronger in his palm. He put it in his coat pocket. He felt as if he'd slipped a small animal in there. He patted it a few times from over the pocket as if to calm it down. *Don't go nuts, be good and sleep.*

What looked like radio dispatch equipment sat in the red car. Koji had turned off the switch. He could learn how to work it if he examined it carefully. He had no intention of putting it to use, though. He had someone to talk to. He wasn't so lonely to have a radio chat with someone whose face he couldn't see.

"Brother, which one is the radio-controlled car?"

"This box."

When Koji handed it over, Hiroshi immediately unwrapped it. A red racing machine. Koji had bought it thinking it would be easy to see even on snow.

"Um, I think I prefer the Porsche."

"Then this one's mine. Why don't we race them? We'll build an amazing course, too. Bridges and tunnels."

"This one looks really fast." Hiroshi rolled the car on the carpet. It wouldn't go that fast. It had a sleek body, but it was cheap. "Can we make a garage?"

"Yes, but after we've eaten. I'm kinda hungry."

He was wondering when to bring out the cake. The birthday was over, and Christmas was the day after tomorrow. It didn't matter. They were going to have a party tonight. A toast with juice and beer.

His coat pocket was heavy. Koji put the gun away at the back of a sideboard drawer so that Hiroshi wouldn't find it. *This is your lair. Don't go nuts, okay?*

He warmed some milk. Milk was better for kids than juice. He tore open the bag containing hamburgers. They were cold now but still tasted quite good.

"It's started snowing!"

Hiroshi went to the window. He looked anxiously up at the sky. He seemed worried about the racing track they'd taken the trouble to make. It was snowing quite hard, and the clouds presaged a blizzard.

"I'll make you another one. It's no fun using the same track over and over again. You won't improve, either. This time, we'll build the bends at angles. Then you can go around them without slowing down much. All the real test tracks are like that."

Snow more. Snow all night, until the traces of that red car, my footprints, and the tracks to this house are all clean gone.

Koji took his time to prepare dinner.

He hadn't cooked much in his life, but he didn't find it that hard. With Hiroshi helping, he chopped vegetables, thinly sliced an apple, and tossed it all in salad oil and pepper. He steamed rice and sprinkled salt and pepper on thick slabs of meat so they were ready to fry.

Koji and Hiroshi were wearing their newly bought matching sweaters. When Koji said it was a present, Hiroshi looked puzzled.

"We're going to have a party and celebrate your birthday and

Christmas in one go."

"When's Christmas?"

"The day after tomorrow."

"Is that why we're making a feast?"

"Christmas is just extra. We're really celebrating your birthday."

"You also promised you'd get a cake."

"I remembered, too. I got a huge one. I'll show it to you."

The plan was beefsteak. Fry them and they'd be edible. He dropped a blob of fat into the pan.

Once the preparations were done, Koji placed the cake box on the table. Hiroshi's eyes were shining.

"Is it really a cake? Such a big one?"

"Open it."

The cake was nearly a foot in diameter. It was ringed with strawberries. Real strawberries. Koji stood the six candles on top of the cake and lit them. Then he pointed to the slab of chocolate in the middle.

"Do you know what that says?"

Hiroshi tilted his head.

"*Happy Birthday.* That's what it says in English. I had them write it for you in the cake store, you know?"

With the lights dimmed, they sat staring at the candle flames for a while. It was a warm, soothing light.

They didn't need anything. Not now, they didn't. What they had was enough.

"Blow them out," Koji said.

"Huh?"

"You blow out the candles. All six of them in one go."

"Why?"

"Why? What, have you never celebrated your birthday? That's the rule. When you blow out the candles, I clap and congratulate you."

Hiroshi gave a bashful smile in the candlelight. *Hurry up,* Koji told him. Filling his small chest with air, Hiroshi blew out the candles in one breath.

Koji put the lights back on. *Congratulations,* he said, and clapped. Faint wisps of smoke still arose from the extinguished candles.

Though slightly tough from overcooking, the meat tasted pretty good. The vegetable salad wasn't bad, either. While scolding Hiroshi for wanting to eat just cake, Koji slowly savored his own cooking.

It had never occurred to him to cook something delicious himself. Until now, when he wanted to eat something good, he just went out. He'd only ever cooked food to fill his stomach.

It occurred to him that this was how a human being was supposed to live. Moreover, doing it alone was pointless. You needed someone to eat with.

"How about your birthday, brother?" Hiroshi asked, his mouth full of steak.

"Mine? Mine's a long way yet."

Koji's birthday fell on the fourth of June. This year he'd completely forgotten about it and only realized he'd turned twenty-one while renewing his driver's license later that month. To begin with, he had no recollection of anyone celebrating his birthday.

"That's no fun."

"Yeah. But everyone's birthday comes around eventually, once a year."

"It's no fun if it's not soon."

Koji laughed. Hiroshi's knife clattered on his plate.

It was windy outside. A serious blizzard was on the way.

This summer house had all the basic things, but for some reason it had no television or radio. The only human voices were those of Koji and Hiroshi. That was enough. Koji didn't want to hear the voice of someone he didn't know.

The model kit was in plastic and of a simple sailing ship. It had been on sale at a toy store. Anything more sophisticated would have been asking too much. Even the sail was made of plastic. He could just make a more realistic one with paper or something.

One look at the parts and Koji knew how to assemble them without consulting the instructions diagram. Most sailing ships had the same sort of structure anyway.

"It's a ship?"

"Yup."

"There's no lake, though."

"This one isn't for lakes. It glides on the sea. With wind in its sails at that."

"There's no sea here, either."

Koji laughed. *There's the sea in my heart.* No point in telling Hiroshi that, he wouldn't get it.

He made a whiskey-and-water. He'd bought two bottles of whiskey.

He took the plastic ship and sandpapered down the parts he disliked. This ship was going to be splendid. If he lacked a necessary part, he could cut up the plastic sail and make it himself. Time, at any rate, was one thing he wasn't short of.

Hiroshi cried out. He was trying to make a toy-car garage from a cardboard box but without much success.

"Here, let me."

Koji took the box and creased it in the shape of a house. When he placed it on the carpet, though, it collapsed unceremoniously.

"We had disposable chopsticks somewhere."

He neatly hewed them with a kitchen knife. Hiroshi gazed at Koji's fingers without a word. Measured out and incised, the chopsticks dovetailed into four pillars and beams. The size was perfect. Tape from the first-aid box on the sideboard served to secure them.

Koji was good at this sort of thing. When he was a kid, his mother used to tell him that he was nimble. Perhaps he'd chosen a technical high school to try to become an electrician because he was good with his fingers.

"One more," Hiroshi said.

Koji hewed the chopsticks and made the incisions but did no more. "You were watching, weren't you? Have a go at it."

Hiroshi began putting together the pillars and beams. "Are you going to the sea?" he asked.

"Why?"

"Because you're making a ship."

"This is just for decoration. I'm not going anywhere. I'll be here. This is our home."

"Me too."

The snow would eventually melt. Money would run out. They obviously couldn't stay here for good, but Koji didn't want to think about that now. Life in this house had just begun.

He hadn't read a newspaper in some time. He didn't even know how his own case was turning out. Maybe the police had a search out on him. But who would notice this house? It was safe here. *A world of just two, me and Hiroshi.*

At last Hiroshi succeeded in putting the pillars and beams together. Koji fixed them to a box with tape.

Two garages sat side by side. Hiroshi steered his radio-controlled car inside. He was getting quite adept with the controls. Though just a toy, for Hiroshi it was a real car. Everything was like that when you were little. A plain old stick was a real katana, slingshots were cannons, and a mound of snow was a true castle.

"Hiroshi, you can practice parking in the garage tomorrow. It's already nine o'clock. Time for bed."

"What about you, brother?"

"I'll go to bed after I've had a bit more to drink. I'm in a funny good mood tonight."

"There's snow all over the course we made."

Outside, it was a blizzard. Hiroshi went to the toilet. Koji poured a little whiskey into his empty glass. Just a little. Just enough so he wouldn't ruin his good mood by getting drunk.

4

Apart from the tea parlor by the train station and the toy store, Mizui's tracks had gone cold. Kuroki trudged in the snow with Makimura until nine, but the most they got was an employee at a meat shop hinting at nothing.

Since the afternoon, there seemed to be even more people in the city, mostly young folk. More than half were men and women about Mizui's age.

"Are they all here to have a Christmas party in Karuizawa? At this rate, it'll be jammed on Saturday," complained Makimura.

They returned to the local police station at ten.

Takao was there, apparently on the night shift. Looking terribly sleepy, he sipped coffee.

They warmed themselves by the stove. Their numb fingers took a while to recover.

"It's impossible," Takao responded without pause.

Kuroki had asked how long it would take to search every single summer house in the vicinity.

"Even if everyone here got on board, it would take many days. Frankly, we're at a loss about the retreats. A weekly patrol is about as good as it gets. If there's a caretaker or a security system, then we have some hope, but if not, any ransacking goes undetected until the owner returns in the summer."

Takao poured coffee for Kuroki and Makimura while he talked. Though it was instant fare, it did a world of good to a chilled body.

"The summer house owners understand this. They don't leave anything valuable. With the power cut off, there's no water. No food, either. In the first place, heating would be an issue. These days they seem to take stoves apart before they store them."

"Kerosene stoves?"

"Mostly, yes. Though it seems some opt for the luxury of logs in a fireplace."

Kuroki finished his coffee and stuck a Short Peace in his mouth. Did Mizui intend to hide out in Karuizawa? If so, how long did he plan on staying? Perhaps he'd procured food before reaching Karuizawa. But not heating fuel.

"Are there a lot of fuel stores?"

"No, most double as gas stands. I don't know about that track. People tend to buy kerosene in bulk in drum cans. The suppliers prefer it that way, too, because they need to deliver across a wide area."

"Does it get cold in the summer, too, for them to use so much fuel?"

"It's for the baths. People use propane gas for cooking, but usually kerosene for bathwater."

Kuroki plunged into thought. Makimura chain-smoked.

There had been no calls from Tokyo. They had two pieces of info about where Mizui had been. They verified that Shibasaki's car had been in Karuizawa. Was that it for today?

"Do you have any basis for suspecting that he's hiding in a summer house?" questioned Takao.

"The cake. He bought a huge cake. It's hard to imagine eating something like that in a car," Makimura answered.

"I see. So you mean Mizui. He even has a kid in tow. Is kidnapping in play here?"

"Kid was abandoned, actually. Mizui's been wandering around with a kid he found."

Kuroki remained silent during this conversation. They began talking about another matter.

"By the way, before noon, someone reported a gunshot. Unreliable info. Could have been a car backfiring or firecrackers. We did check it out but couldn't even pinpoint the location."

"Mr. Takao," Kuroki broke in, standing up. "Could you lend us one of your jeeps? Only at night would be fine."

"I'm sure that can be arranged, but why only at night?"

"I'm thinking of checking out just the summer houses with lights on."

Ah! Makimura exclaimed.

Takao gave a little nod. "It will still be like looking for a needle in a haystack."

"We'll search by night, then check out suspicious points the next day when it's bright out. I can't come up with anything better."

Takao exited the room and returned after a while with some reference documents.

He spread a large map of Karuizawa and its environs on the table. Consulting the documents, he blotted out some places on the map with a red pencil.

"Near locals' houses, dormitories, hotels, skating rinks, retreats with caretakers, relatively dense developments. Those are the areas I eliminated. Even so, it's quite vast, and that's just our jurisdiction. Those dots—they're all summer houses."

Indeed, the territory was more than two people could cover. Moreover, it was unfamiliar to them.

"Too huge," Makimura whispered.

Takao folded up the map.

"Can I borrow that?" Kuroki asked.

"Are you really going to do it?"

"It's the only way. We have no other choice. If we enlist the prefectural police to comb the region in force, he'll catch on and run."

"These aren't houses in the desert. There are mountains and valleys, and on top of it the houses are surrounded by woods."

Kuroki laughed. Takao offered the map.

It was morning. The sky was so clear that the night before's snowfall seemed like a dream.

Just to make sure, Kuroki resumed his canvassing with Makimura, outward from the train station. An employee at a liquor store remembered Mizui. The day before, the witness hadn't been there, out on deliveries.

"Two bottles of Suntory Red," Makimura muttered. "Reminds me of the guy's piggy bank. That bottle was double-sized."

At any rate, Mizui was in Karuizawa. He was hunkering down. He probably didn't intend to come into the city for a while. Two bottles of whiskey. Probably not for the remainder of the year.

There were a lot more people than the day before. Many gaggles of young women.

"We haven't seen or heard a squeak from Shibasaki. There's still a search out for his car, right?"

That was bothering Kuroki, too. No doubt the fellow was trying to steer clear of the police, but he was still obliged to get Mizui. No way he wouldn't make a move.

About that, they received a radio dispatch at one in the afternoon. Kuroki and Makimura headed straight for the summer house.

There were three patrol cars, two jeeps, and one sporty affair with a Tokyo number plate.

"This way."

It was Takao. Instead of a day off after his night shift, he must have received an emergency summons.

They went around to the back of the summer house. In the trunk of a low-frame, crimson Nissan Bluebird was Shibasaki, folded in two.

"The son of the owner came over with some friends to have a Christmas party and found him. About twenty-four hours dead, I'd say. The forensic team should be here soon."

"Strangulation," Kuroki said. The marks on the neck indicated as much. He put on gloves and felt around Shibasaki's body. He searched in the car too. All he found was a knife in the trunk. Its blade wasn't clouded with blood.

"Looking for a gun?"

"We have info that it's an M10, but it's unconfirmed. Yesterday, didn't you say something about a gunshot?"

"The time certainly fits."

Kuroki got into his car. Takao came with him.

"It's some copse at the edge of town. Apparently there was just one gunshot."

Several sites were possible. But they hadn't been able to identify the location, and it remained unclear whether or not the sound had really been a gunshot.

"Would Mizui be on the run again, having killed Shibasaki?"

"I wonder. And there should have been someone with Shibasaki."

Unfolding the map, Kuroki drew a circle where Shibasaki's body had been found. Mizui was unlikely to be close to the spot. Subconsciously, at the least, he would have wanted the corpse to lie as far as possible from where they slept.

"Shall we start tonight with that search?" Takao peered into Kuroki's face.

Kuroki nodded and said, "While it's still light out, it'll be canvassing."

They headed toward a retreat. Here and there stood a lone restaurant, but only a few houses had people in them.

"You haven't had lunch yet, have you? There's a good place nearby for soba noodles," invited Takao.

The noodle shop in Kose hot springs was styled like an old Japanese farmhouse.

When Kuroki called it delicious, Takao looked pleased and opined, "It's no good if the noodles aren't dark."

The local detective went to the back to make a phone call. He got loud. *Wait on that,* he said several times. Kuroki intuited what the conversation was about.

When he returned, Kuroki said, "Tell them that he's with a kid."

Takao nodded.

"What is it?" Makimura spoke up.

"A manhunt. They want to request prefectural HQ for riot police and comb the whole region. It's our station chief. He has a taste for grand maneuvers."

"How long can you hold it off on account of not jeopardizing the kid's safety?"

"Maybe three days. All right, I'm heading back to the station. The way things are, I think we can supply some men for that night investigation."

"Local personnel would really help."

Kuroki finished off the soup and rested his chopsticks. Grinning, the old woman serving them brought over some fresh tea.

When Kuroki tried to pay, Takao blocked his hand. "Don't mind. It's my aunt's place."

The sun was setting.

Takao arrived at the inn in a jeep to pick them up.

"So it's three days after all. They're launching the manhunt on the twenty-sixth. Also, I'm sorry but I could only get the use of one more jeep. There's been another case, and everyone's out."

"Where's that other jeep?"

"Already out there. I've told them pretty straight that they mustn't miss a single one. I took the liberty of picking the areas."

Spreading a map, Takao drew several lines with the train station at the center.

"That looks fine. Do you mind if we open the roof on this jeep? Visibility is critical."

"I thought you would say that, so I've brought winter gear. They're rubber raincoats but don't let the wind through."

They set off. By the time they reached a retreat area, it was completely dark.

The sunlight reflecting off the snow was blinding.

There was no trace of yesterday's racing course. In one night, snow had piled up to the shin.

Hiroshi wanted to go outside right away and build a new track. Koji didn't allow it. He confiscated the radio-controlled car and made Hiroshi help with tidying up after breakfast, cleaning the house, and doing the laundry.

Hiroshi was half in tears. That was fine. That was probably how it went with kids.

"You can cry as much as you want, but no means no."

He was the only adult watching over Hiroshi. Tears didn't justify compromise.

Once it sank in that the radio-controlled car was off limits, Hiroshi began asking for the remainder of last night's cake.

"You can have some cake. But at 3 p.m. In the morning, anyway, you help me out. Kids everywhere are made to help out their moms like that."

"But you're not my mom."

"Of course I'm not your mother. I'm just trying to make you do the things that I think a mother would. I'm the only adult you've got, so I'm responsible."

Hiroshi sulked in a corner. Koji ignored him and went about his chores.

"If you want, you can stay like that forever. I'm not going to spoil you. Absolutely no radio-controlled car until after lunch. You aren't even going outside."

Hiroshi didn't budge from his spot in the corner. Koji couldn't for the life of him recall what sort of chores he did when he was six. Probably none. He just had a vague recollection of being beaten up by his older brother and sobbing in his mother's arms.

But Koji had decided to treat Hiroshi as a man. He couldn't be the boy's mother. A mother was something special. There was only one. Perhaps he couldn't be the boy's older brother or father, either. But he could be his friend—the only friend the boy had in the world. In that case, it was a relationship between men. A punch wouldn't be out of bounds. Just a man whacking another man.

"You and I are gonna live as equals here."

It was easier said than done. It felt like a skirmish of sorts. Hiroshi didn't move from his spot for almost two hours.

The house chores were done.

Hiroshi was still hunched over in the corner. Koji left him alone and stood by the window, cigarette in mouth, looking outside.

Though there didn't seem to be any wind, a small clump of snow fell from the branch of a birch, giving off a faint white cloud. A memory returned to his hands. A neck. The neck of the man he'd strangled yesterday. It had been soft. The only hard thing had been the Adam's apple, and the rest had been as soft as freshly pounded rice cake, just heavy. The Adam's apple at his thumbs, too, got crunched like an empty can.

That guy was dead. There was no mistake, he was dead. Koji had folded the guy's body and shoved it into a trunk. It'd been like a broken doll.

He was unconsciously rubbing both his palms against his trousers. No matter how hard he rubbed, the neck didn't go away.

Why now? When he returned yesterday, he'd almost forgotten about the guy—or, at least, hadn't been bothered much. Watanabe's death, he'd learned about only afterwards. Did the man he stab in the park die, too? He hadn't seen his corpse.

Only Trench Coat died in my hands, his body convulsing. I even stuffed his dead body in a trunk.

This could go on for a couple of days. It wasn't like shaking hands. Eventually, though, he'd forget. He couldn't be bothered about it forever even if he wanted.

He opened the window and flicked the cigarette out onto the snow. A cold breeze blew in.

A subtle anxiety lingered. What was he afraid of? He had no reason to be afraid. The snow stung his eyes. The substance of his anxiety gradually coalesced.

Was that guy really alone? Why was he there?

Maybe his buddies were around. That guy always had buddies with him. Right now, they could be looking for their missing pal.

Koji didn't care if that doll in the car trunk were found. But it meant they might find this house, too.

He couldn't bear just standing there and rushed outside.

He carried out a wooden crate and a shovel from the cellar. He packed snow into the crate. Lifting it up, he climbed the hill.

Putting his body to use somehow quenched his anxiety. The sensation of that neck on his hands dissipated into the cold snow. Panting, Koji went over the hill. He got the crate packed with snow to where the side road began.

The path leading up to the house was about level with the main road and on slightly lower ground than the flanking woods. The piled snow was a little lower, too. Though hidden by the snow, it wasn't hard to discern a path if you were looking for one. If the snow came up level with the woods and was smooth, though, noticing it would be a tall order. Luckily, the side road immediately bent into the woods. There wasn't much distance to cover up with snow.

He made four trips with a crateful of snow each time. He wasn't making much progress. It was taking a lot more snow than he'd hoped. Going over the hill was wearying, too.

A small wooden crate wasn't cutting it, so he took a long plank out of the cellar and nailed down three large boxes. A sled of sorts.

He should have known that snow wasn't light. How odd that he'd tried to carry any. He'd forgotten, living for three years in Tokyo, without snow.

Pulling the sled up the hill with a rope was no joke, but once over the top it was easy. A little push and down it slid.

On his second time uphill, the burden on the rope felt a little lighter.

Hiroshi, his face red, was pushing.

The added strength wasn't much to speak of, but joy surged in Koji's heart. The two of them were working together to ferry snow to defend their living here.

He called out. Hiroshi responded. It felt like the rope had grown much lighter.

He lost count of the round trips. Innumerable times, the sled went up the hill and slid down. It took over two hours to cover up the side road completely. They'd both removed their sweaters and were in their shirts. Still, they were drenched in sweat.

"You can play where you want, but don't go over this hill. Understood? So no one can see us."

Only when Koji said this, the boy looked serious and nodded.

They erased their footprints and the sled tracks from the hill. Now nobody would notice they were here. Koji thought so. It still looked a bit unnatural, but one snowfall would make everything indistinct.

Koji grabbed some snow, stuck it into his mouth, then threw the rest at Hiroshi's face. The boy squealed and fell down, got up, and threw a snowball back. They played like that for a while. Then they collapsed in the snow. To a flushed body, the cold snow felt good.

In the afternoon, as promised, they made a racing track for the radio-controlled cars. Clouds were gathering in force and it looked as if it might snow again.

"Better if it does. It would be boring to run on the same track every day," Koji told Hiroshi, who was looking apprehensively up at the sky. "If it gets buried, then we can build a new one."

"Are you going to make me one every day?"

"Yes. My time after lunch is for playing with you. Not just today, but every day. So you've got to help me with the chores, too."

"Okay."

"Don't just be saying it. If you've said it you keep to it, if you're a man."

Hiroshi was lining the two radio-controlled cars on the snow. Preoccupied with how the track had turned out, he barely seemed to catch a word. "It's going to be easier than yesterday because the road is wider."

"It won't be. This time, just driving it won't be all. We're racing two cars. Overtaking each other, you know?"

On the completed circuit, Koji's red machine took a trial run. Hiroshi's Porsche followed behind. They had packed the snow solid, so the cars ran beautifully. At the bend, Hiroshi's car spun and dove into snow. Hoping to get it loose somehow, he revved it up, merely sinking the car deeper into the snow with every little frustrated cry.

"You need to slow down at the curves. Don't just think about going fast. Yours has a lot of horsepower. You can zoom past on the stretches."

Hiroshi gave Koji a chagrined look and scurried over to his snowbound Porsche.

"Shall we race them? My machine is doing great. It zips along something amazing."

"I want to practice first." Hiroshi started the Porsche again. "Give me some time. You can smoke some cigarettes, brother."

The little body clutching the remote control swayed right and left with the car's motion.

At night it started snowing again.

Koji was putting together wooden planks lopped off at a suitable length. He had taken apart the crate.

It was quiet. The only sound was the hiss of the kettle on the stove. Without a blizzard, the winds were calm.

"Snowy nights are nice, aren't they? The snow absorbs sound. I didn't use to think it was particularly quiet. I took it for granted. But after living in Tokyo for a while, I sometimes badly missed this quiet. It rarely snows in Tokyo, right? Even when it does, it doesn't get as quiet as this."

Hiroshi had a white handkerchief spread on the table. Following Koji's instructions, he was filling in squares with a black marker to make a checkered flag. The boy had gotten to work with great enthusiasm upon hearing that it was used to wave in the winner.

"Make sure you stay within the squares."

"Yeah." Hiroshi's was hardly a deft hand, but he had covered about half the handkerchief with a black-and-white pattern. "Is the garage ready?"

"Just need to hammer in the nails and put on the gate."

The cellar had a full set of workman's tools. The cardboard garages absorbed moisture and had gone bad. It was Koji who'd suggested building a sturdier one. While he was cutting out planks, Hiroshi helped by holding down one end or by searching for hinges.

"Shame we can't paint it."

The garage needed to accommodate two cars, so it was wide rather than long and the roof only sloped in one direction. Koji made pencil marks where the nails would go. Hiroshi came closer and held one end.

"What shall we do tomorrow, Hiroshi?"

"We're going to make another racing track, aren't we? It's snowing so today's is already gone."

"I meant for work, not play."

"I'm not interested in work."

"What kind of talk is that? When all's said and done, human beings need to work. Whether it earns money or not, work is a must. Otherwise, play becomes meaningless. You understand?"

Hiroshi shook his head.

Koji himself didn't quite understand what he'd said. He wasn't one to be giving sermons. He just needed to find them some work to do, and they'd do whatever it was together.

He began banging nails from between his lips into the planks. The three walls and roof of the garage were soon attached to the plywood base. Only the gate was missing. Since the garage was wide, double doors that opened out would be best.

When snow thudded on the ground outside, Hiroshi gave a start and looked up.

"You scared?"

"I'm fine. I just thought someone was here."

"It's okay to say you're scared. It's nothing to be ashamed of."

"I'm a bit scared of the dark. But I'll be fine even if those people showed up."

The kid was afraid of them after all. Not surprising, given all that had happened.

You don't have to be scared anymore. They won't be coming again. I've seen to it.

"We buried the road in snow. Nobody will find this place."

"I'm not afraid of them."

"I know. I'm just saying that nobody will find us here."

Koji tried a gate plank for size. Hiroshi headed for the table. Koji looked for a while at the small back.

204

"There's something I want you to help me with tomorrow, actually."

"What?" Hiroshi asked listlessly, his head still on the table.

"I found old skis in the cellar. We can use them to make a sled."

"Are we ferrying snow again?"

"No, it'll be for you to ride. You can go play on it on the hill out back. A Christmas present, just a day early. Seems like you deserve something from Santa Claus, too."

"Santa Claus doesn't really exist. I know. Mom told me."

Koji decided on the positions of the gate hinges. He hammered them in. The measurement had been too exact. The two sides stuck a bit at their tips. He carefully planed the wood.

"Look, it shuts perfectly." He attached two screws to serve as handles and it was done. Placing it on the floor, he inserted the two cars.

"We can't lock it?"

Nobody will come to steal them, Koji almost said.

To Hiroshi this was a real garage, and within were real cars. Koji bent some wire so that the two handles were hooked together.

"Now it's locked."

Hiroshi nodded. If he could make believe it was real, that was all that mattered.

"What we were talking about earlier," Koji reprised.

"Earlier?"

"About Santa Claus."

"It's true, he doesn't exist. Didn't you know?"

"Of course no one ever comes down the chimney and puts gifts in stockings. But all those kids out there are getting presents. You know what, some grown-up that the kid is living with is the Santa Claus for that kid, that's what I think. Which means your Santa Claus is me."

Hiroshi looked mystified. The gist of it was that Koji wanted to give the kid a present. That was all. But it was making Koji bashful.

"Your present will be a sled. Because you ought to learn other ways to play."

"Is it fun?"

"Yeah, you go flying like the wind. At first, though, you won't be able to slide that well and fall off."

Huh, Hiroshi said and showed no further interest. The checkered flag was nearly done.

It was Koji who was feeling merry. He'd lived his life so far without having anything to do with Christmas. His father used to go out of his way to get drunk during New Year's and at cherry blossom parties, but only while Koji's mother had been alive. After her death, he was an empty shell, and when Koji's brother offered to down some together for a change, he was no good after just a few. Then Koji himself would be asked to join his brother, who'd turn violent and hit him. Koji didn't take it lying down, either.

Yet, even as they traded blows, at times he clearly sensed that his brother didn't understand himself why he felt angry. Koji would feel sad and stop hitting back. At that point his brother ceased his blows, too, and faced away. That was Koji's initiation to alcohol; he'd been a high school student.

"Can you put names on the garage? Yours and mine?"

It was past ten. "Tomorrow. It's past your bedtime."

"What about you, brother?"

"I'll be drinking. I want to work some on my model ship, too."

"That's not fair."

"Uh-uh. Kids need more sleep than grown-ups. You need that time to grow, you see? Kids grow while they sleep. When I was your age, I slept a lot, and ate lots, wanting to get bigger fast."

Hiroshi didn't look pleased. But soon he gave a huge yawn. *See,* Koji gave his head a light poke.

Koji brought out the whiskey, moved a chair to the window, and turned off all the lights.

The blue flame of the stove reflected dimly in the steamed-up window. With the sleeve of his sweater, he wiped droplets from the pane.

There was no moon, but the white snow alone made it light enough outside to see to the back of the woods. Amidst the silence, snow kept falling. The racing track was also buried under snow. Over the snow piled on the road to obscure it, too, more was falling, no doubt. Nobody would spot the way in now.

He stuck a cigarette in his mouth and lit a match. His face, colored

red by the flame, floated for a moment in the glass, then became just a red dot.

The face seemed to belong to a stranger. It suddenly came back to him: *the smell of a beast*, the old man had said.

He struck another match. A face lit red floated in the glass. He didn't put it out right away. He held on until the stick became short. His fingertips burned. He lit another one. The red face was a stranger's. Not because the traces of a fallen scab marked its cheek. Nor because the stubble on its chin was grown enough to pinch. A third, a fourth, he kept lighting matches, but his own face never appeared. The matchbox became empty.

His hand almost moved. It had been about to smash the glass. It stopped in time.

He gulped down whiskey. Just a little to stay in a good mood—that was last night. What did he care. Get stone drunk. Next morning, his face ought to be there in the mirror. He was fulfilled now, he thought again and again. Snow fell from a branch with a light thud. He brought his face close to the window. The pane clouded white from his breath. Once more he wiped it with his sweater sleeve.

Outside there was another thud of snow. The branch regained flexion and wobbled, scattering snow like white powder. Cigarette ash dropped from between his fingers. He was fulfilled. He thought so again. A warm room, food, untrammeled time. He had enough to spare. He even had company to weather the winter with.

Chapter Seven

1

It was still snowing when he woke up.

It only stopped after nine. The clouds were thick, and it looked as if it might snow again at any moment.

The chores didn't take long to finish. There wasn't much to do anyway. Hiroshi helped out without complaining. It was quite a change from the last day's sulking.

It wasn't as if Koji had hooked Hiroshi's attention with something. Simply, in one day, the boy had acquired the habit.

They went outside around ten.

They climbed the hill and examined the side road. It was impossible to distinguish between path and woods. The nightlong snowfall had hidden the unnatural look of the snow they had ferried and piled.

"We're making that sled."

"What about the racing track?"

"I told you. Radio-controlled cars come after lunch. You still don't get it?"

Hiroshi nodded. He didn't look all that displeased.

They brought the old skis out of the cellar.

Koji cut them shorter at their rear ends and removed the binding. There was no suitable box. "Find pieces of wood and bring them all," he told the boy.

Crawling around the cellar, Hiroshi came back with boxes and planks. Koji drafted a blueprint in his mind. Just a simple one would do as long as it was sturdy.

He sawed the planks. With them, he firmly secured the pair of skis. For clasps he used the screws from the binding. Hiroshi began to look interested.

"This is quite something. It might really fly like the wind. Give me the box."

The idea was to attach a box on top for straddling. Koji tried sitting Hiroshi on it. *Ah!* the boy exclaimed.

"I'd fall off backwards. It's dangerous."

"You'll be fine. Look, this is going to slide down a slope. The front part leans forward. If I just stuck the box on, you'd go headfirst into the snow."

"Are you sure?"

"You just see. When I was a kid, I played on one almost every day."

He fastened the box tight. It wouldn't budge now even if a few adults rode on it. He also attached rope to the box. Reins.

"We've a real beauty here, thanks to the skis."

He pulled the rope. The sled obediently followed. With ample space between the two skis, it was stable too.

They climbed the hill behind the house. A few birch trees stood close to the top, but otherwise it was uncluttered slope. It stretched about fifty yards.

"I'll go with you just the first time."

Hugging up Hiroshi from behind, he sat down on the box. The angle was perfect. He gave the boy the reins.

He lifted both legs. The sled began to move, then picked up speed. Wind whooshed by their ears. Fifty yards went by in a flash.

Hiroshi was panting.

"Fun, isn't it?"

Hiroshi silently nodded. Then he showed his teeth. His breath was white.

"Try it on your own now. When you want to turn, slowly tilt your body. Don't let go of the rope."

Hiroshi tried to push the sled up the hill.

"Not like that, dummy. Pull it."

Cigarette in mouth, Koji stood looking up as Hiroshi climbed. The boy arrived at the summit and turned around the sled. He wasn't getting on it. Even from a distance his nervousness was manifest. Koji beckoned with his hand.

Hiroshi sat down. He began to slide. *Good speed, you're not half bad,* Koji muttered. Hiroshi's body lurched. A spume of snow rose. Just the sled came sliding down to Koji's feet. Hiroshi emerged all white from the snow and came running down.

"You crying?"

"I'm not crying."

Hiroshi clutched the rope. He began climbing the slope again.

"Keep your body relaxed. That way, you find a center of gravity. Don't think of it as a sled. Pretend it's a bicycle," Koji advised. The boy didn't turn around.

When Hiroshi arrived at the top, he got astride the sled without the slightest hesitation. He slid. His hair billowed in the wind. Then he fell again.

He repeated the same thing six times without speaking a word.

The seventh try. Koji still stood there, watching. The kid had some guts. It was only right to stand and watch, despite the cold.

Hiroshi began to slide. He picked up speed. His body lurched, but didn't tumble. He came right down to Koji's feet atop the sled.

"I did it."

Koji nodded.

Hiroshi showed his white teeth.

"Once you've done it, the rest is easy. You'll be able to slide in all sorts of ways."

"Thank you, brother."

"For what?"

"My Christmas present."

"Don't mention it."

He grabbed some snow and threw it at Hiroshi. The boy threw some back. As they played snowballs like that, time passed quickly.

"Let's have lunch," Koji said.

Hiroshi took the lead and ran.

Sometimes the jeep got stuck. In one night, the snow had gotten quite deep.

They were heading from the fourth checkpoint to the fifth. Kuroki lit a Short Peace. Makimura was engrossed in the map.

"This winter's going to suck for real. The region isn't supposed to get so much snow," Takao said at the steering wheel. Not surprisingly he was a dab hand at driving a jeep. "The weather's been abnormal. Just when I'd thought it was great having a cool summer, some miserably hot days came around in September."

Last night, from five to ten, they'd driven around looking for lit summer houses. There were quite a few, but most of the occupants had come for Christmas Eve. The parties were full on, the people all drunk. Trying to talk to them seemed a waste of time. Still, they marked about a dozen suspicious places. These were the ones they were checking up on now.

Houses that had their lights on but looked empty, others with just tire tracks—that was all it was for most of them. Moreover, when the detectives dropped by today, they were treated to deflating replies. If the owner hadn't been out drinking all night, he'd merely gone to hang out at a friend's villa. That was normal. Camouflaged somewhere in the normality was Koji Mizui.

"At this pace, it will take at least five days," Makimura said, looking up from the map. Five days even with two local detectives helping out in another jeep.

"What's your other case?" Kuroki asked.

"A robbery at a credit bank. The money taken was negligible, but someone got stabbed. Four from our subsection are on it. I doubt the other subsections can spare people either at this time of year."

"And on the twenty-sixth, a manhunt."

"Our chief does have a point, though. Corner Mizui, persuade him to let the child go. That'd be huge."

Kuroki fell silent. Given the circumstances, relying on manpower to close off the roads and launch a manhunt was only appropriate. If it went smoothly, the case would be solved in a day.

"He's killed three, hasn't he?"

"What do you mean?"

"I'm under the impression that you're wary of cornering Mizui by main force. Don't get me wrong, I'm not criticizing you. It's just that, since yesterday, I've come to sense that for you Mizui isn't just anybody."

"He's the perp. He's killed three people."

"Yes, but there are perps and perps. Some you want to knock down and spit on because cuffing them isn't enough. Then there are those you feel, somewhere in your heart, like letting go. If you arrest them and put them behind bars, you want to look after their families. When they come out you want to shake their hand. I've had one or two of those."

"He was the victim of a wrongful arrest. We made it more than a month ago."

Makimura folded the map.

He ought not to have said that. It was like rubbing salt in his wound. Makimura's eyes fell on the map that lay folded on his knees.

"Given the circumstances," Kuroki added, "the first two could be seen as excessive self-defense."

"And Shibasaki?" countered Takao.

"He too came all the way here in pursuit of Mizui. Though I don't know the circumstances of his death."

"How reliable is the info on the SW M10?"

"It's thinkable. Kansai's Shoyukai were behind him, after all."

"So Shibasaki started it by aiming the gun. He fired one shot but missed. Mizui got in a frenzy and strangled him. Even if he can't claim urgent escape, excessive self-defense might settle it."

"That's just conjecture."

"Another conjecture: the M10 is with Mizui now."

Makimura raised his face. Kuroki had thought as much after searching Shibasaki's corpse.

"Anyway, it would be best to avoid hunting Mizui down like a wild beast," Takao concluded, hitting the brakes.

They were now at the fifth checkpoint. A dog barked. An old man came out.

Makimura clambered out and soon returned.

"He says he spent last night on the mountain out back, watching it snow."

"Strange hobby."

"Apparently he's a painter. He said he's wintering here."

"Okay, next stop."

Takao started the jeep.

Checking out the dozen or so checkpoints took until 3 p.m.

The local station had received a call from Tokyo. The boy who had been with Shibasaki had been apprehended in Tokyo in the morning.

"He went into the city, and when he came back Shibasaki's car wasn't there. Assuming they'd simply miscommunicated, he returned by train."

"Where was the car parked?" Kuroki asked.

Makimura opened the map. It was approximately where the gunshot had been reported two days ago.

"And the heat?"

"An M10 after all. Apparently a battered old piece, but it's a revolver so we can't hope for it to have gone totally kaput." Makimura laughed weakly.

Takao brought some hot coffee.

They left the police station at 4:30 p.m.

An open jeep. Driving around in one in the snow was insanity. Though last night's snowfall had been gentle, it had beaten into their faces like a blizzard.

The wind threatened to be strong tonight.

"Please don't look. Yesterday got to me." Takao took a sip from the miniature whiskey bottle in his pocket.

"Makimura, get treated to some too."

After a moment of hesitation, Makimura reached for it.

It started to snow around eight. For some reason, it was often at night that it snowed. They hit terrain that was difficult even in a jeep. Yet, at the end of such a path, too, a summer house stood, with people in it. A Land Cruiser worth a few hundred million yen was parked at the entrance. There was a chimney, surely for a fireplace. It was a big house.

Inside was a young couple. They were enjoying a swell White Christmas.

The path dead-ended there.

"That's a Blazer Cheyenne, that car. Must be a rich kid, bringing

214

a girl here."

Takao made a brutal U-turn. Indeed, the other car looked like a much more comfortable ride than a jeep.

"Bet it has amazing horsepower, too."

"I don't think I'll ever get to ride in one."

They went back the tree-flanked path. Eventually they got onto a paved road. That was clear from the jeep not rocking as much.

"Weird," Makimura observed, a penlight trained on his map. "There should be two more along this road."

"We must have missed them because the lights aren't on. Make a note of it."

The map had lots of crosses on it. There were some circles, too. These were the checkpoints. They would revisit them in daylight the next day.

"There. More lights," Takao said. Reflecting back from the snow, the light in the trees had a phantasmal aura. Rock music playing at an ear-blasting volume became audible.

"Just young folk having a party." Kuroki removed his gloves and blew on his hands.

The search hit its limit at ten o'clock. After that, even if a house wasn't empty, they might have turned off the lights.

The detectives returned to the police station at half past ten. The other jeep was already back. The two thoroughly exhausted searchers made a curt report to Kuroki: they'd found nothing.

After putting Hiroshi to bed, Koji brought out the model ship kit and placed it on the table.

He intended to go ahead and assemble it. No matter how much care he put into it, cheap was cheap. He could put his efforts into the sail. Stiffening cloth with glue, he'd make it look like the real thing. A slightly worn and discolored cloth, not pure white, would be good. The sail was what made a sailing ship.

The kit was shoddy down to the basic design. While a photo of the four-masted barque *Kaiyomaru* was printed on the box, the kit only contained three masts, and the hull shape resembled a little yacht's.

He attached the bowsprit. It was done. It had only taken an hour.

He put it on the table and, sipping whiskey-and-water, gazed at it for a while. Fine. Once he attached sails, it wouldn't look too bad.

In the garage slept two radio-controlled cars. The checkered flag lay nearby. In that afternoon's racing, not once had the flag come down for Hiroshi's Porsche.

Koji picked it up. He waved it a few times. Then he laughed.

When he walked around the room, the floor creaked a little. He was walking around, nothing more. Another quiet night.

His older brother in Ueda suddenly came to mind. He remembered his father's face, too. His brother would get angry. Or maybe he'd feel sad. The man was brusque but had a kind heart underneath it all. As for their father, best if he'd gone senile. *So senile he won't understand what I've done. If I can have it my way, he's forgotten what I even look like.*

Koji was getting into an odd mood. Wishing for his father to go senile was new to him. Deep down he'd always worried about him.

He tried to clear his mind of the faces of his brother and his father. When he did, Makiko's appeared, laughing. Koji hurriedly took a gulp of whiskey. *It's because it's too quiet.* He'd muttered that out loud, his voice funnily muffled. It didn't sound like his own.

Outside it was snowing again. He gulped down another glass of whiskey. He just needed to get drunk fast.

2

With the help of a wire, Takao was dragging out a car stuck in the snow.

The ordinary passenger vehicle didn't even have chains on its tires. A child was sitting inside.

"We should just leave them. Their fault for driving in the snow in that car." Makimura sound irritated. The manhunt was due to start the next day.

"Stop fretting, Makimura. We just do what we can."

"We haven't even checked a third of the summer houses, sir."

"So?"

"Every second seems precious to a body."

"Even with a manhunt on, we'll have a chance to nab Mizui ourselves."

Makimura put a cigarette in his mouth. The jeep began to move. The green passenger car came crawling out of the snow.

Kuroki looked up at the sky. The clouds were thick. It could start snowing again at night.

"Sorry to keep you waiting."

Takao and the jeep returned. Makimura sulkily climbed into the back.

Kuroki scratched his ear. It felt fearfully itchy since morning. Perhaps it was frostbitten.

"We have seven places remaining." The checkpoints must have been lodged in his head; Takao drove forth without consulting the map.

The villa had been ransacked by vandals still wearing their boots. The furniture was smashed into pieces, too.

"They do it just for kicks. Come summer and we start getting calls about this sort of thing. It's impossible to investigate."

Takao kicked the empty cans that lay on the floor.

Makimura crossed out another spot on the map. "Let's hurry," he said.

"Please don't be in a rush, Mr. Makimura. If the jeep gets stuck, we'll have to walk, and then it'll take hours and hours."

Two in the afternoon. Still quite some time before sunset.

Hiroshi's Porsche overtook Koji's red machine. It was on a stretch.

"Yes!" Hiroshi cried.

Koji went faster. The bend. He'd retake the lead there. The Porsche slowed down. The red machine curved on the outward side.

"How's that!" Koji bellowed.

The two cars lined up. Just as they were entering the final stretch head to head, the red machine's front right wheel fell off the track. The car spun and dove into the snow.

The Porsche came blasting through the finish line.

"Me!"

Hiroshi picked up the checkered flag and waved it. Koji stepped over the track to retrieve his red car.

"I won, brother."

"Yes, you won. I thought you would botch that last bend again. You kept in tight. You held back, more than I could."

Hiroshi laughed. He hugged the Porsche and wiped the snow off the wheels with his palm.

"Want to try again?"

"I'm gonna go ride the sled."

"What, no more racing?"

"Tomorrow. We'll have a new track, and I'll win again."

The boy put his Porsche away in the garage. Koji put his red machine away alongside it and said, "I'll leave them by the front door."

Hiroshi left pulling the sled.

Koji went back inside the house.

He sat down on the sofa and gazed for a while at the flames in the stove. He thought about the race. If he'd slowed down a bit at that bend he would have cleared it, but then the Porsche would have pushed past on the stretch. He hadn't been able to cut inward.

Hiroshi had done what Koji usually did. The kid hadn't been just playing. He'd been thinking and thinking about how to win.

Fresh brat, Koji muttered, and realized that he was upset at having lost. In any match, losing wasn't an option even if your opponent was a kid.

Then he laughed. The kid was a man all right.

He stretched on the sofa. It was still only two o'clock. He'd been ready to play along at racing until four, so he didn't know what to do with himself. There was another pair of skis in the cellar, but the hill behind didn't offer the necessary elevation. Sledding was what it was good for.

He made himself some instant coffee with the hot water in the kettle on the stove. No sugar. He liked it bitter. He picked up the ship with no sails. The masts were weeping. They looked cold.

Koji went upstairs, opened a chest drawer, and pulled out some clothes. He found a beige cotton shirt. He also needed thread to make ropes for rigging the mast. There had to be a sewing kit somewhere. He opened all the drawers in the chest. From the little drawer at the top emerged four photos.

Two of them showed five people. A boy and a girl, the father, and an elderly couple. The second showed the mother instead of the father. The remaining two photos were just of the children. The pictures seemed to have been taken somewhere near the house in the summer.

Koji was about to put them back, but abruptly tore all four in half. Then he clicked his tongue. Why shouldn't they look like they were having fun? Of course they'd be. Tearing the photos, that was just making himself miserable.

He went downstairs with the cotton shirt.

There were no scissors. He cut the sleeve of the cotton shirt with a kitchen knife. Then he loosened the fabric with his nails and tugged out several threads.

He covered the chilly ship with the shirt. He'd make the sails tomorrow. Today, he'd fashion ropes. One thread wouldn't make a decent rope. Better to bundle three or so.

He lifted three threads to the level of his eye. He carefully entwined them, but it was no good. One always stuck out. He tried over and over again.

Hiroshi came rushing in covered in snow.

"Snack time, isn't it?" the boy urged.

It was still some time before three. "Are you hungry?"

"Yes."

"There's some sausages in the fridge. Bring one over."

The snow that the boy shed turned into wet marks on the carpet.

"You still falling off?"

"I can't turn. When I try what you showed me, the sled flips over."

"It's because you're not using the reins. You need to arch your body back hard and lift the front of the sled a bit."

"I'll practice."

The snow on his head was melting into droplets of water and trickling down onto his face. Hiroshi casually wiped them off with his palm.

"You're a real trooper," Koji said.

"I am?"

"I used to think kids gave up easily."

"I'm gonna practice."

"Right. That's why you're a real trooper."

Koji sliced the sausage into two. He gave the longer piece to Hiroshi.

"Why isn't it half and half?"

Koji had only taken about a fifth. Usually they split things equally. "Didn't you say you were hungry? It's your prize for winning the race."

"How about your winning until now?"

"You beat me for the first time. I'd say that calls for a prize."

Seeming to take the point, Hiroshi nodded. He made to rush outside sausage in hand.

"Eat it before you start sledding," Koji called after him. "Get back in the house by four."

He threw his portion of sausage into his mouth. He couldn't tell if the boy had heard him.

Blown off the tabletop, the strands of cotton lay on the carpet. Not a very reliable rope.

Both his shoes and his trousers were damp. He didn't feel too cold, though. Traveling for hours in an open jeep had a way of making one numb.

They had cleared their seven checkpoints and were heading to an eighth.

Kuroki removed his gloves and put his hands to his eyes. Even under cloudy skies, a sheer white landscape was harsh on the eyes.

"And tonight, what do we do?" Makimura grumbled. He'd been sullen. Something was eating at him. He was probably fighting back haste.

"The same. That's all there is."

"Tomorrow it'll be a manhunt."

Makimura's finger drew a circle on the map. Kuroki stuck a Short Peace in his mouth. His throat burned. In the morning he'd thrown five or six packs into his pocket, but there was only one left. He'd smoked too much.

"Sir, could you negotiate with the local station chief?"

"About what?"

"You know."

"Makimura, step down from this case."

"Sir."

"A match against time. Detectives sometimes have to bear it. You don't seem to be able to."

"Are you telling me I'm not fit to be a detective?"

"Take it how you want."

Makimura's eyes glinted. Kuroki looked the other way. He had no time to deal with youthful huffing.

"Well, let's bear it together, all three of us," Takao said soothingly.

The rattling of the jeep suddenly grew more violent. It didn't seem like the jeep itself was acting up. It was the rough ground beneath the snow.

A chunk of snow fell in the woods. A big house came into view. The Land Cruiser from the night before was missing.

"Strange." Takao tilted his head. They were searching for their eighth checkpoint. "Mr. Makimura, you need to be looking at that map more carefully."

Makimura, too, could only tilt his head.

"It's a dead end here. All we can do is make a U-turn."

They drove back, all the while looking carefully left and right. They returned to the paved road.

"Along the way, on our right when we're heading back, there ought to be two summer houses." Makimura pointed to a spot on the map.

"What's the distance from the road?"

"Two hundred yards."

"The other side of the hill, then."

"But we didn't see any side road."

Kuroki leapt out of the jeep. "Let's try walking."

"Wait. You want to walk? It'll take time. The map could be wrong, after all."

"A match against time, Makimura, is all about how much of it you can spend on what may seem like a waste."

"What if the map is wrong? It's already past three. We still have six more places we could check out."

"If the map is wrong, we'll correct it. We'll walk if only for that."

"Sir."

"Well, Mr. Makimura. This is the only place we've investigated so far that's suspicious," Takao remarked, soothingly.

3

Koji went outside.

He wanted to see how the boy was doing on the sled. If he still couldn't turn, Koji could show him again. This kid Hiroshi would sure get the hang of it then.

Hiroshi waved from the hilltop. He came sledding straight.

"Why didn't you try to turn?"

"Because."

"You don't want me to see you fall?"

Koji laughed. Without replying, Hiroshi pulled the sled uphill. Once he got to the top, he stood looking at Koji for a while. Koji beckoned with a gesture.

Hiroshi began to slide. His stiff expression got nearer and nearer. Then he fell off the side. Once again an empty sled came sliding down. Koji stopped it with his foot.

Pulling the rope, he climbed the hill. Halfway up awaited Hiroshi, covered in snow.

"We'll slide together. There's a knack. I'll show you."

He held Hiroshi's small body secure between his thighs.

They began to slide. *Left*, he said, and they turned. Then to the right. The third time they tried to turn, the sled toppled over. Their faces dove right into the snow. The two of them laughed helplessly.

"You see about the knack, though."

Hiroshi didn't reply. The kid wouldn't say he could until he could. He was that kind of guy.

"I'll watch. Try again."

Hiroshi nodded.

Koji lit a cigarette.

Kuroki began walking in the woods. Makimura followed him. Takao advanced the jeep very slowly.

There were plenty of openings between the trees that a car could drive through. This was pretty sparse as far as woods went. Yet digging up the snow with the tip of one's shoe revealed withered grass. It wasn't a road.

Snow fell from the branches at the slightest touch. It was difficult to walk here. Crawling sometimes worked better.

Makimura wasn't talking. He just followed.

Suddenly, one of Kuroki's legs sank knee-deep into the snow.

"Hey," he said and turned around to face Makimura, who'd also lost his balance after stepping into the deeper snow.

"I don't see how there could be so much here," the younger man admitted.

"It's too deep. The bottom could be level with the road."

Kuroki stepped farther in. The woods opened up, the space between trees ample enough to call it a path.

"Anything wrong?" Takao asked. He parked the jeep and got out.

"It's odd. I'm under the impression that this is a path."

Takao, now also knee-deep in snow, silently nodded.

They trekked in. The deep snow went on. When they turned left, the snow became shallow and only reached their shins. A trough that wound between the woods was clearly visible. It continued to the top of the hill.

"He hid it pretty damn well."

"No wonder we missed it," Takao marveled.

"Now don't get in a hurry, Makimura."

"I know."

"Where exactly is this summer house?"

"A hundred yards from the hilltop or thereabouts."

"Let's hope there's cover on the opposite slope."

Both Makimura's and Takao's eyes gleamed. Kuroki led. The snow was shallow now, and it was much easier to walk.

Hiroshi leapt onto the sled. He slid straight but fell over anyway. Clumsy kid. He got to his feet immediately and came running down.

"Brother."

Something had happened—that was clear. Was he hurt? No, it had already happened when he'd leapt onto the sled.

"Someone's coming."

Koji quickly turned around. He saw three human figures on the hill behind him. "Run," he said.

Hiroshi already was.

They rushed back into the house. As they regained their breath, Koji wiped sweat off his face.

He looked outside from the window near the front entrance. The figures were gone. He dashed upstairs. He couldn't see anybody from the upstairs window, either.

He waited.

Who was it? Those guys from before?

Hiroshi was nearby. "Don't worry," Koji assured him. His voice sounded hard.

If it's those punks, I'll chase them off. You just stay still.

It was hard to say how much time had passed. The three human forms appeared again. It wasn't that bunch. Somehow Koji sensed this clearly.

"Is it those people?" Hiroshi's voice was trembling.

"I don't know. They're too far away."

He went downstairs. Hiroshi followed him. He locked the front door. The figures on the hill weren't coming any closer.

"Was it Mizui?" Takao asked.

What Kuroki had seen first was a child standing atop a hill on the other side.

The house had hogged his attention. When he noticed the child, it was already too late to hide. Clearly, the child had seen him.

"Was that a snow boat?"

"The guy at the bottom was Mizui, I think."

"I'm positive." Makimura's voice was a pitch higher than usual.

They hadn't identified the man who'd dashed into the house. He was wearing matching sweaters with the child, not the clothes the tea parlor employee and the toy store owner had described. The proprietor of the ramen shop in Zaimokuza had told them that the child was wearing a check-pattern overcoat.

"We need to make sure."

"He's seen us. Why don't we go nearer?"

"Makimura, I told you not to be in a rush. Look at the lay of the land. He can't get away."

"Shall I ask the station to provide backup?"

"No, Mr. Takao. The three of us should handle this. We can. I'd rather not have some sniper squad sent here."

"Fine with me. It's we three who found him."

They waited for a while on the hilltop.

All three readied their revolvers. A hundred yards. Revolvers didn't cut it at that distance.

"I'd rather not use it."

"The kid is a problem, yes? If he uses the kid as a shield, we can't do a thing."

"Mizui wouldn't do such a thing," Makimura countered.

The slope to the house was only sparsely dotted with trees, not enough to provide solid cover. They needed to get within a hundred feet to identify the man—especially since he was inside a house.

"Let's go. Spread out a bit. Just in case we get shot at."

They descended the slope with Kuroki in the middle, Takao on the right, and Makimura on the left. Kuroki was the only one still on the path; the other two were crawling in between trees.

"Stay away!" a voice came from the house.

It was Mizui's. Though having expected as much, a slight tremor ran through Kuroki.

He gestured to the two men flanking him to halt.

Koji got a clear look at the faces of the three approaching men.

It was that detective called Kuroki and Beanpole. He didn't recognize the third man.

He grabbed the revolver from the chest drawer. He didn't intend to fire it. He could give them pause, though.

They couldn't know that I've got a gun.

He just needed to create an opening for a getaway. The car. Making a run for the mountains wasn't an option, not with Hiroshi in tow. If they could get to the car, they'd manage fine.

He remembered the path they'd filled up with snow. Could he drive on it? Even if he gained speed downhill, the path didn't run straight. It was also narrow. He could crash into a tree.

He quit thinking. What was the use of thinking at a time like this? He had to go for it. But when?

The three men were at the middle of the slope. They were neither closing in nor falling back.

Hiroshi was looking nervously at the revolver. Saying something to the kid was beyond Koji at the moment. He just glanced over and nodded.

The three men began to advance in sync.

"Stay away!" Koji shouted again.

The three men froze once more. They meant to creep down bit by bit, and there was no stopping them.

His hand tightened over the revolver. He pried open his own fingers, laid the gun on the floor, and massaged his right hand.

"Scared?" he asked.

"I'm fine."

Hiroshi had also said so on the boat and when they were being pursued by motorbikes. Yet something in his expression was different this time. Did the gun scare him?

Or is it me with a gun that's scaring him?

"Don't worry. They won't do anything to you. All three are detectives."

"You mean the police?"

"Yes. They've been after me and now they're here."

Hiroshi didn't ask why they were after Koji.

The three men moved again.

"Stay the hell away!"

He wiped his palm on his trousers.

"Damn them… If they come close, I'm gonna butcher them."

He brought his body near the window. The three men were almost at the foot of the hill. Koji went on all fours to the middle of the room and dragged over the table. Grabbing its legs, he hurled it through the window. Glass scattered. A ship without sails lay among the shards. Koji picked it up, looked at it for a moment, then threw it out the window.

Hiroshi was staring at Koji. He looked tense, but there was a strange glint in his eyes. Koji had never seen it before.

It was a gaze directed at a stranger. That did a number on his feelings.

"What's that look in your eyes?" he voiced his irritation.

The boy looked away and then down. *Face me,* Koji was about to say, when out of the corner of his eye he saw the three men moving again.

He picked up the revolver. He tried cocking it. The cylinder swung with a click.

He put a cigarette in his mouth with his left hand and lit it. He smoked one puff after another. He felt dizzy. Slapping the cigarette down on the floor, he stamped it out, leaving a dark stain on the carpet.

Hiroshi was staring at him again.

Damn you, don't look at me like that.

Suddenly, something inchoate rose up in him. It soon took shape. When it turned into a clear will, there was cruelty mixed into it.

"Hiroshi," he said, sticking another cigarette in his mouth. He told himself to calm down, and the words came out. "Could you stand on the window sill?"

Hiroshi's expression changed slightly. "Why?"

"I don't have time to explain. You could save me by doing that."

"What do I do after I'm on it?"

"Tell those guys outside to go home. They're already down at the foot of the hill and are watching us from there."

"Is that all I need to do?" Hiroshi stood up, eerily compliant.

"They're detectives. They might fire their pistols."

What am I trying to test? What in Hiroshi, and what for? Idiot. Stop it. I'm kidding—the words almost came out. They stayed unvoiced.

"I'm fine. I'll tell them."

Hiroshi put his hand on the window. His face was blank. *Stop him.* Koji's hands didn't move.

The boy clambered onto the sill and stood up. His little shoulders were shaking. His mouth moved, but no sound came. After some time, a tiny voice like the hum of a mosquito reached Koji's ears. *Go home.* He heard it again. *Go home.* It echoed over and over in his mind, growing softer, then louder. He almost put his hands over his ears.

It's all right—that, too, didn't find voice. He stood up.

A man was rushing in. He was already close, on the racing track under the window. A gun in hand, clear to see. He was shouting something.

Koji quickly pulled Hiroshi back. Without pause, he thrust out his right hand and pulled the trigger. Maybe he feared that Hiroshi would get shot, he didn't know why himself. Before he knew, his arm was numb from the recoil.

The man collapsed. Koji saw that much. Then he scooped up Hiroshi, who lay on the floor.

The boy was crying. He was looking up at Koji as he sobbed.

What gaze directed at a stranger? No, these eyes follow me, and only me.

"It's okay. It's all right. I'm an idiot. I'm a hopeless idiot."

Under his hands, Hiroshi's small shoulders were still shaking.

Tears welled up in Koji's eyes and threatened to spill over.

"We'll be fine."

Like hell they were going to be caught by that crew. He'd escape for sure, and together with Hiroshi. Then they'd just start from scratch.

There was still hope. They'd been in some dicey situations so far but had gotten out of them.

"Just stay put. Do as I say and we'll be fine, I promise."

The car was it. The chains were still on the tires. He could just step on it, and if the cops dared interfere, he'd run them over.

No one dare interfere with our living.

Carrying Makimura's body from behind, Kuroki retreated. Takao rushed over and took Makimura's feet.

They fell back forty yards to just below the hill.

Neither Mizui nor the child was at the window anymore.

Mizui! Makimura had shouted as he dashed out. There'd been no stopping him. It was when Hiroshi Suzue had appeared at the window. In a moment, Mizui had shown himself as well.

Makimura had collapsed with the gunshot.

"Was he trying to use the child as a shield?" Takao asked, ripping Makimura's trousers open.

It hadn't seemed that way to Kuroki. Hiroshi Suzue had clambered onto the window sill alone. Then he had said something.

How Makimura had seen it was another matter.

"Goodness, that was rash. We knew he had a gun. There was hardly thirty feet between them."

"It went right through," Kuroki said, examining the wound on Makimura's thigh. It was bleeding heavily.

"There's a first-aid kit in the jeep."

"I'm fine," Makimura panted. "Just strap it with a tie. Use mine."

Takao looked at Kuroki, who nodded.

4

The three men didn't move for a while from the foot of the hill.

Had the bullet hit? He hadn't aimed—he didn't even know how. The shock of the recoil remained in his hand.

A bend on the racing track had been trampled over. There was a small red blot, as if Koji's red machine had been totaled.

Two of the men stood up.

They stood somewhat apart and approached slowly. One of the men still lay at the foot of the hill. He wasn't dead. He shifted his upper body and raised his head to look toward the house.

Two more. Then they could escape. But shooting them? If he were to, how many more bullets were in the thing?

He fiddled with the cylinder. It didn't budge. Done right, it popped out sideways. He'd seen it loaded that way at the movies.

He pushed a little harder, but the cylinder still didn't budge. If he got too rough, it might break. Forget that. It was a gamble. He remembered a game where just one bullet was loaded into a six-shooter and a number of men pulled the trigger on themselves in turn. This was like playing that game against those two. Only, Koji was the loser if it didn't fire.

The men came closer. He could clearly see Kuroki's face. They were in a crouch, sneaking from birch tree to birch tree. The other one, on the left, was a chubby fellow.

Koji aimed at Kuroki. He pulled the trigger. A thunderous roar— snow thudded to the ground in the copse. Way off target.

The trigger felt strangely heavy. It had to be because he hadn't cocked the gun first. It had jerked wildly upon firing.

He clicked his tongue. He hadn't expected to be on target, but it could have struck a little closer at least.

The two men were face down on the snow. They didn't attempt to move.

Koji had one thing on mind: how to get to the car. The key was still in the ignition. The chains were still on the tires. Once he got to the car, it would be a rout.

"Let's go."

He grabbed Hiroshi's hand. The boy clasped back tightly.

He removed one of the floor plates in the kitchen.

Sticking the revolver in his belt, he lowered himself. He was by the water pump. On the other side of the partition was the cellar.

He found something to use as a foothold and carefully lowered the boy.

"We're going to the cellar. Don't make a sound."

With snow blocking the sun at the air vent, it was dim inside the cellar.

"Stay here. I'm gonna go take a look."

He opened the door. It was right under the terraced front entrance, and he could get outdoors without using the staircase. Moreover, snow had fallen and piled up from both the terrace and the roof, creating a sort of tunnel. Nobody could see him from outside.

Kuroki raised his head.

The gun had been aimed at him. The bullet, however, had struck far off the mark. Perhaps it had been fired double-action, without cocking the gun first.

"Not even close," remarked Takao, who lay prostrate about fifteen feet to the side.

The M10 revolver could hold six bullets. Two had been fired. Four remaining in the chamber. If a shot had been fired when Shibasaki died, then three.

Go on, keep firing, he wanted to tell Mizui. Only a trained hand could aim true at this range.

230

"Shall I bait him?"

"Yes, please. But don't get close to him. Run to the side."

Takao got up. He ran in a half-crouch. After going about fifty feet he came scuttling back. "He isn't falling for it."

The standard move was to let the guy use up his bullets. But there was also Hiroshi Suzue. Was Mizui planning to use the boy in some way?

"I suppose we should consider the child a hostage?"

"In the worst case, yes."

"What got into Mr. Makimura?"

"His youth."

"'Out of line' would be an understatement."

"Remember I told you we arrested Mizui by mistake. It was Makimura's mistake."

The repercussions were extending this far. Saying that it couldn't be helped wouldn't have kept Makimura from beating himself up.

In not being able to hold back, his heart had been in the right place. But only his heart.

"He's looking this way. He'd do better to keep still," Takao turned toward Makimura and observed.

If he had the strength to do that, then he was going to live.

"Let's move up some."

They advanced fifteen feet. No reaction. Takao tried another baiting run.

Did Mizui intend to watch and wait? Was he calm enough to do that?

Kuroki proceeded another fifteen feet. He put some distance between himself and Takao. Mizui still didn't show up at the window.

Hiroshi, called Koji.

The boy came and clutched Koji's trousers.

"All right, when I say go, run for the car. I'll be running right behind you. Don't turn around. Keep your eyes in front of you and dash straight for the car."

Hiroshi nodded.

Even if they see me and fire, if I'm behind him then Hiroshi won't get hit.

He didn't want to fuss over it. If he thought too much about the danger, he wouldn't ever make up his mind.

He had a pretty good idea of the position of the two detectives. They might have moved some—but probably not far. That shot hadn't been useless. They'd been on their bellies.

Crawling, Koji slowly made his way under the terrace and came to its edge. The car was parked at the side of the house. Sixty feet, maybe. They had to run on snow. It would take more than ten seconds.

"Straight for the car," he whispered by Hiroshi's ear, and took two deep breaths. He'd always come through when it counted. Believe, and luck never failed to turn your way and smile.

"Okay, go!"

He lifted Hiroshi's body onto the snow.

Koji leapt out right after him. Hiroshi was running. The sound of their steps, crunching snow, mingled. It was good. They'd make it.

A shout came from behind. In an instant, as if a knife had been placed against his neck, Koji's hair stood on end.

He turned around—and saw Kuroki. Far closer than he'd imagined, the detective was alone. He was rushing in with a yell.

Hiroshi hadn't reached the car yet. It was no good. Kuroki was catching up. Koji cocked his gun as he ran.

He stopped, turned, and aimed. When he fired the first shot, Kuroki fell flat on the snow then swiftly rose up. At the second shot, the detective leapt headlong into the snow, but rolled over and got up again. Koji tried to fire the third shot. A roar came from somewhere other than his hand.

He felt short of breath. Or so it seemed. The sky spun. Something had happened. He saw nothing but the sky—how come?

Maybe he'd been shot. Yet, he didn't feel any pain. He could get up. He would even be able to run. Was Hiroshi already at the car? He couldn't let himself die here like this, it was absurd. He hadn't lived one bit, hadn't done a hundredth of the living he'd meant to do. His legs were moving, he could feel it. He was running. He was up and running. But where to? All he could see was sky. Was he running toward the sky or what?

All sounds fell away. It was just very bright, and he wasn't even seeing the sky anymore. No, no way he was going to kick the bucket. *Hiroshi, say something. Let me hear your voice. Then I'll run to you. Your voice, just your voice would do.* The bright surroundings suddenly darkened. Why? It wasn't even night. He heard Hiroshi call out: *Brother.* He heard this clearly. *Wait there, I'm coming right now. I'm running, I really am, as fast as I can. See how hard I'm panting, and my heart's clanging like a fire bell. Still I'm running.* Now Hiroshi's call sounded more distant. It was also mixed in with sobbing. *Don't cry, dummy. You think I'm going to die? Don't make me laugh. This body of mine, it's tough. I've never been ill, not once since I was a kid. Sure, I did get hurt more times than I can count. But each time I got hurt, I came back tougher, you know? Don't worry, this one isn't serious. I'm coming right now.*

His heart was pounding frighteningly fast, and his body began to shake. His chest hurt. He felt air seep out from his ears. His heart eased. Instead, he felt drowsy. He almost fell asleep but roused himself. *Dammit!* Suddenly the sea came into view. It was a sea without a single ship. Then the view dimmed again. Something like the flame of a candle was faintly visible. *Hiroshi's birthday.* In the flame, Hiroshi's smiling face gradually receded until it disappeared. That awful drowsiness assailed him again.

Takao wrapped both his arms around the boy, who clung sobbing to Mizui's body, and peeled him away.

Kuroki felt for Mizui's pulse. The skin was warm, but there was none. There wasn't all that much bleeding, just a small stain spreading in the middle of his chest.

Takao wrenched the revolver from Mizui's hand and examined the chamber. "It's got one left."

There was the click of the drum rotating. Kuroki used his fingers to lower the lids on Mizui's staring eyes.

"So it's an SW Model 10, after all. No old lemon, either. It's in good shape."

It had been sudden. He'd first thought that some animal had leapt out from its hiding place in the snow. As if to shield Hiroshi Suzue, Mizui was running with the boy ahead of him. Trying to catch up was all Kuroki could do. Mizui stopped and began firing. Kuroki remembered every move he made in response. As he rolled he cocked his gun and fired when he got up. He couldn't afford to pause for a split second. The muzzle of Mizui's gun faced him.

Should he have gone for the shoulder? No, there had been no time to take aim. Blasting through the body center had been the only option.

"That was close. At any rate, you're a crack shot."

Kuroki lit a Short Peace. Hiroshi Suzue flashed a glance at him that hardly belonged to a little boy.

"You shot him dead..."

The groan came from Makimura, who'd crawled over on the snow. He buried his face in it not far from Mizui's corpse.

"Come on," Takao said, taking Hiroshi Suzue's hand.

The boy showed no signs of moving, his eyes pinned on Mizui's corpse. Takao lifted him up.

"I'll put in a report to the station. Looks like we could use an ambulance, too."

Makimura didn't raise his face from the snow. It looked like there were two dead bodies lying there.

Good thing it wasn't his bullet, Kuroki thought, throwing his Short Peace onto the snow.

Epilogue

He knocked.

A woman officer opened the door, and Kuroki showed her his I.D. She left the room and he went in.

There was a pleasant smell. Etsuko Mitsuya was there sitting atop a bed. Seeing Kuroki didn't elicit any change in her expression.

Without speaking a word, Kuroki sat down in a chair.

When he'd returned to Tokyo, he learned that Etsuko Mitsuya had attempted suicide again. She hadn't had anything with which to do the deed according to Fuse who'd been watching her. She had bitten the flesh off her wrist. On both wrists—and she'd severed an artery on the right.

Kuroki remembered Etsuko's white teeth biting into chocolate in Mizui's apartment.

Without makeup Etsuko's face was that of a girl, after all. A child, Kuroki thought, whose long hair and white teeth suited her.

Still he couldn't fathom Etsuko Mitsuya.

"This perfume smells nice, doesn't it? It's called Mitsuko. I just sprayed the whole room with it."

"Are you glad, or are you grieving?"

"What does it matter now?"

"All in the past, I see."

Kuroki was about to smoke a Short Peace but realized there was no ashtray. This was a hospital room.

"You tried to kill yourself because Mizui died. Isn't that it? But you're still alive. And getting drunk on the smell of perfume."

Etsuko laughed out loud, revealing her white teeth. They remained white, unstained with blood. "You hate me, don't you," she accused.

"I think it's you who hates me."

"He called me Makiko." Etsuko laughed again. "Koji always called me Makiko. Even after he found out my real name."

"Makiko Endo, huh?"

"Right. To him, I was Makiko Endo. And Makiko Endo is dead."

"The one here getting drunk on perfume is Etsuko Mitsuya, I take it."

"You find that strange?"

"No, I kind of understand."

Etsuko lay down and pulled the blanket up to her neck. The bandages on her wrists looked more like a boxer's than an invalid's.

"May I smoke? There doesn't seem to be an ashtray in here."

"Trying to get rid of the smell of perfume? Let me have one, too."

"I guess I won't, after all."

"You're a nasty cop, I've known it."

Etsuko turned to lie on her side. The whiteness above her bosom drew Kuroki's eyes.

As though she'd noticed the glance, Etsuko laughed shrilly.

Kuroki stood up. "Men often die for women. But Koji Mizui didn't die for Makiko Endo."

"What do you mean?"

"Nothing in particular. I wanted to tell that to the woman who used to be Makiko Endo. I came to this hospital thinking just that."

"Without even a get-well present."

Etsuko laughed again. Kuroki lit the Short Peace that he'd been holding between his fingers.

"Leave, you'll spoil the smell of perfume."

Kuroki put his hand on the door.

"It was you who killed him, wasn't it? You shot Koji dead like he was some animal."

Kuroki turned around.

Etsuko's eyes, probing him, shone like an angry cat's.

"You're right. I was the one who shot Koji Mizui dead, not you."

He opened the door, stepped out, and closed it behind him.

A chilly wind was beginning to blow outside.

It was nothing compared to Karuizawa's cold nights. Kuroki held his coat in his hand as he made his way through the year-end bustle. Several times he reached up to his ear. The frostbite felt itchier since he'd returned to Tokyo.

He was off duty but had no desire to head straight back to his room. Walking around the city wouldn't be so bad. He noticed a pleasant fragrance wafting from his clothes. It seemed to be the smell of perfume.

He entered a department store. His ear started itching again. Warm air seemed to irritate it.

Necklaces, handbags, cosmetics—he browsed the booths as he walked. All the time he kept scratching his ear.

He stopped in front of the perfume counter.

Mitsuko, he said. The clerk nodded right away and started wrapping up a box.

"Put a ribbon on, too," he said, scratching his ear. What with the crowd and the heating, his skin was growing moist with sweat. The store speakers called for a lost child. The place was terribly congested.

He dropped the small package into his pocket and stepped outside. The wind felt good.

Kuroki touched the modest lump in his pocket. He felt like he could give someone a present. So he'd bought perfume. Not that he had anyone to give it to. Chances were that the box would sleep awhile in his pocket. Eventually, jumbled with other things, it would become lost to him. And he'd forget the very fact that he'd bought perfume.

About the Author

Kenzo Kitakata is the recipient of many honors including the Japan Mystery Writers Association Award for *The Cage* (also available from Vertical) and the 2009 Japan Prize for Mystery Literature. His U.S. debut, *Ashes,* was a Book Sense 76 selection as well as *Las Vegas Mercury* Best Ten of the Year and *Village Voice* Beach Read picks. Kitakata's works have been translated into multiple other languages including Italian and Russian.